"There [...] Mrs. McGuires. One is my grandmother. The other is Nancy, Eric's wife."

Wife?

The word bounced around Maggie's head, slid down her throat and swirled in her stomach before dropping to the bottom, like one of those penny wishing wells at Wal-Mart.

"Th-that's impossible, I'm his wife."

"Look. My brother's done some pretty crummy things in his life, but he wouldn't stoop to bigamy."

"At least we agree on something."

Eric had been a jerk occasionally. But he'd been a charming, loving jerk. She couldn't believe he would do something to hurt her so badly. To hurt his son so badly.

But doubts tiptoed through her mind. He'd never really believed David was his child. And when she told him he was listed as David's father on the birth certificate, he'd just smiled a sad little smile and kissed her gently.

No. He wouldn't be that cruel.

"Maybe she's mistaken? This Nancy woman."

"Nope. I was their best man. And if there had been a divorce, I would have heard about it."

That's when the second shock seeped in. Everything she'd believed to be true was in jeopardy. J.D. was lying. He *had* to be lying.

Dear Reader,

You may find *The Secret Wife* a slight departure from my previous books. Like many of my stories, the family theme and a journey of discovery are still present. But *The Secret Wife* also contains an element of suspense.

Maggie McGuire's arrival in her estranged husband's hometown sparks a chain reaction of conflict and intrigue, with her nine-month-old son at the center.

As in real life, the opportunity for greatest personal growth sometimes arises from difficulty and heartbreak. Maggie and her new champion, J.D., certainly find this to be true as they search for meaning in a senseless tragedy.

I hope you enjoy my foray into romantic suspense. I found it both challenging and rewarding to write—so much so that I gave one of the characters an important role in my next book.

I love hearing from my readers. Feel free to contact me by mail in care of Harlequin Enterprises, 225 Duncan Mill Road, Don Mills, Ontario, M3B 3K9, Canada. Or I can be reached via www.SuperAuthors.com.

Happy reading,

Carrie Weaver

The Secret Wife
Carrie Weaver

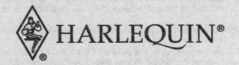

HARLEQUIN®

TORONTO • NEW YORK • LONDON
AMSTERDAM • PARIS • SYDNEY • HAMBURG
STOCKHOLM • ATHENS • TOKYO • MILAN • MADRID
PRAGUE • WARSAW • BUDAPEST • AUCKLAND

ISBN 0-373-71274-X

THE SECRET WIFE

www.eHarlequin.com

Printed in U.S.A.

This book is dedicated to the real Tinker brothers,
Jack and Alex (aka Dad and Uncle Alex), along with
their wives, Mary Ellen and Patty (Mom and Aunt Patty).
Thanks for all your love and support.

P.S. I promise the ladies will receive top billing next time.

Books by Carrie Weaver

HARLEQUIN SUPERROMANCE
1173—THE ROAD TO ECHO POINT
1222—THE SECOND SISTER

**Later this year watch for Nancy's story—from Carrie Weaver
and Harlequin Superromance.**

Don't miss any of our special offers. Write to us at the
following address for information on our newest releases.

Harlequin Reader Service
U.S.: 3010 Walden Ave., P.O. Box 1325, Buffalo, NY 14269
Canadian: P.O. Box 609, Fort Erie, Ont. L2A 5X3

PROLOGUE

FOURTEEN DOLLARS, thirty-seven cents—all that stood between Maggie McGuire and destitution. She slid the change into her pocket, along with the damp crumpled bills.

The Oklahoma rest stop was unusually desolate for a Friday morning. Or so she guessed. Maggie had rarely ventured beyond the Arizona borders.

Peeking through the open car window, she watched David squirm in his sleep. The car seat was too confining. The baby needed room to stretch out and roll.

What kind of mother hauled an infant clear across the country to Arkansas? And for what? The off chance that Eric would surface at his family reunion? Eric, who thought family was an unnecessary drag on his life?

Maggie had told herself it wouldn't come to this, that losing her job wasn't the end of the world. But she'd quickly discovered there weren't many jobs where she could take her baby along, especially working nights. The child-care center where she'd been employed for the past six months had been ideal. But the building was scheduled to be demolished and replaced with a strip mall.

Brushing her hair off her forehead, she figured her ponytail had come undone somewhere in New Mexico. Now it was loose and wild, a copper-colored reminder that she couldn't afford haircuts.

Eric.

She leaned against a primer-gray fender, glancing up at the clear sky. The air was fresh and warm. Innocent.

She'd been innocent once. A long, long time ago.

David whimpered.

Maggie let her eyes feast on the glorious sight of her child. Her David. A wave of protectiveness washed over her.

Eric had sidetracked her dreams, but he'd left her with a precious gift.

A gift that was nearly out of formula and diapers.

Panic hit as she inventoried the contents of the thrift-store diaper bag. Four diapers, four scoops of formula. Her eyes burned as her fatigued mind did the math.

That bought her six hours, tops.

And it was at least eight more hours till McGuire-ville.

As if on cue, the baby's hungry wail echoed through her head. Huge blue eyes beseeched her. As if maternal guilt wasn't enough, she was certain, somehow, some way, the authorities would know the minute the last drop of formula passed David's sweet lips. And they'd take him away. Just like they'd taken her niece, Emma.

Maggie straightened her shoulders and shook off the specter of losing her only child. *Nobody* would be able to say she was an unfit mother once she had a degree in hand and a decent paying job. But until then, the rent was behind, her tuition was due and only fourteen dollars stood between Maggie and the nameless, faceless authorities who haunted her dreams.

David's hungry cry galvanized her into action. She opened the car door and unbuckled the restraint harness. He stilled, waiting expectantly.

She kissed one tearstained cheek, then the other. "Don't worry, sweetheart. Mommy's going to make everything right. Soon."

Only eight more hours to McGuireville.

CHAPTER ONE

MAGGIE SQUARED her shoulders and prepared to do the impossible. Make a scene.

The door to the Grand Ballroom wavered before her eyes. A hunger headache and David's cries made it nearly impossible to think.

"Shhh." She bounced the baby on her hip. "Mama'll make it better, sweetheart." Her voice lacked conviction, and only made him wail louder.

It had to be done. There was no other way.

She flung open the door before her stomach could rebel at too little food and an abject fear of confrontations. A wave of air-conditioning and escalating conversation washed over her.

Lush aromas taunted her. Beef, catfish, potatoes, vegetables. It all made her mouth water, her stomach growl. Even David seemed mollified by the plenty.

She hesitated, but only for a second.

Her gaze swept the room. Searching. She'd know him anywhere. She could be deaf, dumb and blind, and she'd still know if he was near. The mere electricity of his presence was enough to send prickles down her spine.

Nothing.

She eyed the lovely dresses, the summer suits. Her tattered pair of denim cutoffs and worn out tennies didn't even come close.

"I think I'm underdressed," she whispered against the baby's downy hair. "Wish me luck."

It seemed like it took years to traverse the ballroom, even though she knew she must look like one of those racewalkers, elbows flying, intent on the finish line.

Finally, she reached the raised dais at the front. She turned, facing the room full of lovely people.

"Excuse me." Her voice didn't carry to the first row of round dining tables.

"Excuse me." A little louder this time.

They barely paused in their conversations.

Her face burned. She didn't belong here. And if she were really, really lucky, the ground would swallow her up whole.

Then she looked down into her son's bewildered eyes and decided the old Maggie would have to learn new ways.

She would stuff away what little remained of her pride. And she'd make the biggest, noisiest, nastiest scene she could. Until Eric crawled out from under his rock and accepted responsibility for his son.

What she needed was a megaphone. Her gaze swept the dais.

A podium stood nearby, complete with a microphone. Probably for long-winded dissertations on how the saintly McGuires had founded the town. Single-handedly prodded the economy. Provided scions of business.

Except Eric, of course. The black sheep.

She scanned the crowd one last time, hoping to settle this quietly, discreetly. But she didn't see him anywhere.

Probably at the hotel bar, picking up a cocktail waitress.

Well, she'd make darn sure he heard her. Even in the lounge.

The new Maggie stalked over to the microphone and grabbed it off the stand. An earsplitting squeal startled David.

Silence descended on the high-ceilinged room. Except for David's offended screech.

She jogged him on her hip as she tried to attract attention.

"Sorry to interrupt all you nice folks during your dinner. Can you hear me there at the back of the room? No, well let me speak a little louder." Maggie raised her voice until it bounced off the walls and tinkled the crystal chandelier.

"Good. I've got your attention. Just tell me where that lowlife Eric McGuire is and I'll let you get back to your meal."

Her only response was a room full of gaping mouths. Maybe they were all mentally deficient. Maybe Eric had been the sharpest knife in their family drawer.

The thought made her speak very slowly and distinctly, as if they didn't understand English. "I said…where is that lowlife, scum-sucking, lazy, no good SOB, Eric McGuire?"

They must've heard her this time, because they gasped in unison, every set of eyes as big as half dollars.

"You can't hide from me, Eric. I know you're out there. So get your hands off that waitress and come out here and face me like a man."

She watched the double doors, but no lowlife, or anyone else for that matter, entered the room.

An elderly woman in the second row of tables gasped for air. Some guy with a shaved head and shoulders the size of Mount Rushmore handed the woman a glass of water and patted her hand solicitously.

David suckled on her shoulder, leaving a big wet ring on her last clean T-shirt. The baby was hungry and patience wasn't one of his virtues. Just like his daddy.

"Look. This is David. He's Eric's son. We're not here to cause trouble. We just need some…help."

It was nearly impossible to spit out the last word. To beg for what should have been hers.

The old woman gasped, fixed her with a weird stare. The Vin Diesel look-alike whispered something in the woman's ear, squeezed her shoulder and headed for the stage.

The guy was pure enforcer. From the top of his well-shaped head to the toes of his size-twelve dress shoes. He tugged at his crisp, white collar as he ambled toward her. His jacket fit, but just barely.

He moved with graceful control, like the guys she'd seen on televised bodybuilding competitions. The evil glint in his eye told her he'd take great pleasure in throwing her out on her rear.

The man stepped up on the dais and stood in front of her, his shoulders effectively obscuring her view of the assembly and vice versa.

He seemed ready, willing and able to block her only chance at making a better life for her child.

"Eric," she yelled. "All I want is to talk to—"

Her jaw dropped as the enforcer produced a cracker and handed it to David. His baby sobs were muffled by the ecstatic gumming of salt and carbohydrates. Then the man pried the mike out of Maggie's hand and grabbed her by the upper arm.

"But—"

"You wanna know about Eric?" His voice rumbled low in his throat.

She raised her chin. "Yes."

"Then come with me."

"I'm not going anywhere. Not till I talk to Eric."

The man ran a hand over the black stubble on his head and took what looked like one of the deep cleansing breaths she'd learned in her childbirth class. She half expected him to start the hee-hee-hee breaths through clenched teeth.

Instead, he fixed her with a bright, white smile. One

that didn't come close to easing the tight lines around his eyes.

"You'll talk to Eric." His voice was soothing. And totally insincere.

She stood her ground and glared at him. He intended to trot her out the door and hand her over to security.

"Everyone's been through enough." He gestured toward the roomful of silent onlookers. "They don't need this—" His eyes narrowed as he turned to survey the baby. "And neither does the kid."

"He has a name. David McGuire."

The man stared long and hard. Then he glanced over his shoulder at the old woman. When he addressed Maggie, his voice was low, desperate.

"Please. We'll go somewhere, get a bite to eat. There's a diner nearby. The baby...David, is it? He's gotta be tired and hungry."

Her tummy rumbled at the mere mention of food. Her son squirmed on her hip. Dampness saturated her shirt where it was wedged between her body and the baby's. Warm and pungent, it would be only a matter of minutes before the odor of baby urine spread across the stage.

"Only if you promise to tell me about Eric. Promise?"

"Of course."

David cast his vote, by way of an angry screech. The cracker was gone and he demanded more. Now. And a dry diaper, too.

"Okay. But this better not be a trick."

He held out his hands to the baby. David smacked them away. If the man didn't hold crackers or a bottle, he wanted nothing to do with the stranger.

"Follow me."

She nodded, but apparently he didn't believe her. He grasped her elbow and hauled her out of the room. She could feel two hundred sets of eyes follow their progress out the double doors.

Pandemonium broke out before the doors swished shut. Everyone babbled at once. She'd succeeded in making quite a scene.

As she followed the enforcer through the lobby, Maggie couldn't help but wonder how she'd gotten to this point. The point where she'd sacrificed her self-respect and values.

But it really wasn't a mystery. It all came back to Eric. She hadn't had a chance. Not from that first glance.

CHAPTER TWO

THE MAN HESITATED, then held the lobby door for Maggie. His tight expression said he wasn't sure she merited the courtesy.

Maggie held her head high as she passed. She might be broke, but she still had her pride.

"Where's your car?" he asked. His long strides put him ahead of her in no time.

"East lot. Why?"

He turned and raised an eyebrow.

"You've got a car seat, I presume? My truck isn't exactly equipped for kids."

"Oh."

To his credit, he didn't even blink a few minutes later when they arrived at the poor, tired Toyota with the mismatched fenders. He simply waited while she tried to get David into his car seat.

But the baby had fury-induced rigor mortis. His face was squinched up and red; his arms and legs were stiff as boards.

"Do you have any more crackers?" She couldn't

meet his eyes as she begged for food. No decent mother let her child get this hungry.

He patted his breast pocket. "Nope. Didn't think to grab any on my way out. I was busy."

"Maybe we could meet you there. At that diner you mentioned?"

"Not on your life."

She finally managed to maneuver the baby's arms through the safety straps. Leaning forward, her headache went postal as a little fist latched onto a hank of hair. She bit back an oath. Tears threatened as she fought for patience.

"It's okay sweetie," she soothed.

David screamed louder. He didn't want nice words. He wanted food. A bottle. And a nice long nap.

Or was that simply what she wanted?

They'd been together so long, it was hard to separate their needs.

The baby's cries worked on her like fingernails on a blackboard. It underscored how really helpless she was. Her breasts ached with the need to comfort. If she hadn't weaned David a couple months back, she could provide the sustenance and comfort he needed.

The ache intensified. But it was like phantom limb pain, real in her head, but not her body.

"It's gonna be loud," she warned the man.

"Yeah. I noticed. I'm J.D., by the way."

"I'm Maggie. The diner's not far?"

"Nope. Couple miles."

"Get in." *Please don't let me run out of gas.*

He tucked his legs and somehow managed to wedge himself in the front seat. He twisted to the side, eyeing her dash.

He shook his head and grunted.

"I beg your pardon?"

"Gas station. Take a left out of the parking lot. It'll be on your right."

"I don't need gas—"

"Like hell you don't."

"I…um…don't have my debit card."

"They accept cash. Most places still do these days."

Maggie fumbled through her purse, even though she knew there weren't any nickels or dimes left in the bottom. Not even pennies. She'd double-checked a couple hundred miles back.

She laughed uncertainly. "Whoops. Guess I'm out of cash, too."

"I'll buy. Just drive. That kid's giving me a headache."

J.D. SUCKED IN A BREATH of heavy, humid air and thanked his lucky stars for a reprieve from that screaming baby. And from Eric's latest escapade come back to haunt him.

Fluorescent lights bathed the food and sundries in a greenish glow. He looked at the bursting shelves with a new appreciation. The gas station looked like a fully stocked grocery store in miniature. The solution to at least a few of his more immediate problems.

Maggie was flat-busted broke. That much was obvious.

He grabbed diapers, formula and baby biscuits. Baby food? The little boy looked to be about the same age as his buddy Kirk's boy—eight, maybe nine months. Little Brandon ate everything in sight, including mouthfuls of cat hair. Freshly plucked cat hair.

As J.D. juggled jars, cans and diapers, he wondered how he'd gotten himself into this predicament.

The answer was a no-brainer. Habit. A long habit of cleaning up Eric's messes. And this mess wasn't much different from all the rest, except the woman. She was younger, her hair a shiny mass of copper curls. Freckles sprinkled across her nose made her look like a farm girl.

Eric must've digressed from his usual predilections—bleach-blondes with boobs the size of Texas. The last one might as well have had Stripper stamped in the middle of her forehead. Or tattooed on the impossibly huge chest she'd forced into a corset kinda thing.

Nope. This woman was different.

But the same.

Same old story. "Eric got me knocked up. I need money. I'll go away if you help me get back on my feet." This one was lying, just like the others. But it'd kill his grandmother to go through it again. She always hoped it was the truth, even though she knew it was impossible. Hoped Eric had passed along his perfect blond, blue-eyed genes and given her a McGuire great-grandchild to cherish.

J.D. dumped the stuff on the counter.

"This and fifteen bucks on pump three."

David's mom was pumping gas when he returned. Her gaze was fixed on the gas pump, her face flushed. She acted as if she might have some pride and the bundles in his hand eroded it. Interesting.

The sound of pissed-off hollering pervaded the air around the car. The ungodly noise made him sorely tempted to retreat to the relative peace of the service station.

Squaring his shoulders, he opened the door, taking the full brunt of the baby's displeasure. The little guy's face was darn near purple. His hands were clenched, and he squirmed to escape the confining car seat.

"Um…David…shhh." It felt odd to say the name. His own middle name.

Nothing, just more screaming.

He flipped the seat forward and patted a chubby, dimpled leg.

That only made the kid madder.

Then inspiration hit.

He ripped open the box of baby biscuits and offered him one.

The kid gave him a look that said, "It's about time, stupid," and snatched the cookie from his hand.

Furiously gumming the goody, he surveyed J.D. with interest. Waving a little fist, his squirming changed to a happy wriggle. Legs and arms bounced, never still. David cooed his approval.

It kinda made J.D. feel good.

He twisted and withdrew from the back seat, sure he'd need to see a chiropractor the next morning. Straightening, he grinned at the woman.

"I got him to stop crying."

She nodded her head but didn't meet his eyes.

His accomplishment left her monumentally unimpressed.

Silence surrounded them as she replaced the nozzle. Crickets tuned up for their evening encore.

Then she looked up and met his gaze.

Something about her eyes disturbed him. They were green. Deep. Sincere.

"Thank you."

He grunted some sort of reply, Lord only knew what, and got back in the car.

They headed to the diner in silence, broken occasionally by a contented gibberish from the baby.

When they pulled into the parking lot, he gestured toward the back seat. "There're diapers in the bag, if you think he might need a change."

The woman looked away for a moment, brushed her eyes. "You didn't have to do that."

He shrugged.

Charity. Might as well get it over with in one big horse pill to swallow. He didn't like to give it, couldn't imagine taking it and completely understood how hard it was to accept. For a gold digger, Maggie seemed unusually sensitive about asking for help.

"There's formula and some other stuff, too."

Her eyes locked with his, her pretty little mouth turned down at the corners.

He held up a hand forestalling her protest.

"Now that's the way we are around here. Southern hospitality, nothing more. And you can pay me back when you find your debit card."

"Yes. I'll pay you back."

A cold day in hell.

"Why don't you change the baby. I'll go on ahead and order us some food. Burgers okay?"

She nodded. He watched as she flipped the seat forward, contorted her spine and reached for the car-seat latch. Her faded T-shirt inched up toward her ribs. A ribbon of skin peeked out of the gap, pale and vulnerable.

J.D. turned and headed for the restaurant before he did something stupid. Like placing his palm against the warm, bare small of her back. Somehow he didn't think she'd buy his pretext of helping.

He found a booth and watched her lumber toward the restroom door, her child on one hip, an enormous diaper bag banging against the other.

She was thin. Way too thin. Eric didn't normally go for the anorexic type, though J.D. had to admit there was a certain charm to her wide-eyed, heart-shaped face.

He accepted the menu from the waitress while mentally castigating his brother. Disgust and disappointment got all tangled together in one messy package.

Damn him.

Damn Eric for lying. For saying he'd changed. Damn him for putting their grandmother through this. For being the favorite, whether he deserved it or not. And damn him for dumping one more mess in his half brother's lap.

J.D. didn't realize he'd been brooding until the waitress cleared her throat.

He looked up and she flashed a smile. She looked familiar. She'd graduated with Eric. What was her name?

"Darlene," he read off her name tag. "Sorry, guess I was daydreaming."

"No problem, J.D."

How'd she know his name when he couldn't remember hers without reading it?

It was simple really. He was a McGuire, even if only by name and not blood. The McGuires stood for something in this town—they were respected, if not revered. Their money bought a lot of goodwill.

He made a mental note to leave her a generous tip, then ordered cheeseburgers for himself and the redhead. French fries. Coleslaw. Two large sweet teas. Eric's latest mistake looked like she could use some protein. That, carbohydrates and caffeine might get her through what he had to tell her.

J.D. watched her make her way to the table. Dark circles ringed her eyes. She looked like she might blow over with the slightest breeze.

Maggie swallowed, forcing herself to meet J.D.'s gaze as she made her way around the tables. It wasn't a crime to be poor, but the pity on his face said it sure was sad.

Smoothing her hair, she wished she'd had a place to shower and change before confronting the McGuires. Despite splashing her face with cold water and finger-combing her hair, she knew she looked like hell. Her mother would have disowned her.

Maggie stifled a hysterical chuckle as she slid into the booth. Her mother *had* disowned her. But for crimes much more serious than a lack of personal grooming.

The man watched her bounce David on her knee. The cookie was long gone and he started to fuss. Poor thing, it had been a long day for them both.

Pulling the bottle from a side pocket, she said, "I mixed it with warm water in the restroom." Help, so rare and unaccustomed, left a lump in her throat. How different things might have been if… She refused to go there. "Thank you. For the formula and the other stuff."

"No problem. Southern hospitality."

She could get used to this Southern hospitality. And it scared her.

"Give me the receipt. I'm a student and I'll pay you back when…"

When?

When she paid the rent? When she had cupboards

stocked with food and wipes and diapers? When she graduated from college, her mortuary-science degree in hand?

That was the only chance she might have of repaying the man.

"Here. You pay me when you can."

She accepted the folded slip of paper and just about drowned in the kindness in his eyes. Slipping the paper into the diaper bag, she didn't even look at the amount. Didn't have to. She could tell to the penny what he'd spent, allowing for regional differences. Doing without had made her a great comparison shopper. And she knew convenience stores charged an arm and a leg for this stuff. Including the cheeseburger, she owed the guy close to forty bucks.

"You know babies pretty well. You have children?"

He seemed startled at the suggestion. Why? He looked to be in his midthirties. Solid. Kind. Good-looking, in a rough sort of way. A man who should probably have a wife and a few children at home.

"Nope. Couple of my friends do, though. Once they get to that age—" he nodded to David cradled in the crook of her arm sucking greedily on the bottle "—a cracker'll get them to quiet down if they're hungry or bored."

"An astute observation, J.D. I didn't catch your last name? Though with the reunion in town, McGuire would be a safe guess."

His lips twitched. So, he had a sense of humor.

"Yep. You nailed it. McGuire, J. D. McGuire. And you are?"

"McGuire. Maggie McGuire."

His eyes widened at that. Then the frown was back. As if she'd uttered the most despicable thing in the world.

"That's not funny," he said.

"It's not intended to be."

"Passing yourself off as his wife won't help."

Maggie straightened her aching spine. She wasn't ready for this kind of confrontation. Eric, yes. She'd had several thousand miles to prepare for dealing with Eric. But this guy? He made her feel like she was doing something wrong. Something immoral.

"I'm not passing myself off as anything. I'm merely being polite and introducing myself. You draw your own conclusions."

"My conclusions have nothing to do with this. There are already two Mrs. McGuires. One is my grandmother. The other is Nancy, Eric's wife."

Wife?

The word bounced around her head, slid down her throat and twirled in her stomach, before dropping to the bottom, like one of those penny wishing wells at the Wal-Mart store.

"Th-that's impossible. *I'm* his wife."

"Look, lady, I don't know you. But you seem like a nice enough person. My brother's done some pretty crummy things in his life, but he wouldn't stoop to bigamy."

"At least we agree about something."

Eric *had* been a jerk occasionally. Well, more than occasionally. But he'd been a charming, loving jerk most of the time. She simply couldn't believe he would do something to hurt her so badly. To hurt his son so badly.

But doubts tiptoed through her mind. He'd never really believed David was his child. Their argument over his paternity had been intense. She'd started spotting immediately and feared she might lose the baby. After that, Eric had neither accepted nor rejected paternity. He had simply humored her, made sure she ate right, got enough rest, suggested a few names for the baby.

And when she'd told him he was listed as David's father on the birth certificate, he'd just smiled a sad little smile and kissed her gently on the lips. Then he'd taken the newborn from her arms and settled into the hospital rocking chair.

No, he wouldn't be that cruel.

"Maybe she's mistaken? This Nancy woman?"

"Nope. I was best man at their wedding, right after Eric graduated high school. And if there'd been a divorce, I would have heard about it."

That's when the second shock seeped in. Everything she'd believed to be true was in jeopardy. J.D. was lying. He *had* to be lying.

"Look, is this some sort of sick practical joke?" Maggie held her breath, waiting for a camera crew to come out of hiding, hoping against hope that this was a new reality TV show designed to humiliate the unsuspecting.

"Is it? A joke?" she asked.

He couldn't meet her gaze. Instead, he stared off in the direction of the door. As if he would rather have been anywhere in the world but here, breaking bad news to a stranger. "No, it's not a joke."

"If you're telling the truth," she whispered, squeezing the baby so tightly he protested, "that means I'm not married. And David is—"

"A beautiful, healthy child." He leaned forward. "That's all that matters."

"Why are you being so kind?"

The man ran a hand over his head. "I'm not being kind. I'm just stating a fact. My brother is a real asshole sometimes and innocent people get hurt."

Now she realized the man had said he was Eric's brother, not once, but twice.

She slumped against the back of the booth. "You're Jamie?"

"Only to my grandmother. And Eric, if I'm not too pissed off at him."

Maggie eyed him. "You don't look anything like him."

"Yeah, I get that a lot. Same mother, different fathers. Eric's dad was my stepdad."

"J.D.—James David?" She tried to reconcile the man before her with her preconceived idea of what Eric's brother would look like. She'd never even seen a photo of the man, but she'd assumed he would be fair like Eric. Blond hair, blue eyes.

"Yes, that's me. I prefer J.D. though." He nodded toward her son. "Is it coincidence, his name?"

"No coincidence. Eric wanted David named after you. He talked about you a lot. Kind of like you were a superhero."

But it hadn't always been a nice comparison. Sometimes, usually when he'd had one beer too many, the resentment would creep into his voice. The great Jamie, always doing the right thing, always thinking he was better.

"I doubt that. We don't get along very well."

She was silent, watching David's eyes flutter. His daddy had a lot of faults. She only hoped her son inherited the good qualities. His generosity, his zest for life. The way he reached out and grabbed what he wanted.

"I need to talk to Eric. Sort all this out."

J.D. glanced at his watch.

"It'll wait till morning. That way you'll be…um… refreshed before you see him."

"That way you can warn him I'm here."

He rubbed his chin. "The thought crossed my mind."

"No way. I want to see him now."

"Can't. He's racing just outside of town. That's why he missed the reunion dinner. His priorities are kinda mixed up."

"No kidding." Maggie glanced meaningfully at David. "You said racing?"

"Yeah, you know the stuff. Where the guys drive round and round the track until all of them are wrecked or somebody wins."

"Of course I know racing. It's where I met Eric. But he'd given it up. He told me—"

"And you believed him?"

Shifting in her seat, Maggie couldn't decide which was worse, the guy knowing how completely gullible she'd been, or the extent of her desperation.

"No, not completely. I tried to call him when I didn't receive divorce papers, but couldn't reach him at any of the emergency numbers he'd left in the past. Then I checked the Internet at the library. He wasn't registered anywhere on the amateur stock-car circuit."

"And you didn't find him under Eric MacGuire, with an *A?*"

"No."

"How about Johnny Bravo?"

Bingo. His favorite cartoon character.

J.D. had just handed David's lovable, lowlife, scum-sucking, no-good jerk of a father to her on a silver platter.

CHAPTER THREE

MAGGIE SURVEYED the cramped lobby while she swayed from side to side, David's head growing heavy on her shoulder. The motel was neat and clean. Not luxurious, but certainly not a dive—and way off the beaten track.

She watched J.D. set down her suitcase to pull a wad of bills from his pocket. He peeled off several and tossed forty bucks on the counter like it was pocket change. Maybe for some people.

The room was paid up for one night, and one night only. Noon checkout, and Eric's brother expected her to be long gone by then.

He had a lot to learn about her.

What she might lack in worldly knowledge, she more than made up for with grit. How else would she have survived till now?

J.D. handed her the key card. His eyes narrowed as he surveyed her face.

She kissed the top of David's downy head, avoiding J.D.'s questioning gaze.

"Thank you," she murmured.

God, she was getting tired of saying that. Tired of

depending on a stranger. But it couldn't be helped. She'd get her mortuary-science degree, become the best damn funeral director in Phoenix and then she'd never have to rely on anyone again.

"Go get some rest. I'll drop by tomorrow morning and take you to see Eric. They serve juice and doughnuts right here in the lobby, so you don't have to go anywhere for breakfast."

The threat was implicit.

He didn't want Eric's second wife parading around where anyone could see her. Just wanted her to disappear like a wisp of smoke. No ugly scene. No smudge on the sainted McGuire name. Sure, she'd let him savor that little fantasy a while longer.

"Oh, good. I'm really beat. We'll just get settled in, get rested up...."

"Do you need me to carry your suitcase to your room?"

"No, I can handle it."

"I'll pick you up at nine tomorrow morning."

She nodded.

He turned and strode out the door without a backward look. Problem solved. It wouldn't have surprised her to see him dust his hands.

Maggie slid the key card into her back pocket and watched him get into his candy-apple-red pickup. She'd dropped him off to get his truck, then followed him to the roadside hotel. When she'd lagged behind, so had he. There was no way her little Toyota could outrun him, so she'd had to wait for an opportunity to ditch him.

Shaking her head, Maggie had a hard time believing J.D. and Eric came from the same family. He was everything Eric wasn't—solid, dependable, controlled. An accountant hiding out in a football player's body. The kind of guy who should have a four-door sedan, a Volvo station wagon even. Something safe, reliable. Boring.

If J.D. was a station-wagon kind of guy, then Eric was definitely meant for sports cars. Lots of flash and excitement, but never dependable. And her Toyota, where did that fit into the scheme of things?

A little battered, but reliable and good on gas. But underneath the hood, the little import longed to be a sports car.

David shifted in his sleep, settling against her shoulder with a sigh.

But sports cars weren't conducive to children. And if she were one of the little Toyotas in a world of sports cars and SUVs, that didn't mean she couldn't be as successful as the next person. It would simply take more work.

Maggie fought a wave of loneliness as she watched the taillights fade into the distance. J.D. wouldn't be back until morning. Lifting her chin, she shook off the pressure in her chest. Getting sappy wouldn't pay her tuition.

Maggie waited a good fifteen minutes after J.D.

left. When she was sure he wasn't coming back, she settled David in his car seat and continued her mission.

The racetrack wasn't hard to find once she stopped at a convenience store for directions. Straight through town, five miles on the other side, just where the clerk had said.

She swung the little car into the dirt parking lot and wedged the car into a space at the end of a row. In Arizona, the dust would've choked her. But here, it was the mosquitoes. They swarmed around her as she exited the car, ravaged her bare legs when she reached in to remove the sleeping baby from the back seat.

She wrapped a lightweight cotton blanket around David to protect him from the cloud of insects.

Unfortunately, her shorts left plenty of bare skin for the little bloodsuckers. One voracious mosquito died from her stinging smack, only to be replaced by ten more. Finally, she gave up.

Glancing around, Maggie was glad to note that she wasn't late. People streamed toward the entrance gates. She let the crowd swallow her until she neared the ticket booth. There, she split off to the left, following the chain-link fence that separated her from her destiny.

Squaring her shoulders, she headed for the pit entrance. Her face warmed with embarrassment. It wasn't right to avoid paying. But it was the only way.

Maggie raised her chin as she passed the big-bellied guy checking passes. Juggling the baby and the diaper bag, she worked on an innocent fluster—as opposed to a guilty one. The blanket inched down to reveal David's face.

"Aw, shoot. I must've left my pass in the car. Bobby'll skin me alive. He's pittin' tonight and I promised I'd kiss him for good luck."

She didn't know if it was her winsome smile, or the sight of the sleeping baby, but the guy nodded and let her through.

Maggie released a breath. Hurdle number one.

Shielding her eyes from the glare of the stadium lights, she searched the pit area. No number fifty-three. That had always been Eric's lucky number. But number eight was a spanking clean white-and-kelly-green. Eric's colors.

Familiar sights and sounds brought a lump to her throat as she made her way through the pits. People jostled her, the stands seemed to close in. She jumped as an air tool hammered in the area to her left. The din was strange, no longer music to her ears. She didn't belong anymore.

But like his father, David could sleep through it all, the noise a familiar lullaby from the womb. She'd been at the track so much when she was pregnant, it probably seemed reassuring to the baby.

Maggie eyed the green-and-white car. Was number eight Eric's? She cautiously approached, afraid someone would haul her out by the arm. But nobody noticed. They were too busy with their respective jobs, readying the car for the race.

A familiar crouched figure seemed oblivious to the whine of the air gun as he tightened lug nuts. He turned and the light fell on his face. Randy, Eric's buddy and leader of the pit crew. If he were here, then so was Eric.

But there was only one way to be absolutely sure it was Eric's car. Her heart hammered as she scooted behind Randy. She used the surge of the crowd as a shield so he wouldn't see her.

Leaning through the window of the car, she surveyed the dash. Amid all the dials and stuff was a small photo taped to the dash. A wedding photo, circa the late sixties. Eric's mom and dad, or so he'd said. He never started a race without touching the photo for good luck.

Number eight was Eric's car all right.

The battered motor home parked fifty feet away had to be his, too. He insisted on sleeping at the track to be near his car. It looked like a few months hadn't improved Eric's financial position any more than it had hers.

When she'd met him, he'd had only the best—a shiny new motor home and only the finest gear. But he'd dipped into the sponsor's pocket one time too many for bogus supplies and the gravy train had run out. Even an old family friend had a limit to how much he would allow himself to be cheated.

Though the conditions weren't lavish like before, Maggie knew how Eric prepared for every race. He'd be reading his Bible. Maybe on his knees praying.

Funny, he might be a self-centered SOB most of time, but right before a race he always found God.

Maggie sauntered over to the motor home, acting as if she belonged. As if entering Eric's motor home were the most natural thing in the world.

Regret flared, then died. There had been a time when she'd revolved in Eric's orbit. Absorbed his reflected excitement and glory.

Her hand froze on the knob.

Maggie couldn't do it. Just couldn't.

She had vowed never to ask him for anything, but for her son's sake, she'd always accepted the small money orders he'd sent from time to time. Now she was about to beg for regular child support. And have him explain the twisted mess of their "marriage."

Maggie swallowed hard. All she wanted to do was turn around, get into her car and head back to Phoenix. But she deserved answers and a whole lot more.

A chubby little hand patted her cheek.

David certainly deserved more. "Hey, little guy, are you my moral support?" She hoisted him under the armpits so they were eye-to-eye. His wide smile told her she was the most important person in the universe. David planted a wide open baby kiss on her nose.

Pulling him close, she hugged him tightly. Her throat prickled with the enormity of her love for this child. For David, she would do anything: beg, plead, demand.

She grasped the doorknob before she could lose her nerve. The door opened easily, without even a squeak. Tiptoeing inside, she hesitated, allowing her eyes to adjust to the gloom. The tiny light above the stove gave off a weak glow.

The motor home was strangely silent.

Maggie observed the usual mess Eric left behind. Racing magazines, gloves, a sweating bottle of blue sports drink.

But no Eric.

Strange.

He was a creature of habit. And supremely superstitious. He had an unchanging ritual before a race. First, a Bible reading, then prayer. But his Bible wasn't lying open on the table.

She rummaged through what had always been the junk drawer in the other motor home. Her fingers folded around a slim volume of the New Testament, the corners accordion pleated from jamming the drawer so many times.

Weird.

Had he changed that much in the six months since she'd seen him? Two since she'd heard from him?

The bathroom door was closed. Maybe a last-minute bout of nerves?

She tiptoed to the door and tapped.

"Eric?"

No answer.

Opening the door, she leaned in to peer around. Light trickled in through the bathroom window, casting everything in varying shades of gray. The shadows were barely discernible from the objects that created them.

David snuggled close, resting his cheek against her chest. His breathing slowed. Poor baby. They were both exhausted.

The white of the sink glowed pale against the gloomy backdrop. The faucet dripped.

Terrible waste of water. Maggie turned it off.

Black splotches decorated the otherwise pale sink rim, kind of like a Rorschach test, dribbling down the side, to leave tiny specks on the floor.

It was something dark, something liquid.

Oil maybe? It had splattered too much to be grease.

Maggie ran her fingers through it. Thick, crusty and drying around the edges. Definitely not oil. It almost looked like…no, her brain rebelled at the very thought. Not blood.

She searched the gloom for a roll of toilet paper, but came up empty. Typical. Eric could never remember to put out a new roll.

Sighing, she adjusted the sleepy baby a bit higher on her hip and wiped her hand across the leg of her shorts. They'd need washing later in the hotel sink.

The silence surrounded her, intensified by the muffled clanking, banging and hammering outside.

Maggie backed out of the bathroom.

She would come back after the race. If she waited any longer than that she might lose her nerve.

David squirmed in his sleep and made one of his puppylike snuffling noises. He deserved a good night's sleep. In a real bed. And so did she.

Maggie stifled a yawn and headed for the door.

As she grasped the knob, she turned to take one more look at her past. What had once appeared dangerous and exciting, now simply looked sad.

She shook her head. Something white on the lower bunk caught her eye.

There was a lumpy sleeping bag, as usual, tossed over Eric's belongings, as if no one would be smart enough to look there for his valuable stuff. His guitar, his pistol…

The light-colored thing took on eerie dimensions as she stepped closer to check it out. Almost like a—

Hand.

She jostled what she figured had to be his arm under the sleeping bag.

"Eric," she whispered. She didn't want to wake the baby.

She shoved a little harder.

No response.

"Come on, Eric, this isn't funny."

David whimpered in his sleep.

Losing patience with Eric's games, she grabbed the sleeping bag and flung it back.

Time froze, Maggie froze.

She scrambled for the hand she'd seen, grasped the wrist. It was warm.

The wild thumping of her heart eased.

Until she looked at his face.

And knew, without a doubt, her searching fingers

wouldn't find a pulse. She'd been around enough corpses in her embalming class to recognize death.

Her eyes widened at David's shrill screech of baby rage. It rang in her ears, bounced off the fake wood-grain walls, slashed through her to the very core. Only when she slapped a hand to her open mouth did she realize the screams came from her. Then, and only then, did the baby join in.

MAGGIE SHIFTED in the cold, metal chair, David's cries echoing in her head and in her heart.

She could almost feel his terror as he'd been taken from her arms. His little hands had clutched at her shirt, his eyes wide with panic.

And she'd been forced to let him go. Hand him over to strangers. It was her worst nightmare come true. Nameless, faceless authorities taking her son away because she wasn't a fit mother.

Tears sprang to her eyes, but she brushed them away. This was all a big mistake. They would figure out she wasn't capable of hurting Eric, wouldn't they?

She eyed the two deputies as one set down a foam cup of coffee for her. Both wore bland expressions.

"I don't drink coffee."

A half truth. Used to drink the stuff by the bucketful. Back before David, when she'd been a college student with ample scholarship money. These days, generic cola was much cheaper and did a decent job of keeping her eyes open.

But now her nerves jangled and she didn't think she'd ever be able to close her eyes again. When she did, all she saw was Eric. And blood. So much blood.

She should be used to it by now, or she had no business pursuing a profession where it was such an integral part of the process.

"How about a pop?" The scrawny deputy did most of the talking. He wasn't a bad guy, all in all. It was Deputy Wells, the big, beefy, quiet one who made her nervous.

"No, thank you. I just want to get back to my baby."

"He's fine. A caseworker's watching him while we talk."

"There's no need for a caseworker. We'll clear this up, then I'll take care of David."

"Hmm. We'll need your story, from the top."

"I've already *told* you."

"That was an initial interview at the scene. We need your complete story. Details."

Maggie didn't like the way Wells kept calling it her *story*. As if her version were obviously fictitious.

She drew in a deep, calming breath. This guy held her future, as well as her son's future, in his big, square hands.

"Your relationship with the victim was…"

"You know darn well—"

Warning flashed in the deputy's eyes.

"I mean, uh, Eric and I were…"

What were they? Estranged husband and wife, or so she'd thought, until she'd found out about Nancy.

"Lovers," she ended lamely. That at least wasn't in dispute. David was living proof of their intimacy. At least it had been intimacy for her. What it had meant to Eric, she could only guess. And none of the guesses were very flattering.

Anger bubbled up inside and made her face feel hot and swollen, as if her skin might split right open.

"Eric is…was…the father of my child."

"And?"

"I came to talk to him about setting up some sort of agreement about David's care. Child support."

"Yeah, I heard about that little scene at the banquet. It's all over town."

The guy dragged over a gray metal chair and parked his big butt. He leaned back and crossed his arms over his chest. "Eric wasn't what we'd call the responsible kind. What'd he do, laugh in your face? I could see where that might make a woman mad enough to grab a carving knife—"

"I *didn't* grab a knife. I didn't stab him. He was dead when I got there."

"We'll see what the medical examiner says about that. They can determine right down to the minute when a person died, you know. So there's no use lying."

"I'm not lying," she said through clenched teeth. But he was. She knew damn well how many variables there were in determining time of death. There wasn't a decent doctor or coroner alive who would claim to be one-hundred-percent sure. A window of several hours was more likely and that didn't help her a bit.

"Look, lady, you breeze into town and all of a sudden Eric McGuire is murdered. My guess is you didn't know he was married. You got all worked up about it and went out to the track. Eric always was a sweet talker with the ladies. But this time he couldn't worm his way out of it."

"That's not true! I never even talked to him. He was dead when I got there."

The scrawny deputy slipped into the room, his face beet red.

"Uh, there's some guy out front. Says he's—"

"Her lawyer." A tall, silver-haired man pushed his way into the room. He extended a tanned, well-manicured hand to her.

She shook his hand, bewildered. She'd never seen him before in her life. And judging from the cut of his gray summer-weight suit, he looked expensive.

The man handed a business card to the big deputy and motioned for her to follow him.

"We'll discuss the details later, darlin'. First, we get you out of this hellhole."

"But—"

"No buts. Your child is right outside waiting for you."

That was all the encouragement she needed. She followed the authoritative suit out the door without giving the deputies a second glance. For David, she would follow a stranger through the fires of hell.

It shouldn't have surprised her that the devil himself stood on the other side of the door, holding her baby.

"J.D."

He nodded in response. "We're getting you out of here." Turning to the men in uniform, J.D. said, "Deputy, any more questions should be routed through Maggie's attorney."

Her head whirled with unanswered questions. But the most important one had already been answered. David was here, safe and sound, if not totally content.

She held out her arms to him and he broke out in a big, nearly toothless grin. He leaned away from his captor, leaving no doubt where he'd rather be.

J.D. handed David to her and folded his arms over his chest, watching their reunion.

Maggie didn't care who watched. She hugged and cuddled and kissed the soft little boy until he squirmed in protest.

"You done yet?"

J.D.'s voice was harsh, impatient, but his eyes were just a little too understanding.

She nodded.

"She'll be staying at my house, Belmont, if you need to talk to her." J.D. shook hands with the attorney. "Thanks for coming on such short notice."

The distinguished gentleman winked. "It'll cost you, J.D. You know that gazebo my wife's been talking about…"

"Yeah, I know." J.D. winced. "You name the day, I'll be there for measurements."

He shook hands with the attorney, then took her elbow to escort her out of the county jail. As if she needed any encouragement. Intent on putting distance between David and the uniforms, she broke into a jog.

But once outside, her steps faltered.

"Your house? But, the hotel—"

"The hotel isn't an option. Anything you need there?"

"All our stuff is in the car."

J.D. hesitated, "There's someone who insists on meeting you. It's against my better judgment, but…"

CHAPTER FOUR

MAGGIE DIDN'T BOTHER to protest when J.D. asked for her car keys. Her knees shook and her hands were unsteady as she buckled David into his car seat.

J.D. steered her little Toyota out of the parking lot, adjusting easily to the loose clutch and intermittent hiccup on acceleration. Soon, they left the downtown area and houses were fewer and farther between.

Fighting nausea, Maggie closed her eyes and concentrated on breathing. She had no doubt that J.D.'s attorney had saved her from an overnight stay in jail, if not longer. The attorney had also made sure they immediately returned her child.

"Thank you," she murmured.

When she didn't hear a polite response, Maggie opened her eyes and glanced at J.D.

His profile was rigid, his jaw set. "Belmont owed me a favor."

"And now you owe his wife a gazebo. I'll find a way to pay you back."

He nodded.

"Really. I will."

"Look, I didn't do it for you."

"Then who did you do it for?" She doubted he'd considered David. He didn't seem eager to take on the role of uncle.

"It's…complicated. But the last thing any of us need right now is you jailed and the little guy in foster care."

"I won't let them take David."

J.D. glanced in her direction. "I hope you're not thinking about doing something stupid. Like running."

That was exactly what she'd been thinking. Grabbing up David and driving off somewhere, anywhere but here.

"Because that will only make things worse. We were damn lucky they released you today. And that was partly because I vouched for you."

Maggie swallowed her surprise. The car seemed to close in on her. Another debt she owed to J.D., another thread tying her to McGuireville. "I'll try not to get you in trouble."

Avoiding his gaze, she looked out the side window.

But against the backdrop of green, green grass and thick stands of trees, she saw Eric's lifeless body. He was gone, truly and totally, from her life forever. A part of her ached for her first love and all the might-have-beens. All the shared memories that it would be her sole responsibility to pass on to their son.

It was a hard idea for her to accept.

And what effect would David's death have on their son? One of her psychology professors once said that a bad father was better than no father at all. Somehow, she'd hoped that Eric might mature and take an interest in David. Maybe even act like a real father. Now, there was no chance of that ever happening.

"You'll notice we're only a couple miles out of town, but it feels like we're in the country. There's more open space."

Maggie wondered if J.D.'s change of subject was intentional. As if they could pretend she were just another guest in town for the reunion.

Whatever his reasoning, Maggie was relieved to pretend for a few moments that everything was right with the world. She focused on the expanse of green beyond the glass—every conceivable shade from sage to hunter. Once in a while, there would be a cluster of two or three brick ranch houses. Even more rare were elegant-looking two-storied homes that had great white columns creating a front porch. The yards were huge by Phoenix standards and unbelievably green. Some sported large vegetable gardens.

Despite his complaints about the simple life here, Maggie half suspected Eric had made McGuireville his safe haven between adventures. There was something timeless and comforting about the place—or at least she supposed it might seem that way under different circumstances.

"We're almost there." J.D.'s voice interrupted her thoughts.

"It's a nice neighborhood."

"Yes, it is."

J.D. steered into a long, circular drive made up of cinder rock. "Here we are." His voice was light, but she could feel his gaze on her face, as if assessing her reaction.

"It's beautiful," she breathed.

J.D.'s eyes sparked with pride. "I bought it as a repo. The owners defaulted on the mortgage and it stood vacant for a couple years. It's one of the few colonial reproductions in the area."

"The two-story houses with big pillars? Those are colonial reproductions?"

"Yep. I'll grab your bags while you get David."

Maggie got out of the car and stretched her cramped muscles. She felt as if she had walked into a dream. The house, J.D., Eric's murder, it was all surreal.

David rubbed his eyes and yawned when she opened the car door.

"Come on, sweetie. We're going to stay at Uncle J.D.'s house for a while." How long, she had no idea. Maggie tried to pretend this was a normal visit and not the living nightmare she knew it to be. There was no use upsetting David. "And you and I will have a real bed to sleep in. Won't that be nice?"

The baby waved his approval.

Maggie settled him on her hip, pulling the hem of his shirt down over his tummy. She inhaled deeply. The air carried the scent of honeysuckle. It seemed like years since she'd been in Arizona, yet it was only a matter of days. The slow, sleepy pace of the South wasn't all that different from the laid-back Southwest.

The trunk slammed and J.D. came around the side of the car with her suitcase. "Ready?" he asked.

"Yes."

The cool shade was a welcome relief as she climbed the steps to the porch. The atmosphere of old-fashioned homeyness surprised her. Several rustic rockers were grouped together, a perfect spot to watch the sunset and chat.

It was somehow easy for her to visualize J.D. relaxing and enjoying the view, but she doubted Eric had ever joined him. Eric couldn't sit still long enough.

Maggie swallowed hard. Eric had been very, very still the last time she'd seen him. She just couldn't reconcile the body she'd seen with the larger-than-life father of her child.

J.D. opened the screen door and then the simple carved oak door, holding it wide for her to pass.

Stepping over the threshold, Maggie stumbled. Fatigue made her clumsy.

J.D. grasped her arm to steady her. "You okay?"

Maggie managed to right herself by sheer force of will. "I'm fine. Just tired." Glancing at his face, she tried to assess his mood. His expression was remote, polite, not that of a man grieving for his murdered brother. Did he not feel, or did he just not show it? "How are you, um, holding up?" she asked.

Surprise sparked briefly in his solemn eyes. "Don't

worry about me. I'll be fine. But, um, thanks for asking." For a split second his shoulders sagged. Then he straightened, tall, strong, in control. He gestured toward the living room. "Make yourself at home. I'm hoping Belmont can get this mess straightened out quickly. Confirm your alibi with the hotel staff."

"I hope so."

Though Maggie was exhausted, David seemed recharged by his nap in the car. He squealed his approval of the place, wiggling to get down.

Maggie eyed the floor, her protective instincts overriding her exhaustion. Hardwood gleamed, a burgundy Oriental area rug gave a splash of color. But not nearly enough padding should David bump his head. She held him close, which only infuriated him. He screeched and squirmed.

"Go ahead and put him down."

Maggie hesitated. Sighing, she placed her son on the rug. "He's probably too wound up to nap now."

J.D. nodded. "Looks like he's raring to go. How about if I put your bags in the guest room and then we head on over to my grandmother's house? She's very eager to meet you."

"I don't think so. Maybe after I've had some sleep—"

"I imagine you're exhausted, but she was very insistent about seeing you. Immediately, if not sooner." He frowned. "Patience isn't one of her virtues."

"You love her very much."

"Yes, I do. That's why I don't think this meeting is

a good idea, but she wouldn't listen to reason. Eric was her favorite. I hope you won't upset her."

"I'm not a monster, J.D. I wouldn't even think of broaching the subject of David right now." Maggie's heart ached at what the woman must be going through. "You said favorite? Eric always swore he was the black sheep."

"Beloved black sheep, maybe. My grandmother adores him. Always did, no matter how much trouble he made."

"I didn't intend to cause trouble for you or your grandmother. If there had been another way…"

"Why now? Why not right after your baby was born?"

Maggie sighed. "I was in love and I was foolish. Eric was with me the first month or so. He left, but I kept expecting him to come back. It took me a while to realize he wasn't going to."

"If you thought you were married, why didn't you divorce him?"

"Attorneys cost money, Mr. McGuire. I figured he'd file. Maybe I was hoping he'd reconsidered."

"At least you have an alibi. All the sheriff has to do is confirm it with the hotel staff."

Maggie was confused. "I was there. At the track. They didn't tell you?"

J.D. froze. His eyes narrowed. "They didn't tell me anything. Just that you'd been brought in for questioning and had asked them to call me. I figured the only reason you were being questioned was the fiasco at the banquet. I thought you'd agreed not to leave the hotel."

"No, I didn't agree. You assumed."

"Semantics." He grasped her arms, his voice harsh when he said, "Tell me the truth. Did you kill my brother?"

"No, I didn't. He was dead when I got there."

"Why should I believe you?"

"Why shouldn't you? There were certainly enough other people who might want to see him dead."

He glanced down at her arms, where his fingers dug into her flesh. He dropped her arms as if he'd been burned. "But I know them. I don't know you."

"If the sheriff really thought I did it, he wouldn't have released me. Can we argue this another time? I'm about ready to drop."

"No way. We're gonna hash this out before I let you anywhere near my grandmother. Tell me what happened and I'll judge for myself."

Maggie drew a breath and counted to ten. Then she told him everything.

"Okay, your story is plausible. But my bet is that you were hopping mad when you met with Eric. He'd made a fool of you."

Maggie winced.

"Maybe things got out of hand and you grabbed the knife...."

"I did *not* kill Eric. I didn't even get the chance to talk to him. He was already dead."

"So you say. Just like you claim he married you."

"Of course he married me. I have the wedding license to prove it."

He raised an eyebrow. "So prove it."

"The license is safe at home. And filed with the State of Arizona. Check it out if you don't believe me."

"Oh, I will. I've already contacted a private detective."

"You did what?"

"Look, sweetheart, this isn't anything new. You aren't the first woman to breeze through town claiming to have a romantic involvement with my brother. Although, I hope you'll be the last, God rest Eric's soul."

Maggie saw red. "I can prove I'm his wife. And I'm not going to let you brush us away as if we were dirt. David deserves better than that. I deserve better than that."

He eyed her thoughtfully. "Documents can be altered. But one way or the other, I'll figure it out."

"And what if I'm telling the truth? What then? Are you going to welcome me to the family with open arms?"

His mouth tightened. "Sweetheart, if your story holds up and that kid is my brother's, I'll be the first in line. But that doesn't change the fact that both my grandmother and Nancy are going through a difficult time." His voice grew rough. "Eric's death hit us all pretty hard. The last thing we need is you running around telling wild stories."

"Isn't that why you brought me here? To make sure I don't run around telling stories about the sainted Eric McGuire?"

"He wasn't a saint. But he was my brother. And I won't have you upsetting my grandmother. If that means I have to babysit you for a couple days, I'm willing to do it. My grandmother and Eric's wife, his *real* wife, deserve to mourn his death in peace."

"You don't get it, do you? *I'm* his real wife. In here." She tapped her index finger on her breastbone as her eyes filled with moisture, blurring her vision. "And I'm the mother of his child. Yes, it's despicable if he married me while he was still married to another woman. But it's not my fault. And it won't change the fact that he's dead. Or the fact that his son will grow up fatherless."

J.D.'s eyes reflected the loss she described, but only for a second. Then his expression grew closed, as if he were afraid to let anyone see inside.

Her throat tightened. Wiping her cheeks, Maggie drew in a shaky breath. She gestured toward David, sitting near a burnished coffee table. "How can you hold it against an innocent child? He didn't ask for any of this."

J.D. folded his arms over his chest, but his face softened as he watched the baby scoot across the floor on all fours. David's tiny hands made little slapping sounds against the wood as he made a beeline for a corner shelving unit, where some old, rusty tools were displayed. Several had sharp edges.

Unable to get her brain and feet to connect, Maggie watched helplessly.

J.D. was quick on his feet and scooped up the boy in the nick of time. "Oh, no, you don't, buddy."

David giggled.

"You like that, huh?" J.D. grinned, tossing the baby up in the air. His smile grew wider as David laughed and clapped his hands. "You're a little daredevil, aren't you?"

"Just like his daddy," Maggie whispered.

MAGGIE SIPPED HER ICED TEA and wished she were anyplace else but McGuireville. She sat in the sunroom of Eric's childhood home watching his grandmother and brother argue over whether she'd told them the sordid truth about her pseudomarriage to Eric and the circumstances of David's birth. It seemed surreal that the news had superceded Eric's murder, but she supposed it was a way of coping.

Edna McGuire sat opposite Maggie on a wicker love seat and J.D. paced nearby.

"Paternity tests are ninety-nine point nine percent reliable," J.D. said.

The old woman stiffened. Her nostrils flared with indignation. The slight tremor to her hand and bluish tint around her mouth was the only indication that she might not be as hale and hearty as she wanted to pretend. "Nonsense. It's not seemly. No need to draw attention to the fact that Eric's child is a bast…was born on the wrong side of the blanket. Your father must be rolling over in his grave. Anyone can see the baby is a McGuire through and through."

J.D.'s face flushed like a reprimanded boy. His tone was slightly belligerent. "Not seemly? This whole thing isn't seemly. It's just like you to open your heart and your home to some woman with a hard-luck story and a baby she claims is Eric's. You know as well as I do it's not Eric's child."

Maggie swallowed hard. The two had apparently forgotten her presence. How could anyone even think of using such a despicable term as *bastard* to describe David? But J.D.'s insinuation stung as much as his grandmother's assessment. It seemed like a betrayal coming from the man who had rescued her only hours earlier.

"Don't you take that tone with me James David. I know my own flesh and blood when I see it. My great-grandchild will stay with me. Tests or no tests."

"We've been over this before. There's no need for you to undergo the added stress. The funeral will be hard enough. Maggie and, um, David will stay with me until the paternity tests come back. Then, if they come back positive, you can cuddle and fuss over the child to your heart's content. Spoil him rotten for all I care."

The old woman tried to stand, but sank back to the love seat. Her pallor was a pasty gray.

"The funeral," she mumbled. Big, sad tears rolled down her cheeks and plopped onto her lap, leaving spots on her navy shirtdress.

The woman's grief pulled at Maggie. It was an instinctive reaction that went back to her childhood. Grief touched something inside her, some well of empathy that made counseling the bereaved seem more like a calling than a job.

She went to the older woman. Holding David close to her chest, she knelt at Mrs. McGuire's feet and gazed up into her stricken face. "I know this is a hard time and you don't know me that well. I'm grateful that you've invited me into your home, considering, well, the circumstances."

Mrs. McGuire waved her hand, as if she could wave away the pesky details like bigamy, murder and an illegitimate child. "Nonsense. I'm a good judge of character I don't believe for a minute you had anything to do with Eric's death. And you've obviously told the truth about the baby. Why, he could be Eric at the same age."

"Thank you. It means a lot that you believe me."

Maggie thought she heard a snort come from J.D.'s direction, but ignored him.

The woman grasped one of David's waving hands. Blinking back tears, she said, "He is such a handsome boy. Eric was a treasure, too. Such a good, kind child with a smile that could light up a room."

J.D. cleared his throat.

Maggie hesitated, wondering how much to reveal. Certainly not the bad stuff. Now wasn't the time. "I know. That's what I loved about him. Eric was always smiling, always telling jokes." Her heart ached as she realized her words weren't just empty platitudes. She would miss Eric, too, and that really made her mad. Mad that he could still tug on her emotions, even after all he'd done. Even when he was dead.

Mrs. McGuire sighed. "He had such a big heart."

"Yes, he had a big heart." Apparently big enough to love more than one woman at a time. She forced the thought from her mind. Maggie would untangle her marital status later. She rose slowly.

J.D. moved beside her. It made her uncomfortable having him so close. The warning in his eyes told her that was his intention.

Grasping her arm, he herded her toward the door. "We'll get you and the baby settled at my place."

His voice softened as he turned toward his grandmother. "Why don't you go rest for a while? I'll be back later to take care of the...arrangements."

"I still think it would be better if we stayed at the hotel," Maggie insisted.

"And let you out of my sight? No way."

"We don't need your help."

"You're thousands of miles away from home, no place to stay, no money, no food—"

He held up a hand to stop her protest.

"I know, I know. You lost your debit card. But for

the sake of argument, if you were broke, without a roof over your head, no food to eat, how would that look to the authorities? To the Department of Children and Family Services? You know they're going to keep a close eye on you. Wouldn't it be better to show you have, um, friends in the community?"

Maggie swallowed her pride yet again. Nothing was worth risking losing David. "I guess I don't have a choice."

"You always have a choice. But I'm the best bet you've got." The statement was made with the quiet conviction of a man accustomed to calling the shots.

She watched her son grab J.D.'s strong, condescending nose. The guy's eyes widened as the little baby claws sunk in for a better grip. Then yanked, hard.

Instead of the yowl of outrage she expected, the man looked at the baby. The baby stared back. Then grabbed J.D.'s ear with his free hand and pulled.

A smile twitched at J.D.'s lips.

"Quide a grib."

"I beg your pardon?"

J.D. gently removed the tiny fingers from the bridge of his nose.

"I said, quite a grip."

Maggie tried not to smile at his comeuppance. The reserved, very respectable man had five tiny indented half-moons on his nose. She really had to clip David's nails, first chance she got.

"You sure you're ready for this? Us? At your house?"

He rolled his eyes and disengaged his ear from the small fist.

"Lord help me, I better be."

CHAPTER FIVE

J.D. TUCKED HIS GRANDMOTHER'S hand in the crook of his arm and led her to the front pew. He steadied her as she sank onto the polished mahogany seat next to Nancy.

Nancy greeted him quietly. Then she patted Grandma's shoulder and murmured what he assumed was some sort of encouragement.

He bowed his head and briefly prayed for the improbable—that Nancy wouldn't notice Maggie sitting in the back row. Maggie'd almost begged for a ride to the service, her eyes bright with unshed tears. He hadn't doubted the sincerity of her emotion, simply the logistics of keeping a heartbreakingly solemn event from turning into a circus.

He'd finally agreed to bring Maggie on the condition she entered the chapel late, left early and waited in the car for him when it was over.

J.D. resisted the urge to turn around and check to see that she'd honored their deal. Today was about Eric and family. He needed to focus on the important stuff.

So he quieted his worries and simply let the reality

of Eric's death pervade him. All around him, others seemed to be following his lead. The hush of restrained grief echoed in his head. The overpowering scent of flowers made him want to flee. He glanced at the flowers, the decor, his shoes, anything but the casket. Or the still figure inside.

His stomach lurched. His face flushed.

The past and the present meshed in his mind. His dad's funeral had been horrible. The flowers, the heat, the odor of death, barely masked by talcum powder. The fear that life would never be the same again. The sickening knowledge that it would be J.D. and his mom on their own. What would they do without his strong dad to keep them safe?

An uncle had nudged J.D. toward the casket. He hadn't wanted to see or touch his father. But his uncle had insisted. So the five-year-old boy had slowly approached the coffin and the stiff, gray figure inside.

"Give him a kiss," his uncle had commanded.

So he'd complied. His lips had touched the chilled waxy surface of his dad's cheek and it was all he could do to keep from vomiting. There had to have been some mistake. This plastic, doll-like thing was not his father. It didn't even smell like his dad. Maybe the funeral was all some horrible mistake and his dad was alive somewhere in a hospital or something.

He had to know for sure. J.D. tentatively reached inside the casket and touched the jacket sleeve. His dad had a mole on his right wrist. Pulling back the sleeve a couple inches, his mouth filled with hot saliva as he noted the mole. This…this thing was all that was left of his wonderful, laughing dad.

J.D. felt the room tilt and the past fell away, leaving him sweating profusely.

He tried to focus on the present, and paying his respects to Eric, the half brother with whom he'd shared a mother and a grandmother, but not much else in recent years.

Placing one foot in front of the other, J.D. moved beyond the flower arrangements, straight to the shiny wood box. Yellow satin lining, yellow satin pillow.

Not Eric's style. Maybe crimson or black silk, but never yellow. They should have presented him clutching a G-string or lace teddy. Then J.D. would be able to believe it was his little brother lying pale, still and silent in that box. A sad reminder of the little brother he'd watched over, protected and loved. The same brother he'd despised, and, on more than one occasion as a boy, tormented.

It was hard to believe that overgrown Ken doll in the casket was Eric. But he knew it was true.

Closing his eyes, J.D. hoped it was the room swaying and not him. Bright lights spun behind his eyelids.

He had to get out of here.

Turning, he stumbled down the center aisle. It took tremendous concentration to walk slowly to the foyer instead of breaking into a dead run.

Dead run.

J.D. shook his head at his own morbid pun as he entered the foyer and spotted the exit doors. It would be so easy to keep on going out those doors. No, he owed it to Eric to stay. He owed it to his grandmother to stay. He had to get himself together.

So he found a quiet corner and leaned back against the wall, closing his eyes.

Someone pulled at his elbow. A soft, sweet voice sent comforting vibes through the haze.

"Are you sick?"

Cool fingers pressed against his wrist.

He nodded, disoriented and unwilling to open his eyes. "I'm okay. But the guy in the box isn't doing so good."

Damn, more morbid humor.

"Eric's not hurting. But you are."

J.D. cranked open one eye. The woman's features were blurry, ill defined. But she looked familiar, even in his fuddled state.

"Can you walk?"

Finally, the light-headedness dissipated and he opened both eyes to see copper hair and skin so fine it took his breath away. Freckles invited his touch, right there across the bridge of her nose. He reached out, but the angel's voice interrupted him, her instructions gentle, but firm. "There are people here depending on you. Will you follow me inside?"

He shook his head.

"Listen, you can do this. Take a couple deep breaths. In, out."

J.D. followed her instructions and was surprised when the sick feeling eased a bit.

"Ready?"

He straightened his spine and nodded.

"Okay."

The gentle, compassionate woman tucked his hand in the crook of her arm, much as he'd done with his grandmother. She led him into the chapel, stopping a couple rows from the front.

"You can make it the rest of the way on your own. I'll be in the back row like we agreed. If you need me, just signal," Maggie whispered. Then she was gone.

She was right. J.D. was able to make it the rest of the way on his own. He sat next to his grandmother and drew strength from her. He could feel her beside him, back straight as a board, silent in her grief.

Damn. He'd been determined to see her through this the way she always had for him. How could he be her rock, her anchor, when he felt so lost himself?

He forced himself to think of a favorite place in the Smoky Mountains, but his mind turned to Maggie. She'd smoothed her thick, copper curls into some sort of looped braid. And her voice. Why hadn't he noticed the perfect pitch of her voice before? He sighed.

He wished she'd come back and distract him some more. Run those cool hands over his face. Make it all go away.

But she couldn't. Nothing changed the fact that Eric was dead. And no matter how much J.D. wanted to make it all better, it was beyond his control. Him. The big brother who made everything right.

Failure washed over him in waves. He should have been there. He should have protected his brother.

J.D. twisted in the seat, searching for an escape route. Then, in the very back row, a pair of green eyes held his gaze. Maggie's presence reassured him. Calmed him. She understood what he was going through and expected no superhuman effort—just that he get through the funeral.

He idly wondered where she'd secreted the boy while she helped him. The kid was now happily ensconced on her lap.

Shaking his head, he decided the details didn't matter. Knowing she was there made it possible for him to get through the service and even stay behind in the foyer, shaking hands, accepting condolences, making the appropriate responses. And every once in a while, he'd catch a glimpse of Maggie in the background, a constant source of encouragement.

It seemed like hours later when the last guest offered his sympathies and left.

J.D. looked up and saw Maggie.

Slowly, she nodded her approval.

It was humbling, letting a woman see his weakness, yet surprisingly liberating. As if she knew the worst, most cowardly part of his soul and didn't judge him for it. The irony didn't escape him. But it seemed right to have set aside his reservations and offered shelter to

Maggie and her son. In turn, she'd offered him shelter when he'd needed it most.

"There she is," his grandmother whispered, indicating Maggie. "I knew she'd come to pay her respects. She loved Eric. I could tell."

J.D. swallowed a lump in his throat. "Yes, I guess she did."

His grandmother called out, waving to her. "May I hold my great-grandson? It would do me good on such a sad, sad day."

Maggie hesitated for a moment, then stepped forward and handed the sleepy boy to the older woman. "Certainly. You're always welcome to hold him."

"Come here, precious angel," J.D.'s grandmother crooned.

David studied her, frowning. Finally, he reached up and patted her lined cheek.

J.D.'s chest grew tight. It was the first time he'd seen his grandmother smile in several very long days. Hugging the child close, she said, "Yes, you're a precious one."

Then she turned, still holding the baby, and marched out the double doors. "David can ride with me in the limousine to the wake. Nancy is riding with Roy. J.D., you can follow with Maggie," she said over her shoulder.

Maggie's face paled. "No, I can't. Wait, where are you taking my son? Come back. He needs a car seat. He needs me." There was a note of panic in her voice.

J.D. touched her shoulder. "Apparently she's taking him to her house. I bet the limo has a built-in car seat. Come on, I'll drive."

MAGGIE USED J.D. as a human shield as they made their way through the crowd of mourners, many of whom shot her dirty looks. Whispers followed.

Holding her head high, she tried not to think of how she must seem to them. Instead of seeing Eric's estranged wife and mother of his child, they saw The Other Woman. A woman brazenly flaunting herself at Eric's wake.

She grasped J.D.'s arm and halted his progress. "I have to get out of here."

"Tough crowd, huh?" He tilted his head, his eyes questioning.

"I don't belong here." She turned and pushed her way through the press of people, ignoring the hurtful whispers and the realization that no one met her gaze. The truth was, she didn't belong much of anywhere, at least where family was concerned—Eric's or her own.

Another funeral came to mind. Another person she'd loved dying too young. For a moment, it seemed as if she could feel Cassie there beside her, encouraging her to be brave, to fight for her son and her future. Ironic, because Cassie had committed the utmost act of surrender—she'd killed herself.

Maggie felt a hand on her shoulder and turned, half expecting to see her sister. But the person detaining her was very much alive and very much a threat, though he seemed genuinely concerned at times. He was still a McGuire and she'd best remember his loyalties would naturally be to the McGuires.

"Are you okay?" J.D. asked.

"I will be. Once I get my son and get out of here."

Maggie pushed her way through the crowd to reach Edna. Holding out her arms to David, she said, "We have to go."

David grinned at her through a mouthful of crumbs. He clutched a sugar cookie in each hand. But he didn't move.

"He's being such a good little boy," Edna crooned. Raising her chin to address Maggie, her mouth thinned. "Stay just a little longer." It wasn't a request.

"A few more minutes," Maggie murmured and stepped away from the crush of people.

There was a commotion near the front door, where a beautiful blonde dabbed her eyes and accepted sympathetic hugs and handshakes. A short, stocky man followed behind her, cupping her elbow solicitously.

Turning away, Maggie suppressed a pang of longing, wishing she could find comfort in the collective embrace of Eric's friends and relatives instead of rejection and suspicion. Maggie longed for a safe, sympathetic resting place where she could give in to the confusion and grief lodged in her chest. But after that, she feared anger would follow. Anger, betrayal and envy. Emotions she could barely admit to herself, yet they simmered beneath the surface, demanding to be heard, demanding release.

Maggie felt firm pressure on her arm.

She looked up to see J.D.

He nodded toward the baby and his grandmother. "I take it she's not about to give him up yet? At least not without a fight?"

Nodding, Maggie fidgeted with her purse. The room seemed to close in on her. Her breathing grew shallow.

"How about if we wander over to the kitchen? I'll come get David for you in a couple of minutes." His voice was reassuring in the midst of her anxiety. He, at least, was somewhat familiar.

"I—"

"Please? You look like you could use a break." He glanced toward the blonde. "None of this is Nancy's fault. She doesn't deserve a scene any more than you do."

Maggie hesitated, resisting the urge to understand what the other woman might be going through, the urge to understand her own conflicting emotions. Anger rippled through Maggie. Anger at a dead man for putting her in the position of feeling sorry for Nancy. Anger that she felt obligated to hide out because of his sins.

But then the anger dissipated as quickly as it had come. J.D. was right. Nancy was as much a victim as she.

Nodding, Maggie allowed J.D. to lead her to the

kitchen, where she did the one thing guaranteed to give her peace. She watched her son through the doorway.

David gazed up at his great-grandmother with adoration.

Mrs. McGuire bounced the baby on her lap as she accepted condolences from Belmont, the attorney who J.D. had persuaded to come to Maggie's rescue. When he turned, his eyes were shadowed with sadness. Funny, she'd not thought him the emotional type.

As if reading her mind, J.D. commented, "Belmont was like a father to Eric. They were very close."

"Oh," she murmured.

The sound of David's giggle caught her attention. Mrs. McGuire tickled him under the chin, the way Maggie did. Her stomach tightened at the sight. She loved her child so much it hurt. She longed to snatch him from the woman, rush out of the house and out of town, never to return.

David was hers, and hers alone. All she had left since her parents had disowned her and disavowed David.

But now, David had more. A whole family. Wasn't that what she wanted for him? A secure future. A safety net in case anything ever happened to her?

"Thank you."

Maggie started at the deep voice so close to her ear. She turned to frown at J.D.

"What?"

He nodded toward his grandmother, holding court with David.

"Thank you for being kind to her. Letting her cuddle the boy. Letting her remember that life goes on."

"She didn't give me much choice."

"Yeah. Grandma can be that way." His mouth tightened. "I just hate to see her get her hopes up."

"About David?"

He nodded.

Maggie's cheeks burned. "In that case, don't worry. Your grandmother won't be disappointed by the paternity test."

He held her gaze for a long moment. "I was asked to tell you that Belmont wants to see you at his office tomorrow for the reading of the will."

"Eric had a will?"

J.D. tilted his head to the side, his eyes narrowed. "It's pretty common knowledge my stepfather left a trust fund for him. It only stands to reason Eric would have a will. I can't imagine you wouldn't know, after all, husbands and wives share that kind of stuff."

Maggie's heart plummeted. How could she have been so naive? "There was apparently a lot I didn't know about Eric."

She had only herself to blame for accepting a small portion of what a marriage should be. But in her own defense, she had never seen a good marriage, up close and personal. Her parents, though married nearly forty years, certainly weren't a good example. Her father ruled the house with an iron fist—his God-given right, or so he'd said. And her mother had been the dutiful wife. But Maggie had never observed them share a tender moment, or even a smile, for that matter. Life was serious business, obedience paramount.

But Maggie had eventually realized blind obedience got her nowhere. Once she was no longer compliant, her life as Joe and Martha Sinclair's daughter had ended. But Maggie would be damned if she'd allow herself to be another casualty like Cassie. Refused to even consider surrender.

Raising her chin, Maggie said, "You're wrong. There's no way he had access to that kind of money. If Eric had a trust fund, he would have sponsored his own stock car and everything would have been top of the line."

"That's the whole point. He blew half his inheritance the first year racing. He wouldn't have received the second half until he turned thirty. And you claim you never knew?"

Maggie shook her head. "He had a sponsor by the time I met him. Things got really tough when his sponsor fired him. He said nobody in the family would loan him money."

"Exactly. Even Grandma wasn't going to give him more money to throw away."

"Belmont wants me there?"

"I imagine there's something in there that would affect you." J.D.'s mouth tightened. "If I'd known Eric had had Belmont draw up his will, I wouldn't have asked him to represent you. I figured Eric had an out-of-town attorney he'd used for this kind of stuff."

"It shouldn't be a problem, because I had no part in Eric's death. What's more, I had no idea he had a will. You can believe me or not, it's your choice."

"Yes, it is my choice. But until I decide if I believe you, I have family to protect. So you'll excuse me if I'm not in a big rush to make that decision."

J.D.'s intensity made Maggie step backward. Gone was the unemotional man who'd rescued her from the sheriff's office. Gone was the vulnerable guy struggling to function at his brother's funeral. Instead, J.D. was letting her know just what a tough adversary he could be. And she would be foolish to ignore his warning. "I don't know where the meeting is. If you'll give me the address, I'm sure I can find it."

His voice was terse when he said, "You can ride with me. The meeting's at one o'clock at Belmont's office. Be ready at twelve-thirty."

The conversation was obviously finished. But Maggie still needed some answers, needed to know what she would be walking into. "Will the rest of the family be there?"

"Yes. Unless you want to pay Belmont's fee for a private session."

"No, that won't be necessary. I'll be there tomorrow. For David's sake."

"Yes, for David's sake." His tone was flat, his face expressionless. It was impossible to tell if he believed her or was being sarcastic.

"Thank you, I would appreciate the ride." Maggie

managed a tight smile. "Now, it's way past my son's nap time. If you'll excuse me."

Glancing neither right nor left, she entered the living room and headed toward her son. She would keep her dignity even if the women around her whispered behind their hands. Even if the blonde sitting next to the old woman flashed her a killing look.

Maggie reached for her child. "It's time for David's nap. If you need him…us, all you have to do is call."

"Thank you dear—"

"How dare you?" The blond woman's voice was raw with pain. "How dare you show up here? And at his funeral? Flaunting yourself and your child. Embarrassing his family."

"Nancy," Mrs. McGuire chided, "I know you're grieving, dear. But now's not the time or the place."

David squirmed in her lap. Confusion welled in his eyes. He held out his arms for Maggie and this time Mrs. McGuire let him go.

Nancy's face crumpled, tears streamed.

Regret tore at Maggie. Nancy hadn't asked for this crummy situation, either. "I tried—"

"You had no right. *He* had no right," Nancy whispered, tears spilling down her cheeks.

The woman was correct in one respect. Eric had no right to escape taking responsibility for this mess, even through death.

"I'm sorry for your loss," Maggie murmured. Then she turned and walked out the front door.

Maggie didn't realize tears trickled down her face until she was halfway down the block. She didn't know where she was going and she didn't care.

David patted her neck, a frown scrunching up his little baby forehead.

"I can't do it, David. I just can't."

He smiled at the sound of his name. It took so little to make him happy.

Gratitude chased away her tears. She had a happy, healthy, precious little boy. Maggie hugged her greatest blessing close to her heart until he wriggled with impatience.

"I'll try, David. For you, I'll try."

CHAPTER SIX

THE TOYOTA WASN'T FAST, but J.D. figured Maggie didn't have much of a head start. Thank goodness he'd pocketed the keys instead of returning them to her at the funeral home.

Where in the hell did the woman think she was going?

Maybe he should let her go. A part of him wished she and her child would simply vanish into thin air. It would make his life simpler.

But the authorities would drag her back, resulting in certain jail time and a legal free-for-all for custody of David. No, she needed to hang around long enough for the sheriff to determine whether Maggie was all she said to be or if she was a cold-blooded, murdering gold digger.

Shaking his head, J.D. realized he had a hard time viewing her in those terms. The compassionate woman at the funeral was no killer. But was she a gold digger? Or simply delusional?

J.D. squinted into the sun. A tension headache throbbed at his temples and tightened the muscles in his neck.

He slowed when he saw the figure walking along the side of the road.

"Get in."

Maggie turned and frowned. For a minute he thought she might refuse. Then she glanced at David and shrugged. For the boy, she'd accept another favor. Otherwise she probably would have told him to go to hell.

J.D. put the car in Park and set the emergency brake. Once David and Maggie were both settled, he breathed a sigh of relief, refusing to admit he'd been worried.

"Where were you going?" J.D. hoped the question didn't sound as curt to her as it did to him.

"I don't know. Anywhere but back there."

"You don't look much before you leap, do you?"

She raised her chin. "I'm very responsible."

J.D.'s patience was about shot. His head pounded, he was hot and sweaty and definitely not in the mood to humor her.

"What kind of responsible woman falls for Eric's BS and drags her child halfway across the country looking for a handout?"

He regretted the words almost immediately, but it was too late to take them back.

Maggie's face flamed, her shoulders stiffened.

"I'm sor—"

"No, you aren't. And in answer to your questions, number one, I was very naive when I met Eric. He could sell a woman the Golden Gate Bridge if he wanted to.

Number two, people take cross-country trips with their children all the time. Number three, I'm not looking for a handout. I only want what is rightfully David's. Number four, I would give my life for my son."

J.D. sighed. He felt lower than a puddle of snake slobber. "I know you would. I've seen how much you love him. I'm sorry."

Glancing at Maggie, he was surprised to see her eyes fill with tears.

"Now what?"

"It's nothing."

"It's something. Tell me."

"I'm just tired and emotional. And I find it hard to stay mad when you turn around and do something kind."

Clearing his throat, he decided to leave that one alone. Maggie's acknowledgment of his help made him uneasy, wondering how in the heck he could like her one minute and suspect her of murder the next. And made him wish he'd been as kind as she seemed to think. "Where to? My house? A little peace and quiet might help."

She nodded. "David needs a nap."

"Probably wouldn't hurt for you to have one, too."

Maggie nodded slowly. "Maybe I'll sleep while David sleeps. It's been a...hard day."

J.D. nodded. "For all of us. I just hope it wasn't too much for my grandmother."

"She was very good to David."

J.D. recalled his grandmother's absorption with the baby. He reminded himself there was very little reason to believe the child was his nephew. Because, if by some miracle David was Eric's son, that would change everything. Everything he'd worked toward since the day he'd arrived in McGuireville as a six-year-old fatherless kid.

But if David was his nephew, how could he live with himself if he didn't try to ensure the boy's future?

"Um, yeah, she seems quite taken with the kid. He was pretty good through the funeral and wake and stuff."

"Yes, he was. But if he doesn't get some consistent sleep, he won't stay that way. All I want to do is get him home to his own bed."

"In Phoenix?"

"Yes."

"Looks like you're stuck here. At least until Belmont can persuade the judge to give you permission to leave the state."

Maggie gazed out the window. "When do you think that will be?"

"Don't know. We can talk to Belmont about it tomorrow after the reading of the will."

"We?"

"I'd like to see if he knows anything new about the investigation."

Shrugging her shoulders, Maggie said, "I suppose it's okay."

J.D. took a deep breath. "And get a referral for the paternity testing."

J.D. HAD BEEN IN BELMONT'S corner office many times, but never had he been this uneasy. He shifted in the cushy leather chair and attempted to get comfortable. Then he realized nothing short of a miracle would lessen the tension.

As if by some sadistic twist of fate, J.D. was book-ended by both of Eric's wives—Maggie on his right, Nancy on his left. He didn't know whether to be re-lieved or suspicious that his grandmother hadn't felt well enough to attend. *He* certainly would have liked to have been anywhere else.

A soft sniffle came from his left.

"Um, how are you holding up?" he asked Nancy.

Her eyes were red and puffy. "Okay, I guess."

What more could he say or do? Nancy had been his sister-in-law for years and he genuinely cared for her. Yet he'd championed the woman who caused her pain. He was grateful he'd convinced Maggie to leave the baby with his next-door neighbor. If David were in the room, J.D. had the feeling Nancy might spontaneously combust.

Glancing at Maggie, he noted her ramrod posture and the way her hands fidgeted. He resisted the urge to still her restless fingers.

Belmont's arrival broke the silence as he rushed in. "I'm sorry I'm late." He looked tired and sad.

J.D. raised an eyebrow when he saw the second man. It was his own business partner. "Roy?"

Roy nodded. "I'm here to support Nancy." He took the empty seat next to Eric's widow.

J.D. wondered if he'd been hasty discounting the rumors whispered here and there. Rumors that Nancy and Roy spent an awful lot of time alone together, during odd hours of the day and night, and only when Eric was out of town. He generally believed about a tenth of what he heard through the town grapevine, but maybe this time he'd stuck his head in the sand, refusing to consider anyone betraying his brother.

Shaking his head, J.D. couldn't believe his own hypocrisy. Eric hadn't hesitated to step out on Nancy so why should it surprise him if she did the same?

Because despite all else, J.D. wanted to believe in the sanctity of marriage. He wanted to believe with his whole heart that the kind of love his mother and stepfather had shared was more than a figment of his imagination.

Documents rustled as Belmont withdrew papers from a brown, accordion-pleated file. He took a seat behind his polished mahogany desk. Clearing his throat, he said, "I'm sorry we're meeting under such sad conditions. We'll go ahead and get started. The will is fairly simple. Eric made a few small bequests to various racing friends. I'll advise them by mail. And I'll drop by your grandmother's house in the next couple days."

"Thanks. I'm sure she'd appreciate that," J.D. said.

Belmont shuffled papers until he apparently came to the correct page. "'To J.D., my half brother, I leave the following items.'" The attorney handed J.D. a list.

J.D. folded the paper without a glance and slid it into his breast pocket. He didn't give a damn what Eric had left him. He wanted his brother back.

"And the rest will go to Nancy."

Nancy murmured something and dabbed at her eyes. Roy patted her knee.

J.D. resisted the urge to remove Roy's hand. The room suddenly seemed awfully close, the air hot and stifling. He rose. "Thanks, Belmont. I'll be—"

"Wait. There's one clause."

"Clause?" J.D. sank to his chair.

"Yes. Nancy receives the bulk of Eric's estate only if he died without fathering children. It was his wish to have his estate divided equally among his children, with Nancy retaining deed to the house on Maple Street."

J.D. glanced at Maggie. Her face had drained of color.

"What does that mean, Belmont?" Nancy asked.

"It means that if a paternity test confirms Eric fathered this woman's child—" he nodded toward Maggie "—then the boy will inherit the remainder of Eric's trust fund, which, though not a fortune, is a tidy sum. The mother, as legal guardian of the child, would be the administrator."

Nancy stood. "Let me get this straight. If my husband was fooling around and had a son, then I lose everything except the house?"

"Yes, that's right."

"But what if she killed him?" She pointed at Maggie.

"If she is convicted of killing Eric—" Belmont glanced at Maggie "—then the legal guardian of the child would administer the trust. For that reason, I need to meet with Maggie privately to discuss a possible conflict of interest if I represent her. I was remiss in not considering it sooner, but Eric's death was…a shock. My immediate concern was reuniting Maggie and her child as soon as possible."

"I can't believe you're giving that woman the time of day." Nancy pushed past J.D. and Maggie to get to the door, with Roy following closely.

J.D. stood. "Nancy—"

The door closed behind her with an emphatic click.

Running a hand over his head, J.D. felt like a jerk. Divided loyalties weren't something he dealt with much. He was an all-or-nothing kind of guy. This tightrope he walked between the two women in his brother's life was unnerving.

Belmont waved him out. "Go talk to her. It'll give me a chance to discuss a few things with Maggie."

Maggie tried to grasp the import of Belmont's words as she watched J.D. leave the room.

"I'll wait in the lobby," he said, closing the door behind him.

Belmont cleared his throat, a harsh sound in the suddenly silent room. "Obviously, I'm handling the disposition of Eric's estate."

She nodded, not completely sure what she was agreeing to.

"And I handle legal matters for Edna McGuire. As I said, I may have a conflict of interest."

"I don't understand."

"I would be privy to details in your criminal case that might affect the outcome of any civil litigation."

Maggie's heart thudded. "What kind of civil litigation?"

"Oh, for instance…wrongful death, any challenges to the validity of Eric's will, that sort of thing. Your son stands to inherit roughly fifty thousand dollars. Wills have been contested for less."

"Fifty thousand dollars? You're sure?" She couldn't begin to comprehend that kind of money. Why, it would be enough to send David to a good college someday.

"Yes, I'm sure. So you can see why it's important to have another attorney handle your case.'

"But I don't know any other lawyers. J.D. said you're the best."

Belmont's mouth tightened. "He's right. I am the best. But I'll give you the names of a couple local at-torneys who are very competent, along with a few from the next county."

Maggie raised her chin and willed her voice to stay steady.

"I would appreciate that. I'll…ask around about their reputations." She'd almost said she would ask J.D. about them, but then she remembered the tension she'd sensed when he'd been in Belmont's office.

She wondered if his motives toward her were as pure as she wanted to believe. Or was he perhaps operating under a more personal conflict of interest?

Maggie felt more alone than she had in years as she watched the attorney scrawl several names on a yellow legal pad.

He tore off the list and handed it to her with obvious relief.

Nodding stiffly, she said, "Thank you for your time, Belmont."

"Best of luck to you." He ushered her out the door to the reception area.

Glancing around, she was relieved to see that Nancy wasn't there. Her nerves couldn't handle another one of the woman's accusations today.

J.D. stood, hands in pockets, staring out the huge picture window. She walked over and touched his sleeve. "J.D."

"Oh, done already?" He seemed distracted, as if his thoughts were focused on something in the world outside the window.

"Um, yes. It doesn't take long to get fired. I mean if an attorney can fire a client."

"Belmont's not handling your case? Why?"

"Conflict of interest. Something to do with your family already being his clients and the criminal case and wrongful death and civil litigation. A lot of big words that meant I'm on my own again."

"I'll go talk to him."

"No." She placed her hand on his arm. "Don't. He gave me a list of referrals. It's okay."

It surprised her to realize that, after the initial shock, she really was okay with Belmont dumping her case. "It might be for the best."

J.D.'s mouth tightened. "It darn well better be or Belmont will have some explaining to do."

A tiny spark of hope chased away the loneliness she'd experienced in the attorney's office. It had been a long time since someone had stood up for her and here she'd found a protector in the unlikeliest place.

"There's some place I need to go. Would you mind taking me to the cemetery where Eric's buried?" she asked.

He nodded toward her black sandals. "Maybe another day? It's an old cemetery out near the old highway. Sometimes it gets pretty overgrown."

"I don't mind. There are some things I need to sort out. I want to talk to Eric."

His face paled, he cleared his throat. "You're, um, sure you want to do that?"

Maggie couldn't tell if his reaction was because of her odd request to speak to a dead man or his seeming inability to cope with death.

She nodded. "I can handle a little rough terrain. We can pick up David at the sitter's. I don't like leaving him this long in a strange environment."

J.D. nodded slowly. "Don't say I didn't warn you."

J.D. WIPED THE SWEAT off his upper lip and wondered if the day could get any more humid. Late afternoon at the cemetery during the summer wasn't such a good idea. But it seemed important to Maggie, so he ignored the damp shirt sticking to his back.

He also ignored the fact that there were dead people somewhere beneath the headstones and markers. As long as he didn't allow his imagination to go beneath the surface, so to speak, he was okay.

Leaning against an oak tree, he watched Maggie grieve. Should he try to help? Hand her a tissue? What if she never stopped crying? He decided to do nothing. She seemed to have withdrawn into a world of her own that didn't include him.

He glanced around, trying to give her privacy. Eric had been buried in the McGuire family plot where newer headstones appeared relatively unscathed. Others, decades old, were crumbling hunks of granite, inscriptions barely readable.

Tension eased its grip on his shoulders as he relaxed for the first time in days. He shook his head at the irony of it all. He found the cemetery downright peaceful compared to the rest of his life. The deceased didn't bother him as long as they were six feet under. It was just when they were put on display that they totally creeped him out.

Maybe someday he'd come back and have his own conversation with his brother. Just not when there was anyone else around.

As it was, Maggie's crying made him uncomfortable. She held tightly to David while she sobbed. He had to wonder how his brother had managed to elicit such total devotion, even after he'd shown his true colors.

He also wondered why Maggie was suddenly assailed by grief.

A new cry went straight to his heart. It was David's bewildered screech melded with Maggie's sobs.

Stepping up behind her, he touched her arm.

She turned, her face wet, her eyes red. "I'm sorry, I got so wrapped up I almost forgot you were here."

J.D. held out his arms. "Let me take David."

Maggie frowned.

"He and I will take a walk while you…get this out of your system. I think you're scaring him."

She hesitated, then nodded, handing the boy to him.

The child's tears stopped and he studied J.D. solemnly. J.D. turned, patting David's back, and found a path through the overgrown lawn and shrubs.

"See the bird?" J.D. pointed at a flash of red—a cardinal.

The little boy waved his fists and babbled. J.D. supposed there was an approximation of "bird" in there somewhere.

They followed the path and he pointed out various flora and fauna. The child squealed with delight when a squirrel stood on its haunches and watched them. Then, with a quick flick of its tail, it raced up a tree.

"You like squirrels, huh?" J.D. couldn't help but smile at the child's joy. "You know something, kiddo, so do I. Since we seem to be pretty simpatico, maybe you could tell me what makes your mother tick. She's one complicated lady."

David had plenty to say, but none of it was in English.

Sighing, J.D. dusted off a weathered iron bench and sat. With no one watching, he could finally let down his guard, pretend he didn't have the weight of the McGuire world on his shoulders.

And wonder what the hell he was going to do with this colossal mess.

There was nothing he *could* do. Except wait for the paternity test to come back. And hope it came in quickly and in the negative. Otherwise, there'd be a whole new mess to contain.

Searching the baby's face, he tried to find a resemblance to Eric. He smoothed the child's downy blond hair, marveling at the softness. Eric's had been the same at that age. J.D. remembered patting him like a puppy dog, remembered how he had eagerly anticipated becoming a big brother. Little did the child of eight understand the responsibility that went along with the job.

And what a pain in the ass a little brother could be.

It seemed so long ago, the time when J.D. was an only child. He smiled, recalling how hard his mother had tried to make sure he felt included. The baby would be his baby, too, or so she'd told him. And his stepfather, the man he'd learned to call Dad, had perpetuated the myth.

Chuckling hollowly, he realized it was his grandmother who had set him straight. Not intentionally, of course. Making a fuss over the baby and noting all his McGuire features. J.D. had stepped aside, knowing he didn't have a single McGuire feature and, in fact, looked so much like his birth father he could never be mistaken for a McGuire by blood.

For that reason, he almost felt a kinship with the little guy sitting so trustingly on his knee. "Hey, buddy, you're not a McGuire either, are you? It's kind of a crummy hand life dealt you. No daddy. But your mom's really trying, kiddo. She loves you, that much I can say."

David smiled and waved his hands. "Da."

"Whoa. No way. Not even close." J.D. wished he knew games to entertain the kid. But the child seemed perfectly happy to listen to J.D. talk. "But maybe someday you'll have a stepdad. They can be pretty cool. My stepdad was a terrific guy."

"Da, Da." The baby's eyes were wide and trusting.

J.D. felt his insides turn to mush. It was kind of pleasant, like a killer roller-coaster ride, but scarier. Definitely scarier. "Ahem. I think we've had enough male-bonding time. Hopefully your mom has had a chance to work through her…stuff."

He stood and hiked back toward the cemetery proper. Sweat trickled down the back of his neck. Steam rose from the damp earth and a few drops of dew still clung to the shrubs.

"Maggie?" he murmured as he stepped up behind her.

She turned, wiping her face. "I'm okay now."

"Want to talk about it?"

Shaking her head, she held out her arms for David, her mouth set in a grim line. "It wasn't pretty. Stuff I would have said to Eric if he were here today."

J.D. had no clue how he should respond. "Um, there was a provision in the will for Eric's child. That should help some, knowing he thought about David."

"You don't get it, do you?" Her eyes snapped with resentment.

"Get what?"

"Even in death he denied our son. David wasn't mentioned in his will, just any nameless, faceless children Eric might have spawned in his travels."

J.D. shifted. Maybe she needed to know the whole truth about Eric. But it wasn't his secret to reveal. "You're in shock, it's been a rough couple days for all of us. Let's go home." He touched her shoulder, intending to ease her toward the car.

She planted her feet and wouldn't budge.

His face grew warm under the heat of her stare. He couldn't force himself to meet her gaze.

Maggie stepped closer, her eyes wide. The freckles on her cheeks made her seem no older than a teen—a very pretty, troubled teen. "You know something, don't you?"

He swallowed hard. "I promised Eric I would never tell anyone."

Shifting David to her hip, she moved a fraction closer. "Please?" Her hand was warm on his arm, her breath warm on his face.

"I can't."

"Can't or won't?"

"Both. I never broke a promise to my brother."

Maggie nodded slowly. "He counted on that. Said you were the most honorable man on earth." Her laugh was tinged with bitterness. "It wasn't always a compliment."

A sense of loss lodged in J.D.'s chest, a place in his heart he'd closed off long ago. The place he'd reserved for a baby brother who had never lived up to his hopes and dreams.

This whole situation with Maggie made him wonder what might have been. Was there anything he could have done differently to help Eric grow up to be a better man?

Not hardly. Because every time their parents tried to enforce rules, Grandma would come along behind them and give Eric everything he wanted, no consequences, no room to develop strength of character. Just the simple fact that he was a McGuire by birth was enough for her.

And after their parents had died within months of each other, Grandma had taken both boys in. Eric, of course, because he was flesh and blood. But J.D. was different. He might never know what had caused her to take an interest in him—the stepchild of her late son.

"I don't like asking you to break a trust." Maggie's voice was low. "But if you think it might have an effect on David, I'll ask one more time. For his sake. Please?"

J.D.'s gaze dropped to the child resting his head against his mother's shoulder, eyelids drooping. An unfamiliar emotion tugged at him. It was almost… paternal. Definitely protective.

And probably inappropriate. But in that instant, his heart expanded to include David.

He smoothed the hair off the boy's face. Glancing at Maggie, he was startled by the wistful shimmer in her eyes.

"Please?"

Drawing a deep breath, J.D. backed off a step. What he had to say was far too intimate without the added physical closeness.

"Eric was sterile. He didn't want anyone to know."

CHAPTER SEVEN

J.D.'s WORDS RANG in Maggie's ears. The world dropped out from beneath her feet for the second time in less than a week.

"Wh-what do you mean, sterile?"

"He had cancer when he was a kid. Because of the treatments, the doctors said he'd never have children."

"Well, the doctors were wrong." Maggie felt a hysterical laugh building in her chest. "This just keeps getting worse. Why didn't Eric tell me? Are you sure this isn't some kind of twisted reality show?"

J.D. shook his head. "I wish it were. But Eric's not coming back." His mouth turned down at the corners, he swiped a hand across his eyes. "He's not coming back."

She couldn't handle J.D.'s grief right now—her own was too raw. The magnitude of Eric's lies threatened to swamp her. Suddenly it all made sense.

"I'm sorry." J.D.'s voice was husky. His hand was warm on her shoulder.

If he showed any more understanding, she might just break down completely. For David, she needed to be strong. She straightened her shoulders. "Don't be. It's not your problem."

"So, um, does that change your plans at all?" J.D. asked.

"It doesn't change my plans a bit. Though it does explain why you jumped to the conclusion that there was no way Eric was David's father." Disappointment left a bitter taste in her mouth.

He ran a hand over his head. "I don't know what to believe anymore. The doctors said he couldn't have kids. Nancy wasn't able to get pregnant and they really tried, believe me. None of the other women who came forward turned out to be legit."

"Did fertility tests confirm he was sterile?"

"He didn't want to talk about it. Nancy wanted kids in the worst way and that was a touchy subject. But I got the idea the news wasn't good. And Nancy never got pregnant."

Maggie stepped closer, unwilling to let him off the hook. "But what about me? What does your gut instinct tell you?"

His gaze didn't meet her eyes. "That I'm in a whole lot of trouble."

"Nice evasion."

"You're not going to let it go, are you?" J.D.'s voice was low. He brushed a strand of hair from her face.

The intimacy of his touch rocked her, but not enough to retreat from her mission. "Are you willing to take the chance you might be turning your back on your nephew?"

The color drained from his face.

Glancing down at David, she was relieved to see he was sound asleep. "And what should I tell David when he's older? That his father's family met him and just didn't give a damn?"

"Aw, Maggie, that's not fair."

"Nothing has been fair from the moment I set eyes on Eric."

"What more do you want from me?" He spread his hands wide. "I got you a lawyer, bailed you out of jail, brought you to my home."

"I want you to believe me."

J.D. closed his eyes, as if shutting her out. "I can't."

"I know I'm asking a lot. I saw how uncomfortable you were at Belmont's office. You don't want to hurt Nancy by allowing for the possibility David is Eric's child."

"You're putting me between a rock and a hard place."

"I don't want you to turn your back on Nancy. What I'm asking—" she raised her chin "—is for you to believe your gut instinct about me."

HONEY, YOU HAD ME at hello.

The line from the old Tom Cruise movie reverberated in J.D.'s mind as he sanded the lovely piece of maple, admiring the grain. Golden rays of late-afternoon sun highlighted specks of sawdust floating in the air. The place was quiet except for the familiar *scritch* of sandpaper on wood. Peaceful.

The shop in the backyard was the only place where J.D. felt he could be himself. Let his guard down. The wood he worked with had no expectations of him. It was his skill that mattered, his heart. The way he put his all into a pile of wood and made a beautiful piece of furniture.

But peace evaded him this evening, even in the solitude of his shop. He couldn't help but recall Maggie at the cemetery this morning and the way she'd asked him to believe in her. And his honest, knee-jerk reaction was that he did believe her. Where did that leave him?

Shaking his head, J.D. refused to follow that thought any further. It meant divided loyalties and choosing sides in the end. He wasn't sure he was strong enough to do that.

His thoughts skipped to David. Okay, so he liked the kid, big deal. Why should that bother him so much?

Because he liked the kid's mom. She had guts. And grace. And a touch of innocence that even Eric hadn't managed to destroy.

Sensing a presence behind him, he turned.

Maggie leaned against the door frame, smiling. "So is this some kind of mind-over-matter thing? If you stare at it long enough, it'll sand itself?"

J.D. shrugged, realizing he'd forgotten all about sanding—a first for him. "Sure. Think it'll work?"

"If anyone could harness sheer force of will, it'd be a McGuire man."

"I'll take that as a compliment. Though, technically I'm not a McGuire."

"But you were raised a McGuire."

"Richard McGuire adopted me after he married my mom. My real dad died when I was five." His voice grew husky. "But I couldn't have asked for a better man to step into my father's shoes."

"I'd love to hear about him. Richard. He's David's grandfather. But your voice tells me your real father was a pretty special man, too."

"We quit talking about my real dad a long time ago. It made my mom sad and I could tell she wanted so badly for me to fit in with Richard's family. My real father wasn't someone who would be invited to dinner at the McGuires. He was kind of a youthful indiscretion for my mother. They were married and all that, but he was just some poor, uneducated Italian immigrant, trying to find a way to make it in the world as a cabinet-maker."

"Were they happy, your dad and mom?"

"I don't remember much. Just feeling…safe. My dad laughed a lot. He could always get my mom laughing, too. I missed him like crazy after he died, and I think my mom did, too." J.D. didn't know why he was confiding in Maggie. Maybe it was just having her stand in his shop.

"I'm sorry. It sounds like your mother loved him. What about your dad's side of the family? Do you see them a lot?"

He shook his head. "They're scattered around the country. We pretty much lost touch after my dad died."

"That's sad. I would love to have family of my own out there to look up." She crossed her arms. "At least a warm, happy, loving family, the way your dad's family sounded."

"You don't have any family?"

She shook her head. "No. My parents don't want to have anything to do with me or David."

He tilted his head. "Why not? He's a great kid."

"I didn't live up to their expectations. When I started dating Eric, they were angry. He wasn't a nice boy from the youth group at our church." She rolled her eyes. "Then when I moved in with Eric, they disowned me. Completely."

"Surely they want to see their grandson—"

"They want nothing to do with him. I sent a birth announcement, called them, but my mother hung up on me."

J.D. could hear the hurt in her voice. What kind of parents did that kind of thing? Shunned Maggie and their grandchild because she'd disappointed them.

He rested his hands on her shoulders, willing her to understand what he couldn't put into words—how sorry he was that she'd been hurt. "That's too bad."

"I can handle it." Her chin came up, but her eyes were dark with hurt. "I don't need them. Once summer break is over, I'll finish up my last semester at school. I'll have my degree and my son. I don't need anything else."

Her brave words didn't fool him. He wanted to make it better for her, to take away the pain. "It's their loss, Maggie."

She nodded. "Just like it will be your loss if you turn your back on David."

J.D. resisted the urge to pull her close and hold her until she realized he wasn't the enemy. Or was he? He didn't seem to know which side he was on anymore. He was finding it harder and harder to imagine distancing himself from Maggie and David. "You don't pull any punches, do you?"

"I used to worry about making people mad. I don't have that luxury anymore. I have a son to feed and a life to get on with."

"Yeah, school. What're you studying?"

"Mortuary science."

"Why?" J.D. tried to keep the horror out of his voice. He must not have succeeded because Maggie squared her shoulders as if to do battle.

"Pay is above average, hours are relatively good, there are plenty of jobs. People die whether the economy is good or bad. And I love it."

"What about the…bodies?"

J.D.'s question didn't surprise Maggie. Most people were curious about her work. But J.D.'s face turned a funny shade of green.

"The best part of the job is counseling the family. I know how hard it can be to lose a loved one. A good funeral director can make such a difference for those left behind. A bad funeral director can make it a living nightmare."

He chuckled nervously. "So you don't, um, actually come in contact with the, um, deceased?"

"Sure I do. But it's not a major portion of my job. Only about ten percent of a funeral director's time is spent preparing bodies. There are other professionals for that."

"I guess somebody's got to do it."

"Yes, somebody's got to do it." She raised her chin. "Now, I commandeered your kitchen. I hope you're hungry. We can discuss my career more over dinner."

His greenish color deepened.

Maggie suppressed a smile. Oh, he was way too easy to tease.

CHAPTER EIGHT

J.D. STARED AT MAGGIE'S HANDS as she dished lasagna and salads. He tried hard not to think of those same hands embalming a body. He failed miserably.

Shaking his head, he called himself all kinds of a fool. But the truth was, dead people had always scared the crap out of him and nothing was going to change that. Everyone had an Achilles heel and the dead, it seemed, was his. "Where's David?"

"On my bed and out like a light. I hope you don't mind that I took over your kitchen. David was napping and I needed to keep busy, keep my mind occupied...so I wouldn't dwell on all the stuff that's happened."

By sheer force of will, he tore his gaze away from her hands and met her eyes, where concern warred with disappointment.

Picking up his fork, he tried cutting small pieces from his lasagna and pushing them around on his plate.

"Is something wrong with the food?"

"No, um, it's delicious."

"You haven't eaten a bite."

"Sure I have." His voice was a little too weak to be convincing.

"It's me, isn't it?"

"No."

"Don't lie, J.D. Your face was the same shade of green when we discussed mortuary science."

He shook his head as if to deny her theory. He didn't want to be rude, didn't want to spoil the dinner she'd gone to such trouble to prepare.

Maggie leaned forward, her eyes dark and serious. "Have you ever talked to anyone about it?"

"It usually doesn't present much of a problem."

"Hmm. Whether you're forced to face it very often or not doesn't change the fact that there are underlying issues."

"Can we change the subject? I don't want to spoil this nice supper you've prepared."

Maggie hesitated. Relief flooded through him when she nodded and asked, "What do you want to talk about?" She picked up her fork and started eating.

"There aren't many safe subjects for us, are there?" He resolutely pushed his fears away and put a piece of lasagna into his mouth. "Hey, this is good. Like my dad used to make."

"Thank you. A friend taught me how to cook and shared some family recipes."

J.D. savored the melding of spices, cheese and pasta. The flavor meant safety and contentment. Memories of other dinners when he was a kid flashed through his mind.

"Tell me about your dad?"

"Not much to tell. I was only five when he died. But I remember he was a big guy, like me, and used to toss me up in the air and make me laugh."

"Sounds like he was a wonderful man. You said he was a cabinetmaker?"

"Yeah, I guess that's why I have an affinity for making furniture. Grandma would prefer I took up golf as a hobby, but she doesn't understand." He shrugged. "It's something I feel compelled to do. And it relaxes me."

"If that's your hobby, then what's your real job?"

"I'm an architect."

"Do you like it?" she asked.

Maggie's questions should have made him uncomfortable. He wasn't usually inclined to answer probing questions. But with her, he couldn't seem to stop himself. "I love designing buildings. I just wish I could handle a project from start to finish. Design it and build it."

"Combine your craft with architecture. Sounds like a promising idea."

"Enough about me." He changed the subject before the idea caught hold of him. Branching out into uncharted territory with an already successful business wasn't such a good idea.

"The DNA test is scheduled for tomorrow?" he asked.

"Yes, in Fayetteville."

"I put gas in your car today, so you don't need to fill up beforehand."

Maggie's face flushed. "Thank you." Her voice was husky, as if she'd swallowed a big piece of lasagna whole.

"No problem." He held up a hand. "Don't say it. I know you'll pay me back."

And somehow it wasn't a lie. He knew she'd pay him back if it took her a decade to do it.

J.D. didn't like the idea of her driving in an unfamiliar city. "I've got some errands to do in Fayetteville, so how about I drive you?"

"I've inconvenienced you enough already," Maggie said. "I've also got an appointment with one of the attorney's Belmont recommended. I couldn't ask you—"

"It's settled then. You'll need someone to entertain David while you meet with the attorney."

Maggie hesitated. "Thank you. Again."

"Damn, I wish you'd quit thanking me. I'll be in town anyway. It's really no big deal." Except he didn't really have any errands in town. His instincts urged him to keep an eye on her, not because he was afraid she'd bolt, but because he was afraid something might happen to her. For some reason, he'd decided it was his duty to keep her safe.

MAGGIE'S EYES BURNED as she watched the lab technician play this-little-piggy with David. Her son shouldn't have to undergo a paternity test, no matter how much he seemed to enjoy the attention. He should have been fathered by a man who loved Maggie so totally he would never, ever doubt David was his child. A man who believed her when she spoke the truth, despite what the doctors had told him.

J.D.'s revelation about Eric's inability to father children had only confirmed what she'd always known in her heart. David was a living, breathing miracle. Or medical science wasn't infallible. Or a little of both. She didn't really care anymore. Maggie just wanted to make a secure home for her son.

The technician had swabbed the inside of David's cheek before Maggie knew it, and David was happily munching on a cookie.

Maggie was next. The technician had indicated the testing was easier if they could rule out the mother's DNA. She opened her mouth wide as requested and it was over in a matter of seconds.

She exhaled slowly. One anxiety-inducing event down, one to go.

"Let's go find J.D.," she said to David.

He drooled cookie goo down his chin and smiled.

Maggie retrieved a tissue from her purse as she headed toward the waiting room.

It was a relief to see J.D.'s familiar face among all the strangers there.

"How'd it go?" He stood.

"Fine. It's a painless procedure."

"Good. If I'd heard David cry—"

"If you'd heard David cry you would have had no choice but to let them continue. This test is too important, at least for the McGuires."

J.D. flushed. "Yeah. You're right. I just don't like the idea of anyone hurting the little guy."

David wriggled and held out his arms to J.D.

"You want to come to me, kiddo?" He scooped the baby up.

A pang of loss radiated through Maggie's chest. There had been a time when David hadn't wanted anyone but her. She shook her head and willed away the selfish thought. It was good for Eric's family to bond with her son.

So she tried not to let it bother her when the well-meaning receptionist commented, "He looks just like his daddy."

J.D. didn't acknowledge the woman.

MAGGIE LIKED LANE BROPHY the minute she met him. He was young, energetic and had a wide smile that instantly put her at ease.

"I hope you weren't waiting long. The receptionist's at lunch." He extended his hand. "Come on back."

She shook his hand, then glanced at J.D., who held David.

J.D. stood, as if to follow. "I'm J. D. McGuire."

Lane shook his head, his smile not quite as wide. "I'd like to see Maggie alone."

"I don't mind if he sits in," she said.

"Not for this first meeting. I'm sure Mr. McGuire will understand."

J.D.'s eyes narrowed, but his voice was relaxed. "Sure. No problem. David and I will go for a walk outside."

Maggie kissed David and told him to be a good boy. Then she followed the attorney.

His office was comfortable and cluttered. The furniture was nice, solid and inexpensive. Several accordion-pleated files stood sentry on his desk.

He shoved papers into a manila folder and moved it to the side.

In anyone else, the clutter would have made her question his abilities. But the attorney seemed at ease and she felt he had everything under control.

"Coffee?"

"Yes, I'd love some."

He went to the oak sideboard. Grasping a foam cup, his movements were fluid, sure. "How do you take your coffee?"

"Cream, no sugar."

His eyes twinkled as he handed her the cup. "I worked my way through law school as a waiter."

"Thank you," she murmured. His admission only made her more confident. He was a regular person.

With Belmont, she'd felt slightly uncomfortable, as if she weren't quite good enough. His subtle way of talking down to her had given her the impression he believed she wasn't worthy of a McGuire. And probably not worthy of Belmont's time, either.

But without even discussing the case, Lane made her feel as if they were in it together. A team.

She liked that.

"Here, you can fill out this paperwork while we talk." He handed her a clipboard.

For over an hour, he asked questions and she answered, beginning with her relationship with Eric and ending with her temporary living arrangements at J.D.'s house.

"I'll say this as your attorney. Be careful with the McGuires. I've done some asking around and they wield a fair amount of power in the area. I'm surprised Belmont took your case to begin with. The McGuires are apparently among his biggest clients."

"Belmont took my case as a favor to J.D."

Lane paused. "I'm sure he had no unethical intentions, but it's unusual that an attorney as sharp as Belmont didn't anticipate this conflict of interest."

"He came on very short notice. I was in custody, the authorities were threatening to take my child and I needed someone fast. I'm grateful that J.D. was able to find someone. J.D.'s been very decent to me and my son."

"I'm sure he has." Lane frowned. "But it wouldn't hurt to be cautious. I would advise you not to discuss the case with him. What we talk about in this room stays in this room."

"Is that really necessary?"

"Look, you said you didn't kill Eric and I believe

you. That means someone out there *did* kill him. Someone who has a lot to gain by pinning the murder on you. And, statistically speaking, it's usually family or a close friend who is the murderer."

Maggie's stomach ached. "There were plenty of people angry enough at Eric to want him dead."

"Who do you think killed him?"

Shifting in her chair, Maggie hesitated. "His, um, wife was understandably upset about me and my son. She doesn't seem like she'd resort to murder, though."

"I'll send a P.I. down there immediately to investigate the details. That is, if you want to hire me. Even though you haven't been formally charged, there is a lot of circumstantial evidence against you."

"My first priority is protecting myself and my son. To do that, I need to be prepared for the worst." She glanced down at her hands. "It's just that, well, I don't have any money."

"We can work out a payment plan. Say five dollars a month until you're on your feet?"

"Why so little?"

"I take on a few cases here and there where I figure it will take years for me to receive a dime, if ever. It's kind of my way of giving back."

Maggie swallowed hard. The list of people she felt indebted to was growing by leaps and bounds. "What if it takes me ten years to pay you back?"

"Then it takes ten years. Or twenty. I plan to be around for a long while. And in case you think my motives are completely altruistic, the publicity will be good for my firm. You can't buy that kind of coverage." He winked at her.

"Since you put it like that, okay." She extended her hand. "You've got yourself a new client. And I expect to sign some sort of agreement about paying you back."

Lane shook her hand. "Good. I'll send a written request to Belmont for his initial work product on your case. And send a P.I. down to McGuireville. We'll start with Eric's wife. It sounds like she had plenty to be angry about."

It took Maggie a split second to realize he talked about Nancy. It still was hard to hear someone else referred to as Eric's wife. "I don't know if she'd kill him, though."

"It's best to check it out. How did he and his brother get along?"

Maggie hesitated. "They'd had their disagreements, but when push came to shove they loved each other. I think J.D. was very protective of Eric when he was younger."

"Have you ever heard the expression that love and hate are two sides of the same coin?"

"Yes." And didn't that pretty well describe how she felt toward Eric?

"Well, there could have been any number of reasons the brothers might have had a falling out."

Maggie shook her head. "I don't think J.D. killed Eric. He's too…reliable. I can't imagine him losing his temper like that."

"You'd be surprised at what reliable people can do sometimes. Now, let's make an appointment for a week from today. I should have more information and we can map out a strategy."

"A week? I'd hoped to be allowed to go back to Arizona in the next couple days."

Lane sighed. "I know this is tough, but it's gonna take time. Just sit tight and keep your ears open. You never know what you might hear."

Maggie nodded. "I guess I'll see you in a week then."

He walked her out to the reception area, shook her hand and said goodbye.

Her heart warmed at the sight of David ensconced on J.D.'s lap, raptly listening as the man read to him.

"I'm done," she said. She meant it in more ways than one. Her discussion with Lane had reminded her to stay focused on her goal—clearing her name and getting out of town as soon as possible. She was done passively accepting whatever fate handed out.

J.D. rose, closing the children's book and placing it on the end table.

"How'd it go?"

"I hired him." Maggie lifted her chin.

He frowned. "What about a retainer? If you need help, I can—"

"Thank you, but I don't need help with this. We've worked out a payment schedule I can handle."

"Yeah, and probably all the free publicity he can generate at the expense of my family."

His defensiveness struck a chord in her. She recalled Lane's warning about the McGuires. He had seemed to take particular interest in J.D.

But she simply could not imagine J.D. working up the passion to stab his brother.

J.D. took her arm and guided her to the door. "You were in there an awful long time. What did you talk about?"

"Stuff about Eric and me. And all the vital statistics about David."

"Did he say how he plans to defend you, if you're arrested?"

She shook her head. "No. We're meeting again in a week." There, she hadn't lied, but she hadn't told him about the private investigator.

"Hmm. Well, I'll drive you."

"That's really not nec—"

"I want to do it." He tilted his head and studied her. "Is anything wrong?"

"Not at all. Why?"

"You just seemed kind of, well, distant."

"I've got a lot on my mind. I didn't intend to be away from home this long. And now I have to wait at least another week. Surely I can't impose on you any longer."

"No, not a word of that. You'll stay right where you are at my house."

"But—"

"Look, David's comfortable, you're comfortable.

Why uproot everybody when I'm happy to have the company?" His voice was sincere, his gaze direct.

His house had become as familiar as any place in Arkansas. If she couldn't be in Arizona, it soothed her frayed nerves a bit to know she had a place to stay at J.D.'s, homey and secure.

She ignored Lane's earlier warning. After all, she knew J.D. and Lane didn't. "Okay. I'd like that."

CHAPTER NINE

J.D.'S FAVORITE ROCKING CHAIR creaked as he pushed off with his foot. He watched the clouds roll in and listened to the distant thunder. Watching a storm was one of his favorite ways to think. This afternoon, he thought of Maggie.

He'd decided the two days since her appointment with Lane Brophy could have been worse. Realizing she was stuck in McGuireville for at least another week, Maggie could have been a real shrew to live with, but she wasn't. Not that she tiptoed around the house. Far from it. He was aware of her every movement.

If she saw something that needed done, she did it. Like cooking, cleaning, weeding the garden. He'd invited her to make herself at home and she'd taken his advice to heart. He'd expected her presence to be awkward, but instead, he found himself looking forward to talking to her, playing with David, listening to the loving notes of her voice as she sang the baby to sleep.

The front door opened behind him and when he turned, he wasn't surprised to see the subject of his thoughts.

"Looks like it's going to storm," Maggie commented.

"Yep. Probably. Have a seat."

"I don't know if I'll get used to this humidity." She sat in the other rocker. "You do this often?"

"Sit on the porch? Not as often as I'd like. Usually I'm up to my eyeballs in work and when I'm not at work, I'm in the garage creating something new. Roy's taken over a few projects since Eric died."

"You're very good at woodworking. Everything you make is beautiful."

Her approval pleased him more than it should have. His reply was gruff. "Nothing to it, really."

She smiled. "Modest, huh? The way Eric talked about you, I figured you'd have a colossal ego. But then again, I expected you to be able to leap tall buildings with a single bound. Haven't seen you manage that yet."

"No. I just draw tall buildings."

"That's an accomplishment in itself. I can't begin to imagine the patience it must require." Maggie leaned back in the rocker and inhaled deeply. "It's so peaceful out here."

"You've seemed more relaxed the last day or so. Any particular reason?"

"I figured I might as well make the best of a bad situation. If I'm stuck in McGuireville, I intend to be comfortable and learn a little about my son's family."

"That reminds me, Grandma invited us for pecan pie after supper."

"Us?"

"Yeah, you, me, David." It sounded so natural to lump them all together as a single unit. Kind of like a family.

J.D. pushed the disturbing thought away.

"You know, I think I'll pass tonight. I'd like to stick close to home, I mean, um, with the storm…"

He glanced at the sky. "Looks like it might go around us. Besides, an invitation for pie is not optional. It's a command performance. Usually there's a grilling involved."

"Barbecue, I hope?"

"Nope. More like interrogation. Eric would have most certainly been invited to pie after you showed up at the reunion. But, well…he died. She must figure to get the information out of you. And she's eager to see the baby again, too."

"I don't mind if she sees David, but I probably can't tell her a whole lot about Eric. It seems there was a lot about him I didn't know."

"Humor her. She'll enjoy the company."

Maggie nodded. "I better get started on supper then—I'll whip up a quick shrimp salad." She wiped her damp face. "Something cool."

"You've been working too hard for a guest." He exited his rocking chair and held out his hand. "The salad can wait a few minutes. Let's go pitch some horseshoes."

"I really shouldn't."

"Come on. It'll be fun. And I'll help you with the shrimp salad if you're afraid supper'll be delayed."

She hesitated. "I've never played horseshoes before."

J.D. shook his head in mock amazement. "No respectable Arkansas girl would admit to that. Come on. Your education has some gaping holes and I intend to remedy that."

He led her to the side of the house where a horseshoe pit had been dug decades before he'd bought the house.

Briefly, he explained the game to her. "I'll throw left-handed just to give you a fighting chance."

She grinned in response to J.D.'s challenge. "You just hook the horseshoe on that big stake, right?"

"Yes."

"I thought only old, toothless men played. How hard can it be?"

He chuckled. "Wait and see. And for your information, I'm *very* good at the game and I still have all my teeth. Not a gray hair in sight, either. Wanna make a little wager?"

"Sure. I don't have any money, though. And don't even suggest strip horseshoes. Because I don't do that sort of stuff."

"No strip horseshoes, I promise. As a matter of fact, if I win, I'll cook supper by myself. You win, you cook."

"That's kind of a bassackward bet."

"I've got a confession to make." She'd already brushed off his suggestion that she was working too hard. He thought quickly. "I'm not used to owing somebody and it bothers me that you've done all the cooking and cleaning since you arrived. Besides, a bachelor like me can't afford to have his domestic skills get rusty."

Maggie raised an eyebrow. "I didn't have you pegged for a gourmet."

"Nothing fancy. Just good, old-fashioned southern cooking. I can fry chicken better than Colonel Sanders." J.D. realized the thought of pampering Maggie appealed to him enormously. He got the impression not too many people had done that for her. She gave, the world took. Including Eric. *Especially* Eric.

"You're not the only one who hates owing people. Cooking is one of the few things I can do to repay some of your kindness."

"If you feel that way, then you'll be fierce competition. But not nearly fierce enough," he challenged.

Her eyes narrowed as she sized up the competition. "You're on, McGuire. Now, would you please show me how to throw one of those things." She pointed at the horseshoes he held. "My sense of self-worth hinges on winning."

"It would be my pleasure." His grin was wicked.

"You have to be fair, though. I mean, teach me the best way to win and I'll take it from there."

"Of course. I wouldn't think of rigging the game. My honor wouldn't allow it."

Maggie gnawed her lower lip.

He gestured for her to come closer. "Line up here.

It's kind of like bowling. Take a couple steps, pull your arm back, release the shoe and follow through."

The shoe sailed through the air and hit the stake with a clink.

Chuckling, she said, "Bowling with horseshoes. Only a man would think up a game like this."

"Oh, you have no idea the things we can think up to amuse ourselves."

Maggie opened her mouth, then closed it. Her eyes clouded, and he figured she'd been reminded of Eric. She knew full well what trouble a bored Southern boy could create to entertain himself. In his brother's case, he'd created a baby.

J.D. wanted nothing more than to erase the sadness in her eyes. "I'm sorry. That remark was inappropriate."

She hesitated. "Apology accepted."

"Hey, we're supposed to be having fun. Here, I'll show you how to pitch." He handed her a horseshoe and angled himself so that he was behind her and could guide her hand. "Take a couple steps."

She took two short steps.

"Here." He wrapped his arm around her waist so they could move as one unit. A strand of copper-colored hair tickled his nose. "Let's start over."

Pulling her backward with him, he told himself he didn't notice how small and fragile she felt in his arms.

"Okay, let's try again."

Maggie nodded.

He guided her all the way to follow through, her hand smooth and feminine in his. The shoe dropped a couple feet short of the stake. "Not bad. Want to try one on your own?"

"Yes." Grinning, she seemed pleased with herself. Way too pleased for a mediocre pitch.

"What?" he asked.

She tipped her head and smiled, her eyes crinkling at the corners.

J.D. sucked in a breath. She was downright gorgeous, in a simple, girl-next-door way. He wondered, not for the first time, why in the world she'd picked a guy like Eric. Why hadn't she chosen someone who could appreciate her beauty, inside and out?

Someone like him.

The thought had him seriously questioning his sanity. His game was shot after that. He couldn't concentrate and threw short, threw long, everywhere except near the metal stake.

Maggie, on the other hand, was a quick study. She watched, her eyes bright, missing nothing. When it was her turn, her eyebrows drew together in a frown of concentration.

An hour later, J.D. realized two things. One, that he'd underestimated Maggie. And two, her self-worth had been saved, but his had been seriously compromised. Shrugging his shoulders, he decided there wasn't anyone else he'd rather lose to.

She surprised him by saying, "How about if you show me how to make fried chicken?"

"You got a deal."

"OKAY, CHEF, WHERE DO WE start for Southern fried chicken?" Maggie asked, watching J.D. haul a big, cast-iron skillet from the cupboard. He was obviously at home in the kitchen.

He produced a clean painter's apron from a drawer, looped it over his head and tied it at the waist. "What? You were expecting a frilly apron? A guy's gotta draw the line somewhere."

J.D. thawed the chicken in the microwave and mixed together the coating. Then he explained how to dredge the chicken and ensure the skillet was hot, but not too hot. "The grease splatters. For that reason, my lovely assistant and her sidekick, David, are banished until the chicken has been fried."

Eyeing him suspiciously, she mused, "Though I appreciate your concern, I have to wonder why you're so safety-conscious all of the sudden."

"Okay, you found me out. This is a top-secret family recipe, passed down from Grandma's great-grandmother. In other words, it's been around since the beginning of time. There are a few spices I can't add with you watching."

"You're serious?"

"Oh, yes. Only those who have sworn undying allegiance to the McGuires are allowed to learn the secret ingredients."

Maggie didn't know what to make of this new, playful J.D. But she wasn't quite sure he was playing:

"Okay, you win. David and I will go for a walk. Will half an hour give you enough time for secrecy?"

Nodding, his eyes gleamed with amusement. "That should do it."

Maggie lifted David from his swing. She'd placed it what she thought was a safe distance from the stove, but apparently J.D. had other ideas. "Come on, sweetheart, let's go explore."

As she walked out the back door, Maggie watched the sun dip below the line of pine trees. The air was heavy and humid, but somehow refreshing, despite the fact that the storm hadn't materialized.

From what she'd seen of Arkansas, it seemed a sleepy mixture of down-home common sense and refined dignity, a place of roots and restlessness.

She could see where a young guy like Eric could have been eager to leave this place, eager to search for excitement. But to Maggie, it seemed more like a wonderful place to rest. A sense of security stole over her, something she hadn't experienced since before her parents had disowned her. Maybe not even then.

How could they have turned their backs so completely on both their daughters, first Cassie, then Maggie? Where had forgiveness fit into their morality? It hadn't. There was no margin for error in her parents' world. Cassie had sinned by giving birth to a bastard. Maggie had sinned by living with a man outside of marriage, becoming pregnant and marrying after her pregnancy showed.

The consequences had been great. Cassie had lost

her daughter to Child Protective Services and taken her own life. Maggie lived hand-to-mouth but was determined not to fall into the same trap. She and David would do fine all by themselves. Her degree and a good job would protect them. And maybe the ache of losing her parents and sister would subside.

MAGGIE SHIFTED UNCOMFORTABLY, the wicker rocker creaked beneath her. "Delicious pie, Mrs. McGuire."

"Please, call me Edna." She held David, bouncing him on her knee. Occasionally, she'd separate a bite-size piece of flaky crust and feed it to him. He jabbered happily. The sugar buzz alone would probably keep him up half the night.

Glancing at J.D., Maggie wondered when the grilling would begin. They'd been there almost half an hour and simply traded small talk about the weather. Maybe J.D. was mistaken? She could only hope. "You baked this? It's very good, it could have come from a bakery." The pie was so sweet it made Maggie's teeth ache.

"Of course I baked it. Every woman should know how to bake pecan pie. This recipe has been handed down in my family for generations."

Just like the fried-chicken recipe. "I just go to the grocery store. Sara Lee's got to be a Southerner, because her pies are to die for."

Edna sniffed. "Frozen. My men never ate a frozen pie." She nodded toward J.D.

Maggie didn't have the heart to tell her that Eric ate frozen pies for both of the Thanksgiving meals they'd been together. She didn't want to send the woman into a stroke or something.

J.D. cleared his throat. "Thanks for dessert, Grandma. But we need to get going. I have to work in the morning."

"I'm sure no one would notice if you arrived a little late. You're the owner, aren't you?"

"Yes, but—"

"No buts, James David."

"Yes, ma'am."

"Now, Maggie, what about that testing for David?" she asked.

"Paternity testing?" Maggie hesitated, wondering how much of the scientific jargon she should repeat. "They swabbed cells from inside David's cheek and will compare them to Eric's DNA and mine."

"My poor, poor Eric." Edna's eyes filled with tears.

"Um, yeah." J.D. seemed lost in his own thoughts.

"When will we get the results?" Edna glanced down at David and chucked him under the chin. "Not that I need some lab report to tell me what I already know. David has Eric's hair, his eyes, the dimple in his chin."

Maggie couldn't for the life of her remember a dimple in Eric's chin. Could she have forgotten already? Shrugging, she watched J.D. finger the dimple in his own chin. More than a dimple, really, more of a cleft. And he had a stronger chin in general than Eric, though Eric would probably have been considered the handsomer of the two—great bone structure and a quick, wide smile. Whereas J.D. had strength and intensity.

"I want David to come stay with me," Eric's grandmother announced.

Maggie's stomach dropped. It sounded so permanent the way the woman said it. As if she were laying claim to David.

"That's so very generous of you. But David and I are comfortable at J.D.'s house and I hate to disrupt my son's routine again."

"It's not seemly, you staying there. J.D.'s a single man. People will talk."

J.D.'s mouth tightened. "What more could they possibly say than what's already been said? We all loved Eric, but let's face it, he cheated on his wife, committed bigamy and apparently fathered a child with another woman and left her high and dry."

"What I'm saying is all the more reason for you to be circumspect. You carry the McGuire name. David is the only remaining male McGuire by blood, so the family reputation will be tied to you until David is older. I would expect you would do right in deference to your late stepfather. He wanted you raised as a McGuire. He was very firm in that. And he would be even more determined now that Eric's gone." Her eyes filled with tears, her chin quivered.

"Shh, Grandma, it's okay." J.D. set down his plate and moved to her side. "I won't do anything to betray the McGuire name. Don't worry."

Edna sniffed and dabbed at her eyes with a tissue. "I'm just a silly, sentimental old woman."

Maggie caught a gleam of victory in the woman's

eyes and couldn't help but wonder if Edna was as helpless as she led everyone to believe. "We best leave. I'm sure you need your rest, Edna."

"You will move in tomorrow?" Her voice was weak, but the set of her chin was stubborn.

Resentment simmered in the pit of Maggie's stomach. "No, Edna, we won't. Having a small child in the house would be disruptive during an already stressful time. Thank you for your very kind offer, though."

"But—"

"I promise you'll see plenty of David." She grasped her son under the arms and lifted him before Edna could finish her protest.

It seemed to Maggie as if prying David from Edna's grasp was becoming a disturbing habit.

CHAPTER TEN

MAGGIE LEANED BACK and closed her eyes. It was still strange to sit in the passenger seat of her own car, but then again, the whole pie-with-Grandma thing had been strange. She wanted to get back to J.D.'s house and find escape in sleep. She'd been doing that a lot lately.

J.D. turned the key. A whining sound emerged from the dash, but the car didn't start.

"Keep trying. It'll make that horrible noise a couple times and then the car will finally turn over," she instructed.

"It's been doing this long?"

Maggie shrugged. "I haven't really kept track. There was so much other stuff going on."

J.D. mumbled something under his breath. He turned the key and the same thing happened. "Don't suppose you know how to hot-wire a vehicle?"

"No."

"Then it looks like we're not going anywhere in your car."

Groaning, Maggie wished she drove something

new and reliable, complete with a warranty and road-side assistance.

"Don't worry, I'm sure we can borrow Grandma's car. I'll go get the keys and leave her a note if she's already gone upstairs for the night. Wait here."

Maggie got out of the car, willing to risk mosquitoes if it meant a breeze. Leaning against the fender, she tried not to worry about how she would get to Fayetteville in the morning. To keep from brooding, she attempted to piece together what she knew about the McGuire family.

Poor J.D. was a branch all his own of the McGuire family tree, grafted on at an early age. She wondered what it had been like for him growing up. It seemed both Edna and Eric had relied heavily on J.D., but had they really loved him? And what about the rest of the family? Did he have McGuire cousins who welcomed him?

For some reason, she visualized a lonely little boy, lost and afraid after the death of his father. It couldn't have been an easy transition.

"Earth to Maggie." J.D. stood in front of her, jangling a set of keys.

"I thought your grandmother didn't drive?"

"She doesn't. At least not when she can get one of us to cart her around. Keeping the car is her gentle way of letting me know that if I don't give her a ride, she'll drive herself."

"Is she capable?"

J.D. chuckled hollowly, resting his arm against the car roof. "Oh, she can generally get the car from point A to point B, it's just the number of objects she hits in between that has me worried. I'm afraid someday it will be a person."

"And you don't want that on your conscience."

"Exactly."

"You're sure she won't mind if you borrow it?"

"Nah, it'll give her extra leverage when she needs a chauffeur. The ladies at the country club think it's so *cute* that her grandson drives her there and picks her up."

"No offense, J.D., but how do you have a life if you're at your grandmother's beck and call?"

He sighed. "It's really not that bad. She has a few doctor's appointments every now and then. And her weekly bridge at the club."

It was hard to believe this man was related to Eric in any way. He was just too darn responsible. "You're positive you don't leap tall buildings, too?"

A grin tugged at his mouth. "Not hardly. Grandma raised Eric and me after our folks died in a car wreck. She deserves a little pampering now."

Maggie found herself analyzing his statement as she removed David from the back seat. J.D. felt he owed his grandmother something for taking him in and Maggie couldn't find fault with that. It just seemed as if he'd dedicated his whole life to Edna and Eric.

"Let me get the car seat and I'll install it in Grandma's Lincoln," he said. A few seconds later, he emerged from the Toyota and angled his head toward the attached garage. "This way."

Following close behind, Maggie stifled a disbelieving chuckle when he opened the garage door and she saw the Lincoln. "You weren't exaggerating, were you? There isn't a straight piece of metal on that car."

He opened the rear door and quickly installed the car seat. Taking David from her arms, he settled her son in his seat and fastened the buckle.

"Sorry, it's not pretty, but it'll get us home. And, hey, there are advantages."

She could have sworn she detected a wicked twinkle in his eye. "Such as?" she asked.

"When people see this car coming, *everyone* gets out of the way. And fast."

"Edna's reputation precedes her?"

"And how."

Maggie laughed at the mental image of Edna behind the wheel and people diving out of her path, kind of like the crowd scene in *Godzilla*.

J.D. pointed to the crumpled rear bumper. "The Buchanans' mailbox."

He gestured to a long scrape along the driver's side. "The Smiths' new picket fence."

Maggie pointed to the front bumper. "And that?"

"The fire truck that, according to Grandma, 'came out of nowhere' and ran her off the road, into a tree."

Wincing, she commented, "She's lucky she wasn't badly hurt."

His smile faded, his eyes became shadowed. "Yes, she was extremely lucky."

Maggie wanted to reassure him, but she didn't know what to say. Instead, she squeezed his muscular forearm. "You're a good guy, J.D."

He ran a hand over his shaved head. "Sometimes I wonder."

"No need to wonder. You're a genuine hero, in my book."

"What about Eric? Was he a hero to you?"

The blunt question set her back a step. "No, he was the guy who stole my heart and served it back to me, sliced, diced and pureed." Her throat ached, her chest tightened. "It looks like I was just a game to him."

J.D. closed the distance between them. His voice was husky as he touched her cheek. "The more I get to know you, the more certain I am that he cared for you in his own self-centered way. You deserved better than that, though."

She leaned into him, but only for a moment. His sympathy wouldn't change things. Neither would the tears burning her eyes. Slowly, she turned and opened the passenger door.

Struggling for control, she said, "And what about this dent on the door?"

J.D.'s breath stirred the hair at the back of her neck. The warmth of his body so close to hers was reassuring. And subtly sexy, though she doubted he realized it.

"It's something totally new." His voice was solemn.

Maggie twisted to see his face, but his eyes were dark and unreadable. She bit her lip and hoped like crazy he couldn't tell she'd wanted to press against him, not for comfort, but for the sheer, instinctive need to be loved by a man. The need to reaffirm that she was alive and desirable, not just easily discarded garbage.

For a second, she'd even believed his veiled reference to something totally new was an acknowledgment of an errant spark of attraction.

"Maybe you ought to check it out." Her face warmed. "The new dent, of course." Grasping the handle, she opened the door and got in.

J.D. hesitated for a moment. His voice was deep and husky when he said, "Some things are better left alone."

As he closed the door behind her and made his way to the driver's side, Maggie heard him whistle a mournful tune full of yearning for something that could never be.

Maggie shivered, despite the warmth of the evening and the leather upholstery cradling her body.

J.D. NOTED THE FUEL GAUGE and mileage and promised himself he would input the information in the maintenance file later—the new software made it a snap. Might as well change the oil while he had the car, too.

Tonight seemed as good a time as any, since sleep seemed far away.

It bothered him that he'd slipped into an easy familiarity with Maggie. For a moment, he'd forgotten that she'd been his brother's lover. For a moment, he'd thought only of how she might feel in his bed. But it was just a small lapse. His body had responded to the proximity of a warm, feminine body, nothing more.

J.D. shook his head. He was a horrible liar, even to himself. He hoped to heck his instincts weren't getting muddled by hormones. Fighting off his odd mood, he tried to look at Maggie's situation objectively. He had no doubt she'd been involved with his brother. What it came down to was whether he believed she would sleep with more than one man at a time, or in very quick succession. And everything he'd observed about her told him she didn't sleep around. If he accepted that Maggie had been as devoted to his brother as she claimed, then he would have to accept David as Eric's child. The thought made him break out in a cold sweat.

Eric had fathered a child against all medical odds.

His first thought was how the news would destroy Nancy. Close on its heels came a pang of jealousy that caught him unprepared. A part of him envied his brother's relationship with Maggie and the child they'd created.

Where had that come from? Someplace so deep, dark and timeless he wondered if he might be Cain to Eric's Abel. He didn't want to know.

Pacing, he had to do something, anything, to keep his mind occupied.

J.D. walked around the front of the car and popped the hood. It would take a while on a muggy night like this for the engine to cool.

Engine parts blurred as he contemplated his brother's last act of selfishness. Eric had walked away from a beautiful child, his own child, apparently without a backward glace. J.D. shook his head. His brother simply hadn't deserved Maggie or David.

But J.D. did.

J.D. groaned in frustration. He couldn't get away from thoughts that were sure to drive him crazy. Maggie wasn't a prize to settle a rivalry—it was subtle, below the surface, but always between the two brothers. Was his growing interest in Maggie merely a way of one-upping his spoiled little brother, even in death? No way. Because if it was, it meant J.D. was no more than a pathetic loser. A loser because the only way he could win would be out of default.

J.D. slammed the hood shut. He wasn't going to get anything done tonight.

He turned out the lights, then remembered the new dent Maggie had pointed out. Switching the lights back on, he went around to the passenger door of the Lincoln and surveyed the new damage. He didn't have a clue when his grandmother might have inflicted this dent.

He ran a finger down the door. Silver paint. He sent a silent plea heavenward that it was paint from a mailbox or fence post or some other inanimate object and not from an occupied vehicle.

The hair on the back of his neck prickled. There was something he should be remembering, something important.

But then a noise came from the open garage door and the thought evaporated. The evening went suddenly silent, as if the crickets' nightly song had been interrupted in midchorus. J.D. sensed he was no longer alone. He turned and caught his breath at the sight of Maggie leaning against the door frame, her expression soft and inviting. Or maybe he just wanted her to be inviting. "David's out like a light. I thought maybe you might want to sit on the porch. I'm too keyed up to sleep."

He grabbed a rag from his workbench and wiped his hands. Spending more time with Maggie was a bad idea. But undeniably appealing. "Sure. The engine needs to cool off before I change the oil anyway."

"You're going to change the oil tonight?"

Shrugging, he said, "Maybe. I'm a little keyed up myself."

They walked across the yard to the front porch.

J.D. watched the ease of her stride, the way she seemed comfortable in her own skin. He didn't think he'd ever felt that way. At least not after his pops had died.

"Lemonade?" she asked. Without waiting for his answer, she moved to the rustic table.

He raised an eyebrow. "You were pretty sure I'd come, huh? Two glasses."

Maggie turned, her smile tentative. "I hoped."

Her simple, honest answer threw him. J.D. cleared his throat. "Um, yeah, I'd like a glass."

Maggie's movements were graceful as she poured two glasses from the crystal pitcher set on a tray.

They sat in companionable silence, the creak of the rockers and chirping crickets the only noises. Then he realized there was something missing.

The whining complaint of mosquitoes.

That's when he noticed Maggie had lit the citronella lanterns. She'd gone to a lot of trouble to talk to him. It made him nervous and yet it made the blood zing through his veins. A curious mixture very similar to how he'd felt on his first date.

They seemed to be way past the polite conversation stage, so he allowed his curiosity to take over. "What was it like before Eric? Your life, I mean?"

She leaned back in the rocker and gazed at the dark horizon. "Very boring. Tedious. Restrictive. I still lived at home when I met him."

"Saving on dorm fees?"

"No. My parents were, um, very religious. They had certain ideas of what a girl could and couldn't do. They allowed me to attend a couple college classes each semester and work in the church office, but that was about it."

"So you rebelled." It wasn't a question. A woman

as smart and determined as Maggie wouldn't tolerate that kind of environment indefinitely.

Maggie nodded. "I was raised to respect authority. But every once in a while, I'd think about sneaking out, dating like the other girls."

"Did you? Sneak out?"

"No. I respected their wishes and died a little more each day. There was this girl inside me, one who wanted to laugh and dance and sing."

He could see that girl when she teased him about his eccentricities or when she played with David. Her joy was infectious, unselfconscious and pure. He was willing to bet it was her purity that had appealed to his jaded brother. Or the challenge. Or both. "How'd you meet Eric?"

Maggie's body tensed. "At the races. It was one of the few times I lied to my parents. I was supposed to be at the library."

"So, um, were you hanging around the pits?"

"I wasn't a track groupie if that's what you mean." There was a tinge of impatience in her voice.

"I didn't think that for a second. Well, maybe for a second—everyone does stupid stuff sometimes. But I know you better than that."

Maggie cocked her head to the side. "Did you? Do stupid stuff?"

"No. Eric did enough for both of us."

"Hmm. That's too bad. I mean everyone should have some stupid stuff in their past. Mistakes show you're giving life your all. That's what attracted me to Eric, I guess. When I was with him I felt incredibly alive." Her eyes shone with happy memories.

J.D. rubbed his knuckles against her silky cheek, the gesture instinctive and unstoppable. "You're something special."

Doubt clouded Maggie's eyes. "Apparently your brother didn't think so."

His chest tightened. He wanted to erase the pain in her life. He wanted to make her feel "incredibly alive," like Eric had, but he didn't know how. Laughter and love had been his brother's forte. Keeping the world spinning on its axis had been J.D.'s.

He let his hand drop. Clearing his throat, he said, "I'm sorry he hurt you. I'm sorry he hurt Nancy. It makes me wonder if I should have kicked his ass years ago instead of cleaning up his messes. He might still be alive if I had."

Maggie tipped her head to the side, her eyes dark and unreadable. "That's BS. Eric was an adult and he made his own decisions. Hindsight is always twenty-twenty, especially when someone we love does something stupid."

Her voice grew husky, her eyes darkened with emotion. "After my sister committed suicide, I thought of all sorts of things I should have done differently. Would they have made a difference?" Maggie shrugged. "I'll never know. But Cassie was an adult, too. My sister had options. She could have fought for her daughter...or she could have asked for help."

He grasped her hand. "Like you did. It took a lot of guts to drive cross-country and ask for help. I know it wasn't easy for you. I could see it in your eyes every time you accepted something from me. But you set aside your pride to make a better life for your son. That's damn near heroic in my book."

Maggie's eyes were bright. She blinked rapidly and smiled. "Thanks, J.D., that means a lot. But I don't feel very heroic. I wonder if she'll think her entire birth family didn't want her. I'd like her to know I wanted her. I would have adopted her myself if I'd been older."

He rubbed his thumb across her palm, resisting the urge to press a kiss there. "Maybe someday you can look for her."

"I hope so. I'd never try to take her from the only family she's ever known. I'd just like to be a part of her life."

"That's understandable. What I can't understand is someone turning his back on family like Eric did."

Frowning, he tore his focus from their linked hands and concentrated on a theory that allowed him to see his brother as an okay guy, misguided though he'd been. "I don't think Eric intended to hurt you or Nancy. You are both pretty special ladies. I'd like to think he fell in love with two women and didn't have the strength to choose."

Maggie squeezed his hand. Her voice was husky when she said, "I'd like to believe that, too. I *have* to believe that, for David's sake. How else can I tell him about his daddy later and say anything good?"

"Then believe." He returned the pressure of her hand. The simple physical connection of their clasped hands seemed supremely intimate at that moment, as if they shared a bond beyond the usual man-woman mating dance. "Tell me about the night you met."

Maggie shifted in her rocker, withdrawing her hand. She stared at the horizon, avoiding his gaze. "I honestly don't know how I caught his interest. My friend and I were walking through the pits after the race, looking at all the cars."

Even in the dim light, he could tell her cheeks flushed. "Okay, so we were looking at the guys, too," she added.

"No law against that."

"Anyway, Eric started talking to me like we'd known each other forever. He laughed and teased a lot. I wasn't used to that kind of attention. He invited me to a party and I went."

J.D.'s stomach dropped. He didn't think he could handle hearing about Maggie being intimate with his brother. He attempted to keep his voice light as he said, "And the rest is history."

"I tried to introduce him to my parents. Make everything on the up-and-up. But Eric gave me a thousand excuses—now I know why. And when I finally talked him into it, my parents pretty much hated him on sight."

"Hmm."

"Finally, I realized I couldn't do both. I couldn't follow my parents' rules and still have Eric. I wanted to be with him all the time and when he asked me to move in, I accepted. It was love for me." She averted her face. "I have no idea what it meant to him."

"I'm betting you meant a lot. Maybe you reached a part of him others couldn't."

Slowly, she turned her head to meet his gaze. "Even Nancy?"

He cleared his throat. "You have to understand, they'd been together since they were kids. Nancy and Eric were best friends who spontaneously combusted when puberty hit. No relationship can sustain that kind of passion over the long haul, but I'd have sworn they still cared about each other."

J.D. saw the color drain from Maggie's face. He could have kicked himself for being so tactless. "I'm sorry. I know that's probably hard for you to hear."

"It's *all* hard for me to hear. But I need to know what happened so I have a hope of healing."

He nodded slowly.

She was quiet for a few moments, gazing at the night sky. "You know, I never, ever thought bigamy happened in real life, to real people. It's just too dramatic and…well…stupid."

"It sure complicated a lot of lives. Eric left a lot of questions unanswered. I wish I could help sort it out, but I'm beginning to wonder if I knew my brother at all."

"Makes you wonder how well any of us knows the people we love, huh?" Her voice was sad.

Taking a sip of lemonade, he pushed the rocker. There wasn't a damn thing he could say to make her feel better. Except that maybe she was the best thing Eric had ever fallen into.

Maggie leaned back and lapsed into silence, rocking and staring at the sky.

Was she looking for answers there? Wondering about heaven and hell and what really made the universe spin? Or wondering where Eric's eternal soul rested?

One thing was for certain, she didn't seem in any way affected by the same vortex sucking J.D. in. Her calm acceptance would not have been possible if she'd felt the same undeniable attraction he did.

Maggie caught her breath and nudged him with her elbow. She pointed to the sky. "Did you see that? A shooting star."

"I missed it." But he didn't miss the way she shut her eyes tight. Even after all the crap life had handed her, she still wished on falling stars.

A shred of Quixote-like gallantry prodded him to try to make her dreams come true. Fortunately, he was able to ignore the call. But not before the question leaped to his lips. "What did you wish for?"

Opening her eyes, Maggie glanced up at the sky. She hesitated. The slice of a half moon bathed her upturned face in an otherworldly glow. Slowly, she shook her head and met his gaze. "It won't come true if I tell."

J.D. released the breath he hadn't known he'd

been holding. As if he'd really expected her to beg him to slay her dragons. No, as fragile as she looked, there was an inner strength to Maggie. A depth way beyond anything Eric would have been capable of appreciating.

A memory flitted at the edge of his consciousness. Of being held tight in his mother's arms while his pops pointed out the constellations. "I used to wish on falling stars when I was a kid."

"But you don't anymore?"

Shaking his head, he fought off a wave of sadness as the loss of those starry nights enveloped him. "Wishes and miracles are for kids."

"Oh, no, J.D., you're wrong. Miracles are for everyone." She reached over and clasped his hand again. "Never doubt that."

For a minute, with his hand cradled in hers, he could almost believe. But who would slay the dragons and change the oil and make sure nothing interfered with the McGuire way of life if he focused on miracles?

He suppressed a pang of longing so intense he wanted to cry out, howl at the unfairness of it all.

Withdrawing his hand, he tried to ignore the disappointed tilt to her lips, the hurt he imagined shining in her eyes.

"I never doubted. Until my pops died. That's when I knew miracles didn't exist and prayers were never answered." Years of yearning for what might have been tinged his words with bitterness. "So you make your wishes and believe with all your might. But don't expect me to share them."

With that, he stood, his heart heavy, his footsteps even heavier. He placed his glass on the tray. His voice was husky when he said, "Thanks for trying though."

Because nobody had tried in a very long time.

CHAPTER ELEVEN

CONVERSATION at the breakfast table the next morning was strained. Even David was unusually quiet. He'd had a fretful night and very little sleep, which meant Maggie got very little sleep. She felt as if sandpaper lined her eyelids.

J.D. seemed to be in his own world. It was as if he'd forgotten Maggie was there. She wondered if his revelations from the night before made him uncomfortable. The wounded little boy she'd seen beneath his bitterness had surprised her. Eric wasn't the only one who thought J.D. just about walked on water. J.D. seemed so collected and together. But last night, he'd simply been a man hiding from pain. And his distress had reached her in a way she'd never anticipated; she'd longed to comfort him.

Good thing he'd shut down on her or she might have done something embarrassing. Like tell him he was twice the man his brother had been. And explain that loyalty, tenderness and sacrifice could be sexier than Eric's empty charm.

Maggie flushed at the very thought. J.D. had been

nothing but respectful and kind. Her reaction to his kindness was understandable. She was starved for compassion, particularly from a man. But there was absolutely no reason to let J.D. know that her admiration for him was threatening to cross a very scary line.

Reminding herself of her mission today, she sucked in a deep breath and exhaled. "I have to ask a favor."

He glanced up. "Hmm. Were you talking to me?"

"Yes. I have a favor to ask."

"Shoot."

"I'd call Edna and ask her myself, but it's still early and, um, I was wondering if she would mind if I borrowed her car to go into Fayetteville? I'm a good driver and I'll be very careful."

"She probably wouldn't mind at all. But I'd rather you took my truck, so I can change the oil in her car."

Maggie was reluctant to borrow his truck—it was big, new and expensive and she didn't want to be responsible for it. But there seemed to be no other option. "Thank you. I'll be very, very careful. I've got another favor."

He raised an eyebrow.

"David has been fussy. I think he's teething. An attorney's office isn't the best place to have a teething infant—"

He smiled and his shoulders relaxed. "I'll work from home this morning. You can leave the little crumb-catcher with me."

"You're sure?" Maggie asked. "I don't want to interfere with your work."

J.D. winked in David's direction. "Nah, he won't interfere. We'll have some male-bonding time. You go, we'll be fine. Maybe just pick out what he'll eat for lunch and leave the jars on the counter. I can play 'here comes the choo-choo' with the best of them."

"Thanks so much. You're a gem." Maggie sorted through jars of baby food and selected peas and bananas.

"You remember the way? There's a map in the glove box if you're not sure."

"Thanks, that'll save me time. I've gotta run."

She kissed David goodbye, admonished him to be a good boy and made sure J.D. knew where to find the teething toys in the refrigerator. Leaving David and J.D. behind as she headed toward the garage felt strange, as if an important part of her were missing.

But she had to admit the drive gave her a few moments to herself, time she sorely needed to think.

J.D.'s denouncement of miracles the previous night rang in her ears. *I never doubted. Until my pops died.*

He had stuff from his past that obviously still bothered him. Emotions that ran deep.

Shaking her head, Maggie reminded herself not to get too involved. She had plenty of her own problems. The upcoming meeting with her attorney, for one. The question of what to do with her apartment in Arizona for another.

She'd expected to be home and current on her rent by now. The landlord had been understanding to a point but he'd made it clear in her recent phone conversation with him that his patience was at an end. It would be so much easier to ask her friend Gina to store her things, tell the landlord to rent the apartment, and start new when she returned. But the apartment was the only home David had ever known—babies needed stability even more than adults.

Maggie sighed at the uncertainty of her immediate future. She should be grateful to J.D. for making their extended visit a little less traumatic. But a part of her didn't want to admit how well David had adapted to Arkansas and staying at J.D.'s home, or how easily *she'd* grown accustomed to the place.

Finding her attorney's office turned out to be easy. She was a bit early for her appointment, but the receptionist ushered her right in.

Lane rose, reaching across the desk to shake her hand. They exchanged pleasantries and discussed the weather while he got her a cup of coffee.

When he was seated once again, he said, "My P.I. did some initial work in McGuireville. Spoke to the staff at the banquet hall. You really know how to make an impression."

Maggie flushed. "Um, yes, I guess I do. I couldn't see any other way."

"Fortunately, your presentation left an indelible mark in the wait staff's minds. They were able to remember quite accurately who left shortly after your announcement."

"The people who left might have had time to go to the track and kill Eric before I got there?" she asked.

"Exactly. Now, J.D. left with you." He flipped through his notes. "Let's see, you waited a couple minutes before you left the hotel. And stopped at a mini-market for directions?"

She nodded.

"I asked the private investigator to time the drive from your motel room to the racetrack. I find the time line troubling. With your delay in stopping for directions, J.D. could have feasibly gone immediately to the track, killed Eric and left before you got there."

"J.D. wouldn't do something like that."

Lane held her gaze. "You seem very sure."

"I'm relying on instinct." She'd hoped for good news at this meeting, not a dissection of J.D.'s character. "Let's leave J.D. out of it for now. Did anyone else leave the reunion early?"

"Most of them were too busy raking Eric over the proverbial coals, in absentia." Lane raised an eyebrow. "You certainly made a dramatic entrance to McGuireville."

Maggie refused to be sidetracked. "Anyone who might have wanted Eric dead?"

"Eric's widow, Nancy, left immediately, escorted by Roy Abercrombie. Edna McGuire complained of feeling faint and Belmont Kincaid took her home. Nancy obviously had motive to murder Eric. And the way Eric was stabbed, it appears to have been a crime of passion, hence the overkill. I'll leave J.D. on my list of suspects, despite your opinion that he wouldn't hurt his brother. A couple of sources told my private investigator Eric and J.D. argued frequently."

Maggie opened her mouth to protest, then clamped it shut. Her instincts told her J.D. couldn't have done it, but her track record judging male character was seriously flawed.

Lane paged through a thick document. "The P.I. canvassed the racetrack, too. One of the pit crew thought he saw Nancy at the track. Of course, he saw you, too, but then again you've never denied being there."

"I was there, but Eric was already dead. You know that. Or don't you believe me?"

He raised a hand. "Oh, I believe you. But that means we need to know who else with motive was at the track before you were."

"It was crowded. There were so many people coming and going."

"Yes, but not so crowded that you weren't seen leaning inside Eric's car." Lane frowned. "How do you explain that?"

She felt as if she'd somehow betrayed her attorney by doing something stupid. Her face grew warm. "It had a different number and I wanted to make sure it was his."

"Still, it could look suspicious to a jury."

"Jury? I haven't been charged."

"And it's my job to see that you aren't. Believe me,

I'll do everything I can to keep you out of jail. But we have to consider all eventualities."

Maggie's breathing grew shallow at the thought of jail, the thought of being separated from David. "I'll help you any way I can."

"Good. We're on the same team."

"I know."

Lane's gaze was intent. "I need your complete trust."

Warning bells went off in her head. A man demanding trust was automatically suspect in her book. But she couldn't let her caution in romantic relationships cloud her judgment when her life was at stake. "I do trust you, Lane. But I also have to follow my conscience. I won't serve up one of the McGuires just to take the heat off me. I would need solid proof before I would even consider it. They *are* my son's family."

"Maggie, let's get one thing straight. You are my client and therefore I will aggressively defend you, but not at the expense of truth and justice. Sounds corny maybe, but I believe in those things."

Tipping her head to the side, she said, "Good, we understand each other. We should work well together."

Lane nodded and grinned. "Yes, I think we will. Now, I'm going to have the P.I. interview Nancy. Anything else you think we should pursue?"

"What about Roy Abercrombie? Was he seen at the track with Nancy?"

"No, but that doesn't necessarily mean anything. I

have to admit I've heard rumors that Nancy and Roy spent a lot of time together when Eric was out of town."

"Can anyone really blame her? It doesn't sound like Eric was there for her any more than he was there for me."

"No, but if they are having an affair, that gives Abercrombie motive, too."

Maggie shook her head. "What in the world do they put in the water in McGuireville? It sounds like a soap opera."

Lane chuckled. "You've never lived in a small town, have you?"

"No. That reminds me. My landlord in Arizona expects me to pay rent, but I can't leave Arkansas. I'd like to find a temporary job if it looks like I'll be here much longer."

"I wish I could tell you you'll be able to go home soon. Fact is, this investigation could drag on for a while. Getting a temporary job might be a good idea."

"I'll have to check the want ads. In the meantime, we're waiting for the paternity-test results. Have you received any word?"

"We should have them any day now. J. D. McGuire was more than happy to pay the rush fee. The waiting and wondering probably has the whole family stressed."

"Edna's the only one who believes David might be Eric's child. Apparently, everyone assumed that Eric was sterile. They're in for a big surprise when the results come back positive."

Lane leaned back in his chair and smiled. "I'd sure like to be a fly on the wall when they get the news."

J.D. PLACED DAVID'S SWING where he could keep an eye on the boy and still tinker with his grandmother's car. As long as David had something cold to chew on, he was a pretty happy camper.

Changing the oil would only take a few minutes, but he hadn't felt like working on the car after his discussion with Maggie the previous night.

She'd seriously disturbed his equilibrium, making him think about dreams and miracles and all the hokey stuff he'd stopped believing years ago.

But her enthusiasm engaged him and he didn't want to be engaged, darn it. He had enough on his plate keeping the McGuire family from going up in flames without adding more complications.

Turning to David, he asked, "So are you going to enlighten me on what makes women tick?"

The baby merely kicked his feet and gnawed on a plastic pretzel.

"You don't have any idea, either, do you?" J.D. shook his head. "I didn't think so. It has something to do with the whole double X-chromosome thing."

It didn't take long for J.D. to change the oil and filter, though he had to stop twice when David dropped his teething toy and started to cry.

J.D. rummaged around in the cubby on his workbench where he kept the notebook for recording mileage—he'd input the data in his computer later. Frowning, he double-checked the odometer. He found it hard to believe his grandmother had been out driving again when he made every effort to take her wherever she needed to go.

He shrugged, tucking the notebook in his back pocket. "Maybe she loaned the car to one of her friends."

David smiled in agreement.

"Come on, kid, we better get you some lunch."

MAGGIE STOPPED JUST INSIDE the kitchen doorway. J.D.'s back was to her and David seemed mesmerized with the spoon in J.D.'s hand.

There was a hint of desperation in the man's voice when he said, "Okay, we've established you don't like trains. How about airplanes?" He made swooping motions with the spoon while adding the drone of an engine.

The sight tugged at Maggie's emotions, kind of like the sappy commercials that made her cry. But this was the real deal. J.D. wasn't an actor and he related to her son as she'd dreamed Eric would.

It was somehow touching to see his strong, calloused hands grip the tiny baby spoon with such dexterity. J.D.'s denim shirt cuffs were rolled back, revealing tanned wrists with a sprinkling of dark hair. "The airplane's gonna have to make a crash landing if you don't open your mouth, kiddo."

Maggie chuckled. "It's a game. He hates peas, so he won't open his mouth."

J.D. turned, raising an eyebrow. "You're a cruel woman, you know it? You left me here to feed the kid veggies, knowing he wouldn't touch them."

"Oh, he'll eat them. It just takes patience."

J.D. snorted. "His or mine?"

"Definitely yours. He could play this game all day."

"So what's the secret?"

She briefly thought of letting him dangle a while longer, but took pity on him. He was doing her a favor by watching David. "Scoop a dab of peas, then a dab of bananas. The banana is what he sees and smells first."

J.D. followed her instructions and succeeded. "Hey, you're good."

Maggie suppressed a laugh, realizing she was the only one in the room who heard the double entendre in his observation. "I'm a very good mom."

He studied her for a moment, then nodded. "Yes, you are." Did she imagine the trace of wistfulness in his voice?

She wondered what his life had been like as a child. Eric had barely remembered their parents. "You were pretty young when your mother died, weren't you?"

"Ten. Eric was just a toddler. We were lucky we had family to take us in." His statement was flat, as if he repeated it by rote, having heard it recited to him over and over.

"Yes, you were. It was still probably a rough transition though."

He shrugged.

"Other than feeding, did everything go okay with David?"

"Yep. He's a good kid. How'd your meeting go?"

Maggie longed to tell him everything she'd found out, but Lane's warning rang in her ears. "Good, I guess." She hesitated. Lane couldn't complain if the information was common knowledge, could he? And she had no doubt Nancy's shenanigans were probably already common knowledge. "Did you know Nancy was at the track the night Eric died?"

J.D. wiped David's hands and face with a wet towel, then wiped his own hands. "Yeah, I heard some stuff. Just rumors. It wouldn't surprise me if she was there. Eric made a fool of her in front of two hundred people. She had to have been mad as hell."

"Mad enough to kill him?"

He shook his head. "I just don't see it. I think it's more likely to be a jealous husband or someone Eric cheated out of money. Don't let Nancy's Playboy bunny exterior fool you. She's normally a pretty sweet girl."

Maggie didn't want to hear about sweet Nancy. She wanted to hear that Nancy was a murderous bitch who had never deserved Eric. Then Maggie wouldn't have to feel sympathy for her. Or a twinge of guilt about unintentionally playing the role of home wrecker, even if the only home that had been wrecked was Maggie's.

J.D. lifted David from his high chair and handed him to her.

"Is that what the private investigator dug up?"

"How'd you know about the investigator?"

Raising an eyebrow, J.D. said, "It's a small town. Word gets around." He stepped closer. His voice was husky. "What I want to know is why I had to hear the news through the grapevine. Why didn't you tell me?"

"Lane said I shouldn't."

"Why?"

Maggie turned, picking up the damp towel and wiping down the high-chair tray. "He, um, said Eric was probably murdered by someone close to him."

"Was my name mentioned?"

She hesitated. "He didn't specify. It was merely a precaution, I'm sure."

"Yeah, I bet. What matters is what *you* think."

"J.D., I know you wouldn't hurt Eric."

He stepped up behind her, his breath warm on her neck. "Do you? Really?"

She shivered. Goose bumps prickled her arms. Turning, she used David as a shield against J.D.'s nearness. "I believe it with my whole heart."

J.D. brushed a strand of hair from her forehead. "I'm glad," he murmured. "I just don't want your attorney fabricating stories to suit his purposes. It's been known to happen."

"I wouldn't allow that to happen. Plenty of people saw Nancy at the track. It shows I'm not the only one with motive who was there that night."

"Oh, I imagine there were several people. There are no secrets in this town."

CHAPTER TWELVE

J.D. DROVE THE LONG WAY to his grandmother's place, enjoying the less-traveled road past Big Lake. It was a drive he took when he needed to think, though he preferred his truck over Grandma's Lincoln.

Something Maggie had said kept bothering him. How well does anybody really know a loved one? He'd known his little brother inside and out, or at least that's what he'd thought. But toward the end, he hadn't known him at all. Hadn't known about Maggie or David or God knew what else in Eric's life. Though his brother had always seemed easygoing, there was a part of him he'd held apart, covered with laughter and games. But every once in a while, J.D. would see regret in Eric's eyes, quickly camouflaged by jokes. Mostly, it had been when his little brother watched Nancy and thought nobody was looking.

J.D. didn't doubt for a minute that Eric had loved Nancy. But apparently he hadn't loved her enough to stay home or resist temptation.

One thing was for sure, when J.D. met and married the right woman, wild horses wouldn't drag him from home. He couldn't think of anything more important than family barbecues and baseball games, or the joy of watching his wife breast-feed their infant.

Whoa. More wild thoughts. He'd never felt like life was passing him by, until Eric's death. Now, there was a new urgency to living life to the fullest and savoring every day.

And what did that mean to him? He worked, hung out with a few friends and kept an eye on his grandmother. It was a safe existence, but at what price? He felt almost as if he were an observer instead of a participant. On the outside looking in.

On the outside looking in. It was a concept J.D. knew well. He remembered vividly the first time he'd met Grandma McGuire and the rest of the family. He'd only been seven, his hair slicked back, his shirt tucked in. Beside him, his mother fidgeted with his collar, Richard McGuire chucked him on the shoulder. This was an important event. Their future hinged on the McGuires liking him, accepting him as one of their own. Mama had never put it into words, but the knowledge hung in the air as they stood on the porch. A golden glow emanated from the huge picture window. Inside, there was lots of food and everyone was laughing and talking. And somehow, J.D. sensed he wouldn't fit in. He wanted to simply press his nose to the glass and watch from the safety of the shadows.

Instead, Richard opened the door, waiting while J.D.'s mother gently propelled him inside.

Once there, a hush fell over the room. Then everyone talked at once, as if to cover the fact that he didn't belong. Whispered comments about his daddy reached J.D.'s tender ears and it felt as if his heart were broken with each revelation. Words he'd never heard before, like *dago* and *immigrant* were used to describe his father. But it was the blue-collar part that really confused him. He'd never seen his dad wear a shirt with a blue collar. But it was obviously a bad thing.

So J.D. had sneaked away as quickly as he could, curling up in a rocker on the front porch. On the outside looking in. And there he'd remained for twenty-eight years.

Shaking his head, J.D. guided his thoughts to the present. The past was over and done. He'd earned his place in the world. It seemed like a hollow victory, though, compared to the riches Eric had acquired and tossed away.

He swung the Lincoln around and headed for his grandmother's house.

After parking the car in the garage, he tucked in his shirt as he took the front steps two at a time.

The door swung open before he knocked.

His grandmother extended her hands. "J.D., what a nice surprise."

She seemed glad to see him. But he wondered if she was one of the people who had looked down on his father. The faces and voices blurred in his memory and he knew he would never sort them out. God, he hoped she hadn't been one of them. It hurt to think the woman he loved so much might say such cruel things about the birth father he'd adored.

J.D. cleared his throat. "Hi, Grandma. I brought your car back. Thanks for letting me borrow it."

"You're welcome to use it anytime."

"It was overdue for an oil change, though I'd thought it was good for another month or so."

She waved away his concern as she opened the door. "You know I don't pay attention to those things. Come in."

"Hmm. Maybe I transposed a number or something last time I checked it."

She beamed at him as if he'd discovered a cure for cancer. "I'm sure that's it. You take such good care of me, Jamie. Please say you'll join me for a piece of pie."

Uh-oh. What had he done to warrant a pie inquisition? Nothing that he could recall. "I'm in kind of a hurry. Maggie's got a job interview and I need to fix her car first."

"A job interview? Whatever for?"

"The usual reasons, I guess. She's still got an apartment and bills in Phoenix and it doesn't look like she'll be allowed to leave the state soon."

Grandma wrinkled her nose. "She's not working as a mortician, is she?"

"She's interviewing at the Tinker Brothers Mortuary over in Confederate City. Maggie wants to be a funeral director. It's what she does." It felt odd to be defending her profession when he didn't completely understand her choice himself.

"Hmm. Well, it doesn't seem like the right job for a woman. She needs to stay home with David. Maybe if she remarried…"

"You mentioned pie, Grandma."

"Oh, yes, pie. Make yourself comfortable in the sunroom and I'll get our plates."

J.D. didn't have long to wait. Grandma was back amazingly quickly, as if she'd had the pie and iced tea already arranged.

She didn't waste time coming to the point, either. "Have we received the paternity-test results?"

"No. But I'll call this afternoon and see what the holdup is."

"I want to know immediately, dear. Not that there's any doubt in my mind."

J.D. chewed slowly, savoring the extraordinary sweetness of caramelized pecans. "I'm beginning to agree with you. Maggie's not a bad person. She just got in over her head with Eric."

"You like her, don't you?"

"Yes, I do." He wiped his mouth with a napkin. "She has a good heart."

"I'm glad to hear it. You know, in the old days, especially after the war between the states, it wasn't unheard of for a man to marry his brother's widow."

J.D. inhaled pastry crumbs and coughed. Her

suggestion came out of nowhere. Was her mind slipping because of grief?

But Grandma seemed bright and alert as she patted his back solicitously and pressed a glass of tea into his hand.

After a couple of swallows, his cough subsided. "Me? And Nancy? I don't think so."

She made an impatient noise. "No. Not Nancy. Maggie."

Fortunately, J.D.'s fork was suspended midair, so he didn't inhale more pie. "Maggie?"

"You have to admit, it would be the perfect solution. Maggie would forget all about returning to Arizona and taking Eric's son with her."

"You're kidding, right?"

"I never kid about something this important. You seem to get along with Maggie and—"

"And what? I'm to be the sacrificial lamb? Keep it all in the family?"

"Nonsense, Jamie. You like Maggie, don't you? And I think she likes you."

"There are a lot of things I'd do for you, Grandma. Marrying my brother's, um, girlfriend, isn't one of them. Where in the heck did you get such an idea?"

"I was chatting with Belmont—"

"*Belmont* suggested it?"

"No, dear. I was consulting with him about the possibility of gaining custody of David."

His heart sank. Great. Just great. He'd been afraid of

something like this. She was grieving and adopting David probably seemed like the perfect way to heal. He knew better. Adopting David might help his grandmother in the short term, but a custody battle would end up hurting everyone involved, especially Maggie and David.

And if his grandmother succeeded? J.D. didn't think he could stand by and watch her ruin another child. He'd always secretly thought Eric might have grown up to be a responsible adult if she hadn't constantly indulged him.

J.D. wasn't cruel enough to point that fact out to her. From what Belmont had told him, his grandmother's excessive indulgence and overprotectiveness started after her only son died. From that point she held on tightly to Eric and excused him from the rules J.D. was expected to follow.

Trying to get the older woman to see reason, he stated the obvious. "David doesn't need a guardian. He has a good mother."

"Yes." Grandma sighed. "Maggie seems to be devoted to the boy. Belmont said we'd have to prove she was an unfit mother to have any chance of gaining custody."

"This whole conversation is ridiculous." J.D. started to rise.

She gestured for him to sit down. "Jamie, I didn't say we would do it. I'm merely letting you know that I would not be averse to a match between you and Maggie. It would be—"

"Expedient."

"James David, I will not allow you to interrupt. It's very rude."

If it weren't such a difficult conversation, he might enjoy watching her masterfully deflect blame. Was it any wonder Eric had acquired the same trait?

He took a deep breath. "I'm sorry for interrupting. But my answer is no. If you'll excuse me, I need to fix Maggie's car. And please don't mention this crazy idea to her. She might find it…insulting."

"Of course I wouldn't broach the subject with her. I imagine you can be much more persuasive."

J.D. prayed for patience. She was an old woman grieving for her favorite grandson. But deep down, he wondered if she'd always been this manipulative and he just hadn't noticed.

MAGGIE CAME OUT of the interview thanking her lucky stars. The job was perfect. She would fill in temporarily while the receptionist/office manager was on maternity leave.

When she arrived at J.D.'s house, she hesitated before getting out of the car. The wonderful old colonial seemed so familiar, almost like a real home, where a family might laugh, argue, forgive and pull together. It was the kind of home she'd always wanted.

Pushing away the momentary wistfulness, Maggie went through the unlocked front door without knocking. She found J.D. in his office, drawing what looked like blueprints, while David watched from his swing.

Scooping David up, she kissed his cheeks. He smiled from ear to ear. So did J.D. when he glanced up from his paperwork.

Maggie reminded herself this was only a temporary solution. They would be back in Arizona soon. Why was the idea of returning home suddenly so unappealing?

"How'd it go?" he asked.

"I got the job."

"Wonderful. That'll ease your financial situation, I imagine."

"Yes, it will. And Mr. Tinker said David could come to work with me for at least part of the day. They planned to set up a playpen when the regular office manager returned anyway. And Mr. Tinker has a teenage niece who would be willing to babysit a couple hours a day."

"A baby at a mortuary?"

Maggie sighed. "Only in the office. It's not like he'll be crawling around the embalming room."

"Sounds like it's coming together for you. I'm glad." He smiled slowly, but his eyes didn't reflect any happiness. "Um, so the office is baby proof? No danger of David getting into chemicals?"

Maggie frowned. "No. None of the chemicals are kept in the office. And he'll be in his playpen, safe and sound."

"Good. Glad to hear it."

"Is something wrong?"

"No. I'm sure you don't want people to get the idea you might be neglecting David in any way while you're at work."

"J.D., I thought you knew me well enough now to know I would never endanger my son."

Sighing, he leaned back in his chair. "I told my grandmother you were looking for a temp job and she was...concerned."

"Maybe we should invite her over for pie and I'll re-assure her." Reassurance was the furthest thing from Maggie's mind. The woman was seriously overstepping her bounds and Maggie intended to politely tell her so.

"No." J.D. tensed. "That's not necessary. I explained it to her."

"If you're sure..."

"Positive. When do you start?"

Maggie decided not to press the subject—yet. "To-morrow. The office manager's been on early maternity leave for a week already. They seem pretty snowed under. I should be able to start paying you back a lit-tle when I get my first paycheck."

He waved away her offer. "Take your time, I'm in no hurry."

The phone rang. J.D. picked up the receiver and frowned as he listened. "How in the heck could some-thing like this happen?"

Foreboding settled in Maggie's stomach.

"Isn't there any other way?" he asked. After listening for a few minutes, he said, "Okay. We'll be there as soon as possible."

When he hung up, Maggie asked, "Is something wrong?"

"Yeah. That was the lab."

"The results are in?"

J.D. shook his head. "The test was no good. Something about bad gel or something. I didn't understand half of the terms he used. The gist is the test needs to be redone."

"Redone? Haven't we all been through enough?"

Swiping his hand over his face, he swore under his breath. "I thought for sure we'd have the results today. But apparently these things happen. You and David will need to be retested and they'll have to see if another, um, sample from Eric was preserved."

Maggie groaned. "What if there isn't another sample?"

"Then it's me or my grandmother they compare to. I guess it's more complicated since Eric and I didn't have the same father."

"Let's hope they don't have to do that."

"Yeah. They want us down at the lab right away to retest."

Maggie's sense of accomplishment faded. Just when she was excited about starting her new job, the past jumped in to remind her how badly she'd messed up.

David patted her face and grinned, a solid reminder that good sometimes came out of tragedy.

CHAPTER THIRTEEN

J.D. WATCHED AS MAGGIE OPENED her mouth and allowed the technician to scrape an oversize cotton swab against the inside of her cheek. Resignation lurked in her big, green eyes.

He resisted the urge to tell the technician to go to hell for doing his job so damn clinically and efficiently. J.D. hadn't realized how much he'd been depending on having the results today. Disappointment and frustration made him restless. Holding David, he paced. "I bet this is kind of confusing, huh, kid?"

The baby didn't seem to mind though. There was plenty of strange equipment to keep him fascinated. When they brushed close to the counter, David leaned over and reached for a medical instrument. "No, you don't, buddy."

J.D. grasped the small hand and moved a safe distance from all objects.

David screeched.

"I know, I spoil all your fun, don't I?"

The kid quickly forgot his anger, though, too busy looking for something else to get into. J.D. chuckled.

"Maggie, you're going have your hands full once this one starts walking. He'll be into everything."

Maggie rolled her eyes. "Don't I know it. He's already into everything."

J.D. fleetingly wondered if he'd be there to see the boy take his first steps, say his first real words, ride a bike.

"David McGuire?" the technician read off a clipboard.

"This little guy here." He nodded toward David.

"You can hold him while I take the sample."

"Sure."

David apparently decided he didn't like the guy's bedside manner. He clamped his little lips shut and turned his head.

The young man tried to demonstrate to David how he should open his mouth wide, but the baby would have none of it.

"Last time they gave him a cookie," Maggie suggested.

"It's better if there's no food in his mouth." The man's tone held a note of impatience. "Here, set him on the exam table."

The lab guy reached for David and J.D. instinctively backed up a step.

"I don't think so," J.D. said. Protectiveness surged through his system. He didn't know where it came from, but it was an almost uncontrollable urge to guard the child at any cost.

Maggie must have seen it, because she stepped toward the technician. "Let's try a cookie, please? I have one in the diaper bag. Just hold it where he can see it and ask him to open his mouth."

"If you'll bring the cookie," J.D. said, "I'll do it." He wasn't at all sure he wanted to let this guy anywhere near David. But how much damage could he do with a cotton swab?

Maggie produced the treat and handed it to J.D.

"Okay, buddy," he told David. "Open your mouth wide for the nice man and you get the cookie. Like this." J.D. demonstrated, as he opened his mouth as wide as he could.

He could have sworn he heard Maggie giggle, but he ignored her. His mission was too important.

David eyed the stranger, eyed J.D., and imitated J.D., his gaze locked on the treat J.D. held out of his reach.

"Better be quick," he muttered to the lab guy.

The technician didn't need any urging. "Yeah, man, these kids'll bite a finger off if you don't watch them."

"*I'll* bite your finger off if you don't get a good sample. There's absolutely no way this child or his mother should have to go through a third testing."

The test was over in a flash and David was overjoyed to have the cookie in his grasp.

The technician peeled off his latex gloves, washed his hands and put on another pair of gloves. Glancing at his clipboard on the counter, he said, "Let me guess, you must be J. D. McGuire. You're next."

J.D. obligingly opened wide without urging.

The lab guy hesitated. "I took a good sample from the kid. You're not gonna bite me are you?"

"No, I'm not going to bite you. It was an idle threat. Now get on with it."

J.D. felt like cursing his brother while the technician rubbed the swab against the inside of J.D.'s cheek. All this trouble and heartbreak because of Eric.

When they were done, he said, "Maggie, go on ahead to the waiting area. I'll be there in a minute."

She tipped her head to the side, but didn't utter the question he could see in her eyes. She nodded, took David from him, and did as he'd suggested.

"I want to speak to the clinic manager," he told the technician.

"You're not filing a complaint, are you?"

"No, but I might be tempted, if I don't get to speak to the manager immediately."

After J.D. explained the first botched paternity test, the manager assured him the results would be delivered within forty-eight hours.

Satisfied, J.D. shook her hand and joined Maggie and David.

"Ready?" he asked.

"More than ready."

"Let's go grab something to eat before we head home." Hot, damp air settled over him when they exited the clinic. "There's a place not far from here that serves catfish and chips that'll melt in your mouth. I'm not sure if there's anything on the menu David can eat, though. I don't suppose you have any baby food in that suitcase you call a diaper bag, do you?"

"Of course I have baby food. I've noticed you have a magical pantry at your house. David eats and eats, but the supply never dwindles."

J.D. rubbed the back of his neck. "I hoped you wouldn't notice, what with all the other stuff going on."

"Oh, I noticed. And I think it's incredibly sweet of you." Her eyes were warm with admiration. She made him feel like he had done something really outstanding. "And it was sweet of you to stand up for David back there."

"No big deal."

"Yes, it is a big deal." Her voice was husky. "And I appreciate it." She kissed him on the cheek.

He didn't know how to react. So he didn't. Just stopped in the middle of the parking lot.

Maggie blushed. She rubbed his cheek with her thumb as if to erase the gesture as well as any residual lip gloss.

Grasping her hand, he stilled it.

Her eyes widened, her pupils dilated, her lips parted.

And David fussed, apparently tired of the inaction.

J.D. pressed a kiss to Maggie's palm, holding her gaze and making a silent promise. He had no idea what he was promising, but he knew on some level it was essential.

She glanced at her palm, at him, then at David, as if the three were linked.

He feared she was right. They were linked. Not by blood or marriage, but by a tentative connection with a dubious future.

David started to cry, breaking the spell. J.D. cradled the back of the baby's head with his hand, marveling at the fragility. "My nephew. I will always be there for you, little one."

Maggie inhaled sharply. "J.D.? What happened back there?"

"Nothing and everything. Things became very clear to me all of a sudden. I don't need a test to tell me what I already know in here." He tapped his chest. "You're telling the truth. You and my brother created a miracle together."

David's cries of frustration seemed like beautiful music, almost like a newborn greeting the world. Because as far as J.D. was concerned, David was being reborn as the child of his heart.

THE FISH-AND-CHIP JOINT doubled as a pool hall, but J.D. led them to a secluded alcove more conducive to dining. They'd been nearly silent in the ride from the clinic. Maggie was still processing J.D.'s admission. He believed her. She found it both reassuring and scary. Their friendship had shifted and she had no idea what that meant.

A part of her feared she would open herself up to more hurt and disappointment if she accepted J.D.'s change of heart at face value. The other part breathed a sigh of relief that she was no longer alone.

The aroma of fried catfish intruded in her thoughts. Maggie decided to enjoy their meal and leave the analyzing for later. "I didn't realize how hungry I was."

"I'm starved." J.D. found a high chair along one wall and carried it to their booth.

She placed David in the chair and scooted into the booth. The table was made of rustic planks, initials carved here and there.

After they ordered, Maggie retrieved a jar of bananas from the diaper bag and started feeding David. "He's hungry, too."

J.D. smiled slowly. "Eric and I used to eat here when we'd come to Fayetteville. It was one of his favorite places."

"Maybe that's why he always wanted to eat at Ralph's Fish and Chips in Arizona." Taking a bite of the steaming fish, she thought she'd died and gone to heaven. "No wonder he said it never held a candle to what he got back here."

"You know what, we always talk about Eric. I want to know more about you." His gaze was intent.

Maggie blushed. "There's not that much to tell. I'd rather hear about your work. Tell me what it's like to be an architect."

J.D. didn't call her on the obvious attempt to change the subject. "It's a good job most days."

"What makes the other days bad?"

"Sometimes being cooped up inside gets old. Sometimes I just itch to get tools in my hand and create something without drawings and plans. Something completely free-form. Goofy, huh?"

"No. Creative." *And sexy.*

"I create when I design a project. But this is different. This is hands-on. I don't know—freer somehow."

Maggie's gaze was drawn to his hands. He seemed just as comfortable holding a baby as holding a power tool. She wondered what his hands might feel like skimming over her body.

Her face flushed, her entire body flushed, with the mental image of J.D. focusing his considerable concentration on making love to her.

Almost knocking over her glass in her haste, Maggie clasped it with numb fingers. The water trickled down her parched throat.

David banged on the high-chair tray with a spoon, giggling at the noise he made, and Maggie managed to get past her embarrassment while J.D. filled the silence with small talk.

When she didn't think she could eat another bite, Maggie leaned back against the cushioned booth and sighed. "That was wonderful."

J.D.'s eyes twinkled. "It's good to see you relax. Sometimes I wonder what you're like when you're in Arizona and not in the middle of this mess."

His admission touched her. "My life's not very exciting. Work, school and David."

"Tell me about your job."

"I was the evening day-care director for a child-care center. It didn't pay very well, but I got to take David with me. I loved being able to spend time with him and with the other kids. And David loved all the attention from the older children. It was pretty much a win-win situation."

"What happened?"

"The owners sold the lot to a commercial developer and moved to Payson. They're in their sixties and the summers in Mesa were too hard on them. So they jumped at the chance to move. I can't blame them. But it's been difficult for me to find a job where I can take David and still work around my school hours."

"I've been wondering. Most people would be a doctor or a nurse or a social worker even. Why'd you decide on something a little less traditional?"

Maggie shrugged. "It's a stable profession and I knew I could make a difference. Besides, I really don't think of it as nontraditional. There have been professionals in charge of preparing bodies as long as man's walked the earth. Though the procedures and ceremonies may differ, all cultures have rituals for dealing with death. In essence, what I do is the second-oldest profession."

J.D. grinned. "Point taken. But I still get the feeling there's more to the story."

Maggie adjusted David's bib and gave him a cracker. Stalling wouldn't make it any easier. Taking a deep breath, she said, "I told you my sister Cassie committed suicide…." It was still so hard to say the words. "I kind of fell apart."

"I'm sorry."

"Me, too. But it's what ultimately brought me to my true calling." She hesitated. "My folks had disowned Cassie, but I'd still sneak over to her apartment to see her and my niece, Emma. After Child Protective Services took Emma, I should have known Cassie was more than a little depressed. I had no idea she might hurt herself. For a while, I blamed myself. I should have been there for her more or tried harder to understand what she was going through. Lots of stuff."

J.D. clasped her hand. "That must've been terrible."

Nodding, she didn't trust herself to speak. She closed her eyes for a moment, trying to remember Cassie when she'd been so full of life.

"I'm the one who found her," Maggie whispered, opening her eyes.

"Aw, sweetheart. I'm so sorry."

"It was pretty rough. I started having nightmares. Couldn't eat, couldn't concentrate."

"That's only natural, I'm sure."

"Yes, it was. But I didn't know that. I thought I was losing my mind. Fortunately, the funeral director was a wonderful, wonderful man. He counseled me for hours. Helped me to see that Cassie had made a terrible, tragic choice, not thinking of anyone but herself because she was in so much emotional pain. Her choice didn't mean someone had to be at fault, or that anyone could have stopped her if she was truly determined to take that way out."

J.D. nodded. "Sounds like a pretty smart man."

"Yes, he was. He helped me forgive myself and forgive Cassie. For that, I'll always be grateful."

"He helped you like you helped me at Eric's funeral." Awe tinged his voice.

"It's as much a part of me as breathing. I'll never know if I would have found my calling if he hadn't helped me. I get so much satisfaction from counseling. It's my way of giving back."

"So, it's kind of like being a shrink, only a specialized shrink?"

Maggie smiled. "I guess you could put it like that."

"Your folks? Did they go to the funeral?"

Nodding, she was surprised by an errant spark of anger. "Yes. They wouldn't help when she needed them most—when she was a scared, lonely, single mother with no one to turn to. But once Cass was dead and didn't need them anymore, they showed up at her funeral." She wiped at the tears trickling from the corner of her eye.

David started to fuss. His eyes were wide with confusion.

"Mommy's okay honey." She stroked his cheek. Turning to J.D., she murmured, "I wonder how people with half a heart could turn their back on their own child."

"Maybe half a heart isn't enough. Maybe kids need to be loved wholeheartedly, even when they disappoint their parents."

Maggie's vision blurred as his words touched her somewhere deep inside. "Yes. That's it exactly. Not just when they do the right things, but when they do the wrong things, too. I felt like my parents quit loving me when I couldn't live their way anymore."

"I don't know how anyone could *not* love you." J.D. reached across the table and cupped his hand around her cheek. "It was because something was missing in them, not you. Don't ever forget that."

Covering his hand with hers, Maggie absorbed his tenderness. His simple gesture of comfort touched her more than any of Eric's grand, empty displays. Tears trickled down her face. "Thank you." Maggie saw that she'd been waiting a long time for someone to convince her she deserved to be loved.

CHAPTER FOURTEEN

THE NEXT TWO DAYS were the most surreal of J.D.'s life. Everything had changed now that he believed he had a nephew. He found himself simply watching the little boy, awed that his brother had created something so perfect.

And he watched Maggie, too, but that caused more questions than answers. The whole idea of his place in the universe was shifting. He was now an uncle. An uncle who had the hots for the child's mother. Like his grandmother had pointed out, it wouldn't be the first time in history for something like that to happen. But it would be the first time for J.D.

He and Eric had been far enough apart in age that they hadn't hung out together, hadn't fought over girls. And J.D. honestly hadn't been attracted to the same kind of woman as Eric had. Until Maggie. It was unsettling, somehow, to even contemplate dating a woman who had dated his brother—worse yet, a woman who had been *intimate* with Eric.

The doorbell rang and J.D. went to answer it. Seeing the big, white FedEx van through the window,

J.D.'s stomach started to churn. He signed to acknowledge receipt and accepted the packet.

The return address was for the lab conducting the paternity test. It seemed as if the results were finally here.

Should he look at them? Should he wait till Maggie got home from work? Although he was pretty sure he knew what the report contained, it still would be reassuring to see it in print.

He grabbed his keys and headed out the door. Surely Maggie could take a short break, even if it was her first week of work.

Parking in the shaded lot, J.D. inhaled deeply. The office was the only place he'd see. There wouldn't be any bodies there. He wouldn't even be close to a body. The thought reassured him and he headed for the office of Tinker Brothers Mortuary.

A small bell dinged when he opened the door. The office was apparently designed to make people feel at home, as if that were possible in a mortuary. There were comfortable love seats and chairs grouped around a large coffee table.

Maggie's desk was at the far end. She looked up from her paperwork and smiled. Her desk was small and loaded with papers. "Hi. What brings you here?"

Not far from her desk was the playpen. "Looks like David's asleep," he whispered.

"No need to whisper. He's getting used to the phones and lots of stuff going on while he sleeps. What's up?"

"The test results are in."

"Good. It's about time."

"Do you mind if I go ahead and open it here?"

"Please do."

He peeled the strip of cardboard away where indicated. Withdrawing the report, he took a deep, fortifying breath.

Maggie, on the other hand, seemed cool as a cucumber. "I thought you believed me."

"I did. I do. It's just so…final."

"What does it say?" she asked.

He read the cover letter. "It says David is Eric's child." J.D. got a lump in his throat. The report confirmed that he was an uncle.

Maggie smiled. "See, I told you."

"Yes, and I believed you, too. But it was nice to have it confirmed."

"When should we tell Edna?"

He'd almost forgotten his grandmother. She would undoubtedly be overjoyed by the fact that she now had a great-grandchild by blood to carry on the McGuire name.

A tiny stab of jealousy caught him by surprise. David was a McGuire by blood, J.D. was not. Where did that leave him? Almost instantly, he was ashamed of himself for being jealous of a nine-month-old baby. An innocent who hadn't asked to be in the middle of this complex situation.

"J.D.? Should we call your grandmother? I don't

like giving this kind of news over the phone, though."

"Um, no. I'll call her and we can plan to go to her house when you get off work, if that's okay with you."

"That's fine. Her reaction will be good, won't it?"

"Good? She'll be dancing on the lawn. I can't think of anything that would please her more."

Maggie nodded. "Okay. I'll be home about five-thirty. Do you want to grab something quick to eat at home first?"

"If I know Grandma, she'll have her housekeeper help her whip up a special dinner. Let's play it by ear. I'll let you get back to work." But instead of leaving immediately, he tiptoed over to the playpen and looked at the sleeping baby.

He'd worked from home today and had missed not having the little guy around the house. Placing his palm gently on David's back, he was awed by the peace and purity of the sleeping child. "Sweet dreams, little nephew."

He couldn't quite meet Maggie's eyes as he turned. He probably sounded like a total sap, but something about David choked him up. "I'll see ya at home."

Gathering his courage, he met Maggie's gaze. Instead of ridicule, her eyes were suspiciously bright and she blinked rapidly. "Yes, we'll see you at home."

MAGGIE GLANCED UP what seemed like only minutes later to find Charla, the boss's niece, coming through the door with David. Charla was at that gawky stage— tall, thin with straight brown hair. She also had a beautiful smile and loved children.

"Wow. That time already?" Maggie asked.

"Sure is. David's a great kid. We had fun."

Maggie accepted David from her and kissed him on the cheek. "Hey, sweetheart, were you a good boy for Charla?"

He jabbered in response, waving his arms and smiling.

"Same time tomorrow?" Charla asked.

"Yes. That would be great. Your uncle would like me to take a few appointments tomorrow helping clients make arrangements."

Maggie said goodbye to Charla and gathered her diaper bag and purse. Peeking in the door to Mr. Tinker's office, she poked her head in to say goodbye.

He was also tall and thin, tanned by all the time he spent outdoors. Photos on the walls showed him whitewater rafting, hiking and rock climbing. For a man in his late fifties, he seemed younger. His brother, Alex, was reportedly exploring the Himalayas.

"Mr. Tinker, I've got your receivables up-to-date and I'll work on the payables tomorrow. Then in the afternoon, I've got two appointments with clients."

"Maggie, I can't thank you enough. You've been a real godsend. And please call me Jack."

"I'll see you in the morning, Jack."

Her step was light as she took David out to the car. She couldn't have asked for a better temporary job.

It wasn't until the drive home that she had time to think about the test results. They didn't change a thing for her, but she realized the changes for the McGuire family could be astounding.

She was nervous about meeting with J.D.'s grandmother. The woman could be intimidating in the best of circumstances. But she seemed genuinely fond of David and had been nothing but kind to Maggie.

J.D. was sitting on the porch when she pulled up. His welcoming smile warmed her. She'd very rarely had anyone to greet her with a smile when she got home and it would take very little for her to get used to coming home to J.D.

Maggie was glad he couldn't see very well through the windshield. He'd been very kind to her and the last thing she wanted to do was misinterpret his signals. But all signs pointed to the fact that he enjoyed her company as much as she enjoyed his.

Shutting off the engine, she cranked down the window and asked, "What time are we supposed to be at your grandma's?"

J.D. came toward her, his stride confident. Amazing how a man that muscular could be so, well, graceful. "She wants us there ASAP. We can leave now, unless you want to freshen up first."

"Let's go ahead and get it over with. That way we

don't have to take David out of his car seat and put him right back in again. Hop in."

J.D. made himself comfortable in the passenger seat, moving the seat back to accommodate his longer legs. He twisted around to see David in the back. "Hey, kiddo. What'd you do today, besides sleep?"

David gurgled and pulled on his foot.

"He played with Jack's niece, Charla. It seems like they had a pretty good time," Maggie supplied.

J.D. frowned. "How old is she?"

"Fourteen. She's very responsible."

"I hope so. I wish you worked in McGuireville, then I'd know her. I've asked around a bit, though, and Jack Tinker is supposed to be a pretty good guy."

"Yes, he is."

"Single?"

"I believe so."

J.D. grunted.

"He treats me as a professional."

"He better," J.D. muttered.

Maggie found it amusing that J.D. took such an interest in her new job, especially whether she and David were being treated well. And she found J.D.'s touch of jealousy surprising. It meant he cared more than he was willing to admit.

"You still think you're going to like it?" he asked.

"It's the perfect interim job. In the past two days, I've been able to jump right into the administrative side of the business. It's given me a terrific view of the day-today workings. And tomorrow, I'll meet with a few clients."

J.D.'s face paled slightly. "Not in the embalming room, I hope?"

Maggie chuckled. "No, one client is planning her arrangements in advance and the second is a son whose eighty-year-old father died. The process is pretty much the same, but the bereaved generally need more gentle handling. Particularly, in choosing caskets."

"Hmm. And you learned all this stuff in school?"

Nodding, she said, "This job is a wonderful opportunity to practice what I've learned. Kind of like an informal paid internship. I'll have to see if maybe I can earn some college credit for it, too."

"Have, you, um, seen any bodies there?"

Maggie wondered if it was morbid curiosity or if J.D. was trying to work through his aversion to dead people. With J.D., she was pretty sure it was more than just curiosity—he usually had a good reason for everything he did. "Not yet. I toured the preparation room, but there were no clients in there at the time."

Maggie steered into the circular driveway at J.D.'s grandmother's house, pulling up behind a BMW convertible.

She turned to J.D. and asked, "Whose car is that?"

"Belmont's. I wonder what he's doing here."

Maggie shut off the engine and went around to remove David from his car seat. J.D. stepped behind her, frowning, when she straightened and turned.

"What's wrong?"

"I hope Belmont isn't planning on staying. This is a private, family matter."

"He probably just dropped in. Maybe he'll leave soon."

J.D. knocked on the door. His grandmother answered and ushered them in.

"I asked Belmont to be present. There is some legal work he will need to get started on."

"You're awfully certain you know what the results are," J.D. commented.

"I am. Plus, I believe in being prepared."

J.D. stood in the doorway, crossing his arms. "Being prepared is a good thing, but I think it should be only family when we discuss the paternity results. You can consult with Belmont later."

"I don't intend to waste a minute. Besides, he's almost family anyway."

Shrugging, J.D. grasped Maggie's elbow and steered her toward the settee.

"Hello, Edna, Belmont." Maggie smiled weakly. Belmont usually made her feel as if she'd just crawled out from under a rock. It wasn't so much what he said, but the superior way he looked down his nose at her.

Belmont nodded in response to her greeting. Turning to J.D., he said, "Hello, J.D."

"It's so good to see you, dear." Edna held out her arms to David. "And especially good to see this little one."

"I'd like David to stay with me for a few minutes, until he gets settled in," Maggie said. The truth was that Edna's constant pawing of the child made her uneasy. If the woman was so proprietary toward him before she knew for certain he was her great-grandchild, how would she act once she knew for sure?

Edna patted her hair. "Oh, well, if you think that's best, dear."

"I do."

"Maggie's right, Grandma. She's his mother," J.D. said.

Maggie thought he placed extra emphasis on the *mother* part, as if reminding the woman of an indisputable fact.

Edna took a seat in a cushy, antique wingback chair. She looked a bit like a queen reigning over her subjects. "Supper will be ready in about thirty minutes. Shall we go ahead and discuss the results?"

"Grandma, no disrespect intended, but I don't think it's necessary to have Belmont here. You're not considering Maggie's feelings."

"Oh, dear, I'm so sorry." Edna frowned. "I didn't even think."

Maggie squeezed J.D.'s forearm. "I don't mind."

"Are you sure?" His gaze was warm and reassuring. She nodded.

"Okay." He handed the FedEx envelope to his grandmother. "Here's the report."

Edna's hand shook as she removed the sheaf of papers. Putting on her reading glasses, she scanned the first page. She clasped the papers to her chest and closed her eyes. "He's ours," she breathed.

Maggie thought it was an odd way to phrase it, but was too busy trying to keep David occupied to comment. The baby squirmed in her arms. He wanted down on the floor to crawl and Edna had way too many fragile things within his reach. "No, honey. You can't get down now."

Edna crossed the room, but before she could scoop up David, J.D. held out his arms to him. "Come here, buddy."

David leaned toward J.D. "Da."

J.D. blanched, but grasped him under the arms. "Hey, slugger."

Edna's tone was overly casual when she said, "J.D., have you given any further thought to our conversation the other day? Especially in light of recent developments?"

"What conversation?"

Edna pointedly glanced at J.D., then to Maggie, and back to J.D. "You know, those Confederate brothers we discussed."

Maggie could feel J.D. stiffen. Glancing at him, she was surprised to see his eyes narrow and tense white lines bracket his mouth.

His voice was low and emphatic. "No, I haven't, Grandmother, and I don't intend to. You're out of line to even suggest it."

Maggie couldn't recall seeing J.D. this angry. Whatever their discussion had been, it must have been a doozy. Funny, J.D. hadn't mentioned a disagreement.

Edna sniffed. "There's no need to be rude, James David."

"I'm not being rude. I'm merely stating a fact."

Belmont cleared his throat. "Maybe I should go."

Maggie resisted the urge to fall in behind him to escape whatever awkward power play was happening.

"Nonsense, Belmont. Supper should be ready soon." She turned to Maggie. "Dear, J.D. tells me you have a job."

"Yes. It looks like I might be stuck, um, I might be here a while, so I'm doing some temp work at Tinker Brothers Mortuary."

"That's very…admirable. But who takes care of David?"

"Jack Tinker has allowed me to keep him in the office with me during the morning. Then in the afternoon, his niece, Charla, watches David."

"How interesting." Edna's smile was stiff. She turned to Belmont. "Isn't that interesting?"

He nodded, his expression thoughtful, as if he were mentally taking notes.

"David is being well taken care of, Grandmother. I visited today and he was asleep, safe and sound." Now J.D.'s voice was more forceful, as if he were reacting to the undercurrents in the room.

The friction in the air was enough to make the hair

on Maggie's forearms rise, as if a storm were brewing. She wanted to jump up and scream at them to stop talking as if they were all in on something she didn't understand.

Taking a deep breath, she somehow remained calm. "J.D.'s right. David loves it at the office. And having him there allows me to spend more time with him."

"I'm sure it does, dear." Edna's voice was placating. "But wouldn't it be better if he were with family while you're at work?"

Maggie's heart sank. Her breathing grew shallow as the walls closed in on her. It was the same feeling she'd had when the people from Child Protective Services had started asking too many questions. It was also the one she'd gotten when she had found her sister Cassie's body.

J.D. must have sensed her distress, because he reached over and clasped her hand.

Drawing strength from his support, she managed to slow the racing of her heart. "David is fine with me at work, Mrs. McGuire."

"I didn't mean to imply he wasn't. It's just that I could care for him while you work and then he'd be with family. It would mean so very much to me." Edna's voice quavered, her eyes clouded.

Maggie felt like she was being maneuvered into a corner. "I don't know what to say." That at least was the truth, while she stalled for time, her mind working furiously. How to graciously decline without offending her son's great-grandmother?

"He will be with family, Grandmother. I'll be working from home the next couple weeks. I'd intended to broach the subject with Maggie in private. But anyway, Maggie, if you don't mind, I'd like to watch David while you're at work." Something that looked an awful lot like pity flashed in J.D.'s eyes. But his grin was sincere. So sincere, she almost believed him.

CHAPTER FIFTEEN

J.D. DIDN'T LIKE THE TURN the conversation had taken. So he did what came naturally—he tried to protect Maggie and David. He didn't know which bothered him more, the fact that he viewed his grandmother as a threat, or her machinations. "Maybe tonight isn't a good night for us to stay for supper. Maggie has to work in the morning."

"Nonsense. Maggie is perfectly capable of speaking for herself."

Maggie smiled. "Yes, I am capable of speaking for myself. Dinner would be lovely. J.D., we can discuss your kind offer to babysit later."

He could tell from the lift of her chin that she wouldn't accept. She wasn't about to let his grandmother change her plans. A part of him applauded her spunk. The other part wished she'd just take him up on his offer, so they wouldn't have to worry about Grandma doing something stupid.

Changing the subject seemed to be the best course of action. "Belmont, I was going to call you later to set up an appointment for initial measurements on the gazebo project," J.D. said.

"Excellent. Grace would like to have it done in time for us to renew our vows in September."

"How lovely for you," Grandma said.

"We had a rough patch there for a while. But it's only brought us closer together. We both thought it would be a nice statement to renew our vows."

"I should be able to have it finished by then as long as you're not wanting a three-thousand-square-foot gazebo. Or too much hand carving."

"You'll have to talk to Grace about that." He scratched his head. "I think she has some very specific ideas of what she wants."

"I'll sketch something out for her this weekend."

"Good deal. I appreciate it." Turning to Maggie, Belmont asked, "How is Lane Brophy working out? I apologize again for having to decline the case."

"Fine. He seems very nice."

"Yes. Crackerjack attorney, too. Was it his private investigator in town asking questions?"

"You'd really have to ask Lane," Maggie murmured, shifting uncomfortably.

She'd been very circumspect when discussing Lane Brophy and J.D. had to wonder why. Was she just being cautious? Or did she have feelings for the man?

J.D. suppressed a pang of jealousy. These proprietary feelings about Maggie weren't good for him. But Lane Brophy was young, successful and handsome. J.D. couldn't help but wonder if the attorney had put the moves on Maggie.

Grandma's voice was sharp when she said, "Belmont, I still don't understand why you couldn't help Maggie."

Belmont sighed, as if they'd had this conversation many times before. "It was my ethical obligation to step aside."

The older woman sniffed. "You have an ethical obligation to this family, too."

Belmont ran a hand through his hair. "Yes, and sometimes those two things are at odds. That's why they call it a conflict of interest."

"It's fine," Maggie assured Belmont. "I understand completely."

Turning to J.D.'s grandmother, Maggie said, "I hope you won't hold it against him. I'm sure it's for the best."

"You're very understanding, dear. I know you didn't have a thing to do with Eric's death, no matter what Sheriff Andrews says."

"What did he say?" J.D. asked.

"Nothing really. Just that Maggie had means, motive and something else, I can't remember."

"Opportunity," Belmont supplied.

"Yes, that's it. Opportunity. But I told the sheriff his time would be better spent checking into some of the unsavory characters on the racing circuit. Our Maggie wouldn't hurt a fly."

Though her reference to Maggie as *our Maggie* seemed overly possessive, he had to agree with her sentiment. "Yes, I'd like to see them look into other avenues. They're wasting precious time investigating Maggie."

"I'm sure Sheriff Andrews has protocol to follow. Now I believe supper should be ready soon."

As it turned out, J.D. was uncomfortable the whole way through supper. The pot roast was delicious, as was the rest of the meal. But something had him on edge. He wished he knew what it was.

Maggie was unusually quiet, too. He decided to get her the heck out of there as soon as was reasonably possible.

"Lovely dinner, Edna," Belmont commented.

Maggie folded her linen napkin and placed it next to her plate. "Yes, it was lovely. Thank you. Your mashed potatoes and gravy were a big hit with David." She nodded toward her son, sitting in a high chair next to her.

David smiled a big, goofy grin, with mashed potatoes from ear to ear. Table food didn't seem to be doing him any harm. Maggie always double-checked to make sure it was nothing he would choke on.

Edna beamed at the compliment to her cooking. "It's so nice to have family suppers again. Now, who wants peach cobbler?"

They all declined for various reasons: J.D. because he needed to get out of there, Maggie because she couldn't eat another bite, and Belmont because he was watching his carbs.

His grandmother was disappointed, but she didn't push the issue—a first for her.

They retired to the living room, where they chatted about mundane things like the weather and the latest baseball scores.

The doorbell rang and his grandmother got up to answer it. Her voice was tight when she said, "It's so good of you to visit, Nancy, but now isn't the best time."

Nancy. Great. As if the evening hadn't been weird enough already.

J.D. strained to hear Nancy's reply, but it was muffled by the door Grandma had only opened a fraction.

He didn't know why his grandmother bothered to prevaricate. Nancy probably knew Belmont's car and realized he was here. And had guessed by now that the little Toyota belonged to Maggie.

"Well, come in, dear." She sighed with resignation and opened the door wide. "We certainly don't want you to be alone if you're having a tough day."

"Thank you, Edna," Nancy said as she walked through the door. "Belmont, good to see you."

Then she scanned the rest of the room. "J.D., I didn't see your truck—" and her gaze came to rest on Maggie.

"Would you like a nice piece of peach cobbler?" Grandma offered, her voice tinged with desperation.

J.D. folded his arms over his chest and waited for the fireworks to begin. There was no avoiding it now.

Nancy took a few steps toward Maggie.

Though J.D. didn't move a muscle, he prepared himself for breaking up a catfight.

Nancy lifted her chin and, though her mouth wobbled a little, she was still able to keep her voice level as she extended her hand and said, "I'm Nancy. I don't believe we've been properly introduced."

Maggie's eyes grew wide, but she accepted Nancy's handshake. "I'm Maggie."

"There are some things we need to discuss, Maggie. Would you consider having lunch with me on Saturday?"

Maggie turned to J.D., a question in her eyes.

He nodded almost imperceptibly. Nancy had never been a cruel woman, so whatever she wanted to discuss must be important.

"Yes. That would be, um, fine." The color drained from Maggie's face, telling J.D. it wasn't really fine, but she'd deal with it. Just like she'd dealt with all the other curveballs life had pitched her way.

"My house, then? At noon?" Nancy suggested.

Maggie hesitated, frowning.

"I'm not asking you to my home to make you uncomfortable. It's just that there are some things I'd like to show you and I'd rather not meet in a public place."

Maggie nodded. "Then, your house it is. Thank you."

Nancy turned to Edna. "Since you have company, I'll leave. I'll call you tomorrow."

"No, please stay," Edna protested weakly.

"No. It's better if I go. Goodbye everyone." She quietly walked out of the house leaving stunned silence behind.

MAGGIE LEANED HER HEAD against the headrest and closed her eyes. She so didn't want to face any more complications. And lunch with Nancy would definitely be a complication.

"You okay?" J.D.'s voice was deep and tender as he drove.

Opening her eyes, she sighed. "Yes. I just wish the world would stand still for a minute. I can't even get used to one change before another wallops me upside the head."

"Yeah. I was pretty much stunned when Nancy invited you to lunch."

"You don't think it will get nasty?"

"I wouldn't bet my life on it. But I know Nancy and she must have a good reason for wanting to meet with you."

"Sure. To rip my hair out one follicle at a time for ruining her life."

"No, that would have been in the heat of the moment. You gotta remember that her life has changed, too. She might be adjusting a bit now."

"You're probably right." As much as she tried to resent Nancy, she couldn't. Much.

"I was serious about babysitting David while you work." J.D.'s eyes were dark and unreadable as he glanced at her, then back at the road.

"I know you were. But it's not necessary. The arrangement I have is perfect."

J.D. hesitated. "I know on the surface it seems to be, but people who don't know you might think you couldn't properly care for him at work."

"Other people? Or you?"

"I've seen you in action. I know you're a terrific mother no matter where you are. I'm thinking more of, um, the child welfare people."

Outrage warred with fear. Outrage that someone would even think to say she was an unfit mother simply because she took her son to the mortuary every day. Fear that her worst nightmare might come true—that her child might be taken away, just as Cassie's had been taken.

"David is the most important thing in my life. I can't make every decision based on what the majority thinks is the best way to raise my child. It's better for us to be together and I'll continue to take him to work with me."

"Okay, okay. Point taken." J.D. pulled the car into the drive at his house and parked. Turning to her, he said, "The offer is always open if you find out it's not working to have him at the office."

"Thank you. I appreciate your concern." She knew it came out stiff and slightly belligerent, but she really was grateful. "I'm just angry that some folks in the world seem to think they have the right to tell the rest of us how to raise our children."

J.D. grasped her chin. "Hey, I didn't mean it that way."

The gentleness in his voice brought tears to her eyes. She brushed them away. "I know." Maggie reached up and smoothed his worried frown. "Really. It's okay."

His eyes darkened. He caught her hand and pressed a kiss to her palm. "I wouldn't do anything to hurt you."

Unable to express her tangled emotions in words, Maggie pressed a kiss to his lips. Then she pulled away and got out of the car.

When she opened the door to remove David from his car seat, she realized J.D. was still sitting in the same position in the front seat, motionless, apparently stunned.

THE NEXT AFTERNOON AT WORK, Maggie glanced up from her desk when she heard the front door shut. It was the big, beefy deputy she'd disliked on sight the night Eric had died.

"Miz McGuire." He removed his hat. Although his words were somewhat more respectful than the last time she'd talked to him, his gaze roamed over her as if she were up for grabs for any man who had the inclination.

Maggie refused to rise to the bait. Losing her cool wouldn't help matters. "Deputy. I didn't have you pegged for the type to plan your funeral arrangements in advance, but I guess I was wrong."

"I'm here to talk to you."

"Oh?"

"Word has it that the kid of yours—" he glanced toward the playpen where David was just awakening from a nap "—was fathered by Eric McGuire."

"Just as I told you."

"That you did. But you failed to mention the little tyke will inherit Eric's trust fund now that he's dead."

"I was as surprised as everyone else." She clenched her hands until her nails bit into her palm. "I haven't really been able to process that fact."

"I bet. My guess is you knew all along. You figured getting your hands on the trust fund might be easier than squeezing the money out of Eric a dollar at a time."

"I beg your pardon?"

"That's the way my ex-wife does it. I get a dollar ahead and she wants two. It just ain't right."

Maggie thought the woman deserved every penny she got from the deputy and then some, just for putting up with his sorry butt for any length of time. She managed to bite her lip and refrain from telling him so.

"Was there anything else, deputy?" She gestured to a stack of invoices. "As you can see, I'm busy."

He grunted. "I just wanted to let you know I'm still keeping an eye on you."

Maggie suppressed a shudder. "That's very comforting, Deputy, thank you for your concern."

His eyes narrowed. "Oh, you won't be thankin' me once I gather all the evidence. Good day, Miz McGuire."

"Good*bye*, Deputy."

He strolled outside.

Maggie shivered in spite of her vow not to let the man get to her.

MAGGIE PARKED ACROSS from Nancy's place and double-checked the house number. Yes, this was the house in which Eric and Nancy had lived for God knew how many years.

Turning off the engine, she rested her forehead against the steering wheel and tried to gather her courage. Her emotions were raw and all over the spectrum. How in the world could she go into that house?

How could she not?

Maggie sat upright, drew a couple deep breaths and got out of the car. Raising her chin, she headed toward the redbrick ranch-style house. The white trim was fresh and bright. Flowers bloomed in pots and beds. The grass was lush. This house was well loved.

Had Eric enjoyed mowing the lawn or gardening on a Saturday afternoon? Oddly enough, she could see him doing that. And could visualize Eric and Nancy going to Edna's house for Sunday dinner, or worse, for a dreaded pie summons.

She almost smiled at the thought. In a strange way, it brought a little peace imagining Eric here.

Maggie rang the doorbell and Nancy answered almost immediately.

She was immaculately groomed, from the top of her

beautiful blond head to the freshly pedicured tips of her toes, displayed to perfection in her strappy sandals.

"Come in."

Maggie stepped across the threshold and tried not to imagine Eric carrying Nancy on their wedding day. "How lovely," she murmured.

"Thank you."

The decor was such a hodgepodge that it worked in a funky way. Antiques alongside Danish Modern, an old quilt thrown haphazardly over an Andy Warhol–style sofa designed to look like huge red lips. And there were photos everywhere.

Eric and Nancy smiled at her from every conceivable angle. It almost made her dizzy. He'd certainly *looked* happy with Nancy.

"I thought about taking those down before you came over." Nancy laughed uncertainly. "But I thought you might wonder about all the empty spaces on the walls."

Maggie was oddly touched by her thoughtfulness. Nancy wasn't a horrible person, just a horribly wounded person. "I'm glad you didn't. I needed to see these."

She wandered around the room. With each photo, it felt like another piece of her heart died. It was probably similar to amputating a gangrenous limb. Maggie needed to see the extent of the infection she'd been dealing with and then cut it out.

But she couldn't cut it out completely. Eric was David's father and she would always remember the good stories to tell him. And there had been plenty of good times.

"How long were you married?" Maggie asked.

"Eleven years."

"Wow."

"Yes, wow."

"Nancy, you have to know it wasn't my idea to attend the wake—Edna practically shanghaied David and it was the only way I could stay with him. I tried to be inconspicuous at the funeral. I—I just needed to say goodbye to Eric I guess."

Nancy shrugged. Her teeny pink T-shirt revealed a taut, tan stomach and a belly-button ring. Her shorts were low slung and sexy.

Standing next to her, Maggie felt like a scrawny, ugly duckling. No wonder J.D. said Maggie wasn't Eric's usual type.

"J.D. explained when I talked to him a couple of days ago, honey. Why don't you go ahead and fix a plate and I'll bring in the tea." She gestured toward an antique sideboard set up buffet-style with all sorts of cold salads, meats and cheeses, along with an assortment of breads and rolls. A beautiful red-velvet cake resided on a crystal cake plate.

"I hope you didn't go to any trouble."

"It's what I do best. Humor me." Nancy's smile was wry as she brought in a tray loaded with a pitcher of iced tea, two glasses, a small ice bucket, lemon wedges and fresh mint.

Maggie's spirits sank as she viewed all the perfection that was Nancy's life.

"I was mad as hell at you," Nancy stated as she scooped three-bean salad onto her plate. "I hated you for showing up here. I blamed you for Eric dying. And most of all I hated you for having what I wanted most in the whole world. A child."

"Eric's child," Maggie murmured.

Nancy nodded. "Yes, J.D. told me the test results. But I could have hated you just for being in Eric's life and having a child."

"So why the olive branch?"

"J.D. got me thinking. He said you didn't ask for this situation any more than I did. That if we were guys, we'd go out, get drunk, throw a few harmless punches and then be buddies."

Maggie laughed. "J.D. has some twisted logic."

"He's a guy." Nancy shrugged, as if that explained everything. "Then later, I found some stuff of Eric's. It explained things for me a little. I thought it might help you understand, too."

"What stuff?"

"Some letters and pictures and things. I'll show you when we're done eating."

Maggie's mind whirled. What on earth could he have left behind. "Um, where did you find this 'stuff'?"

"In his bottom desk drawer. It was locked and I normally wouldn't have opened it. Eric was pretty particular about his privacy. Now I know why. Anyway, I was looking for an insurance policy."

"You never, um, suspected about me?"

"No. There was always talk about Eric, but I didn't listen to much of it. Didn't want to. I knew he loved me, in his own way."

Was the woman certifiable? Or was this the way worldly women discussed their mutual bigamist husband?

"I know, all of this sounds strange. I've had several days to get used to the idea. Reading some of Eric's letters helped me forgive him a little. And made me understand that you weren't some home wrecker luring a married man."

"It wasn't like that at all."

"Maybe someday we can sit down and drink sangria and swap stories about him." Nancy's eyes clouded. "But it's still too raw for me. The guys must be more evolved than I am."

"Somehow, I can't see J.D. forgiving and forgetting if he'd been the one betrayed."

Nancy laughed. "No, definitely not. J.D.'s a sweetheart, but not real big on sharing confidences. But I do know his feelings run deep."

Nodding, Maggie bit into her sandwich so she wouldn't have to answer. She flushed under Nancy's scrutiny.

"He's a good guy, Maggie. I've seen how he looks at you. I'd hate to see him hurt."

Maggie almost laughed aloud. This had to be the weirdest conversation in the history of womankind. Then a scary thought hit her. "Are, you, um, and J.D., um, I mean…"

"No. I'm just a concerned bystander." She dabbed her mouth with a napkin. "I'll cut the cake. I think a sugar buzz is definitely going to be needed. It's not sangria, but almost as good."

Maggie shook her head in wonder. Nancy McGuire was nothing like she'd expected. And Maggie suspected that, had they met under different circumstances, she and Nancy could have been good friends.

Nancy set a dessert plate in front of Maggie. "I'll be back in a sec."

She returned carrying a shoe box. Placing the box in the center of the coffee table, she stepped back.

And staring up at Maggie was a photo of herself cradling David in the hospital.

CHAPTER SIXTEEN

MAGGIE CLUTCHED THE BOX to her chest. It seemed like days since Nancy had set the box in front of her, but in reality, it had only been two hours. The time had flown as she'd sifted through the contents while trying to carry on a normal conversation with her hostess. Maggie could hardly wait to get home, where she could read the bundle of letters she'd refrained from opening in front of Nancy. There was no need to hurt her more than Eric already had.

Touching Nancy's arm, Maggie said, "Thank you, Nancy. You could have destroyed these things and I would have never known."

"Eric's son deserves to know his daddy loved him."

"And David will know." She hesitated, unable to phrase the question she knew she had to ask. "Nancy?"

"Yes?"

"I've heard you were at the track the night Eric died."

Nancy stiffened. "Nothing's a secret in this town. I told Deputy Wells that I went to see Eric, but he wasn't there. Or, at least I thought he wasn't there." She shivered. "The deputy figures I scared off the killer."

Maggie tipped her head to the side.

Nancy crossed her arms over her ample chest. "And no, I didn't kill him. God knows I felt like it. But I didn't get to talk to him." Her voice trailed off with regret.

"For some reason, I believe you."

"You believe me because underneath it all, we're more alike than you think." She placed her hand on Maggie's arm. "Take care of yourself, you hear?"

Nodding, Maggie swallowed the lump in her throat. "One more thing. Did Roy go with you to the track?"

"No. He was way too angry for me to let him get anywhere near Eric. Roy is very…protective."

"He seems, um, very fond of you."

Propping her hands on her hips, Nancy raised her chin. Her eyes flashed. "I know what people say about me and Roy. It's not true. He's always been a perfect gentleman to me. He knew I was devoted to Eric."

Maggie had only observed Roy firsthand a couple times, but he'd been very solicitous with Nancy. He might have always been a perfect gentleman, but it probably wasn't due to lack of interest.

"I don't always believe what I hear, Nancy. I prefer to decide for myself. Thank you again for lunch. I'll take good care of Eric's things so someday David will have them."

In her rearview mirror, Maggie could still see Nancy standing on the porch a few moments later.

Maggie's mind worked furiously as she drove to

J.D.'s. She wanted time to absorb the implications of the box, but her sense of self-preservation told her she needed to figure out who had killed Eric. The deputy's visit the day prior had seriously spooked her. Although they'd interviewed Nancy, the authorities apparently weren't looking very hard at anyone but Maggie. It was probably easier to believe an outsider was capable of murder rather than one of their own.

As she approached the old colonial, Maggie couldn't help but appreciate the beauty of J.D.'s house. The soaring white columns were pristine, the porch wide and inviting. She was almost disappointed to note the rockers were empty, bobbing slightly in the breeze.

J.D. walked out the door as she turned in the driveway. Hands in his pockets, he wore navy-blue chinos and a plaid, short-sleeve shirt. His smile was warm and inviting, but there was a glint of curiosity in his eyes.

Maggie turned off the engine and went around to the passenger side to get the box.

"Need help?"

"No, I've got it."

"How'd it go?"

"Better than I expected. You're right, Nancy is nice. If we'd met under different circumstances, we might have been friends."

"That's what I figured. I couldn't help but worry a little, though."

"She said you pretty much paved the way for us to

talk. I appreciate that. I have a question though. Do men really forgive and forget as easily as you told her?"

He laughed. "It depends on the man and depends on the grievance. Bigamy's a little too serious to be settled in a bar fight."

"Thank goodness. And here I was afraid men were more highly evolved than women."

"Oh, we are. We just hide it well."

Maggie snorted, climbing the steps.

J.D. reached to take the box from her, but she elbowed him out of the way. "Huh-uh. This box stays in my possession at all times."

"I was just trying to help." His tone was aggrieved.

"You weren't the least bit curious what was inside?"

"Okay, you caught me." His grin was lopsided and almost boyish. "I'm *very* curious about what's in the box."

"I need a little time by myself. But after that, I promise I'll show you everything in the box."

"So how long is 'a little time'?" He followed her into the house. "Five minutes? Ten? Surely no more than ten?" He sounded aghast at the very thought.

"It will take as long as it takes. I never realized how curious you are."

"You oughtta see me at Christmas and on my birthday. I'm good at finding my presents. Even better at guessing."

It was strangely endearing to think of him as a little boy, searching out his presents. She wondered what his life would have been like if he hadn't been burdened by the responsibility of watching out for his brother. Probably something like he was at the moment—mischief sparkling in his eyes, grinning from ear to ear.

"Is David asleep?"

"Yep. Poor little guy's tuckered out."

"You've been such a godsend, J.D. I can't thank you enough for all the times you've stepped in and watched David for me." When this was all over, she intended to do something nice for him. Maybe brush up her rusty crocheting skills and make a throw for his family room.

"It's no big deal. We had a good time. I enjoy being with David."

"What'd you do while I was gone?"

"A little of this, a little of that. He watched me hand-sand a dresser while he bounced in that little saucer thing. I think that's what got him tired. We went to the hardware store, too."

Maggie was relieved she'd had the presence of mind to leave the car seat with J.D. Taking David to the hardware store was the kind of thing a dad would do. She knew J.D. would always stay in touch, for David's sake, if nothing else.

J.D. frowned. "I ran into Deputy Wells. How come you didn't mention he questioned you again?"

"He didn't question me. He simply came to the mortuary and made a couple insinuations. I get the impression he doesn't like me."

"The deputy doesn't much like anybody. Pretty women are guaranteed to tick him off."

"Like his ex-wife?"

J.D. nodded. "Yes. She was a pretty redhead, too. And to hear him tell it, she wiped him out in the divorce."

"Anyone who stayed married to that man would have to be a saint."

"Oh, his ex wasn't a saint. But she wasn't as bad as he paints her, either. But he might think you resemble her and that's why he's on your case, though he'd never admit it."

"What did he say to you?"

"Wanted to know if I locked up the steak knives at night."

Maggie shook her head. "Oh, that man. I should sue him for slander."

"Good luck. He's related to half the law enforcement in the state."

Then his description of the deputy's ex-wife sank in. J.D. had said she was a pretty redhead, *too*. Could that mean he thought Maggie was attractive? She wanted to ask him to clarify, but there was absolutely no way to phrase the question casually.

Dragging her errant thoughts back to the deputy, she said, "He made me kind of nervous, like he wasn't investigating anyone but me. So I'm going to try to do some digging, see what I can find out. If you could ask around a bit, that would help. People would be more inclined to talk to you."

"I think you're smart to do that. It may not turn out to be necessary, but better safe than sorry. I'll help any way I can."

"I asked Nancy a couple of questions."

"Oh?"

"She admits she was at the racetrack the night Eric was killed. Said she'd gone out there to talk to him but he wasn't there. Then she said the deputy told her she probably scared off the murderer."

"Nancy's been my sister-in-law pretty much her entire adult life. Yes, she's got a heck of a motive but I don't see her flipping out like that."

Maggie nodded. "I don't see it, either. What about Roy? How did he get along with Eric?"

"Roy's my business partner and I've known him for a lot of years. But anyone with eyes can tell he's crazy about Nancy. Roy used to sponsor Eric's race car, and I often thought it was to keep Eric out of town. But then he quit sponsoring him for some reason."

"I know. I was with Eric when he lost his sponsor. He'd padded the parts invoices and some of the other expenses. I guess his sponsor was livid when he found out."

J.D. shook his head and frowned. "I never knew. Roy didn't say anything about it."

"Nancy said Roy didn't go with her to the track. Is it possible he could have dropped Nancy off at home and made it out to the track before her?"

"Sure, it's possible. But I have a hard time seeing Roy getting that riled."

"Nancy volunteered some interesting information. She denies ever having an affair with Roy. Says he was always a perfect gentleman, but I've seen the way he looks at her. Do you think maybe he was trying to clear the field in a more final way?"

"Hmm. I wouldn't necessarily have blamed Nancy if she'd stepped out on my brother. But if she says she didn't have an affair, I believe her. She's loved Eric since high school and nothing ever changed that. I imagine Roy would jump at the chance to marry her. It would be interesting to know if he's still a gentleman now that Nancy's free."

"We'll leave Roy on the list of suspects and take Nancy off for now." She nodded toward the box and said, "If you don't mind, I'll go up to my room and look at some of this stuff before David wakes up. I promise I'll share when I'm ready."

"Hey, no pressure. I was wrong to bug you about it. My curiosity got the better of me. The box is private, something between you and Eric. Go ahead."

She reached up and hugged him. Then she hurried off to her room.

Closing the door behind her, Maggie placed the box on her bed, then tiptoed to the playpen where David slept. J.D. had said he'd borrowed the playpen from friends, but it looked brand-new.

She stood and watched her son sleep. His baby cheeks were rosy, his little arms flung wide. Maggie held close the knowledge that someday she would be able to truthfully tell David he'd had a daddy who loved him.

Maggie blinked back tears at the incredible gifts Eric had given her. The first was David, the second was proof that he'd loved both Maggie and her son.

Turning, her gaze fell on the box. She went to the bed and sat down. She removed a small bundle of letters. They were letters Eric had written to her without sending, explaining why he couldn't be sure David was his child. And describing how torn he'd felt between her and Nancy—how he'd wanted to do the right thing, but somehow hadn't been able.

Tears streamed down her face as she remembered her time with Eric. She cried for the young Maggie and the life she'd anticipated. And she cried for Eric, the little boy who'd never completely grown up. And she cried for the lies and misunderstandings that had tied them together and, ultimately, torn them apart.

But she didn't cry for David. Because he would someday know he was conceived in love.

Maggie retrieved a tissue from the nightstand. She'd only just begun to come to terms with what she'd found in the box, but she didn't want to be alone anymore. She wanted to share what she'd learned with someone who'd loved Eric, too.

She returned everything to the box and replaced the lid. Tiptoeing to the playpen, she tucked the lightweight cotton blanket around David so he wouldn't get chilled. Gathering the box, she headed downstairs to find J.D.

But he wasn't anywhere in the house.

She knew he wouldn't leave without telling her or at least leaving a note. He had to be in the workshop.

Maggie walked out back to the shop. Sure enough, she saw the overhead lights were on.

She stepped inside and watched J.D., deep in concentration, carving an intricate design. It was amazing that his large, calloused hands could create such detail. His head was bent, his face taut with concentration.

It was as if Maggie were seeing him for the first time. Not just the guy who'd been there for her during a rough time, but the man who understood her well enough to anticipate her needs. To help her without appearing to help. To build her confidence, not by flattery, but by his strong, abiding presence.

In whatever he did, J.D. had a quiet confidence, a strength of character that allowed her to simply be Maggie, without judgment or labels.

She'd always thought Eric's ready smile and infectious laugh had made him the sexiest man alive. Now she knew it had concealed perhaps the unhappiest man alive.

A sexy man was one who made a woman feel loved and accepted no matter what. Maggie longed to step up behind J.D. and put her arms around his waist, rest her cheek against his broad back. What would he do? Turn and wrap his arms around her or tense up and find an excuse to move away?

She'd never learned to ask for what she wanted, simply accepted what was offered. How differently would her life have been if she'd made decisions based on what was right for her?

"Hey, how long have you been out here?" J.D. asked.

Maggie's face heated. How long had she been standing staring at him? "A couple minutes."

"Still got the box, huh?"

Nodding, Maggie didn't know how to get from where she'd been to where she wanted to go.

Simple. By asking for what she wanted.

"I'm ready to show you." She held out her hand to him.

He held her gaze for a moment, his eyes full of questions. Then he removed his painter's apron and accepted her hand.

Maggie inhaled sharply. She felt like a virgin again, holding hands with a boy for the first time. It was new and sweet and real. "Wow," she murmured.

J.D.'s hand tightened on hers. He rubbed his thumb over hers. "Did you say something?"

Shaking her head, she felt suddenly shy. And very, very feminine with her small hand enfolded in his. She led him into the house and to the family room.

Sitting cross-legged on the floor, she placed the box in front of her. J.D. sat down next to her and waited, his gaze intent.

Her hands were shaking slightly as she removed the lid. It contained her past and, just possibly, her future.

"This is when Eric and I went to the state fair." She handed him the black-and-white photo strip. "Goofy, huh?"

J.D.'s mouth curved in a smile. "You both look so young."

"We were young."

He carefully set aside the photo.

"And this." She offered him the precious lock of golden baby hair, silky, soft, tied with a blue ribbon. "Is David's hair. I gave it to Eric to take with him on the circuit, so he'd have a part of David with him always."

J.D. cleared his throat. "He kept it? I didn't, um, know Eric was the sentimental kind."

"Apparently he was a lot more sentimental than any of us realized. Did you know he thought he was dying?"

"What?"

"He was convinced he'd die young, that the cancer he'd had as a child would recur. I think that's why he was such a daredevil, almost tempting fate. But not so much a daredevil that he wouldn't pray before each race."

"I never knew. The doctors assured my grandmother that he was in complete remission."

"Hmm. He must have misunderstood then."

J.D. picked up the photo of Maggie holding a newborn David in the hospital. J.D. stared at it. When he looked up, Maggie's breath caught in her throat. His bittersweet smile tugged at her heart. She could have sworn she saw a hint of longing in his eyes.

"Wait here," she told him. "I've got something else to show you."

Maggie walked quickly to her room and went to the dresser. She removed the photo she'd brought with her from Arizona. It was a companion to the photo in Eric's box—only this one showed the proud daddy holding David.

Handing the picture to J.D., she watched his reaction closely as she sat down next to him. His eyes clouded and his voice was husky when he said, "You can tell he loved David. It's there on his face."

"Yes. It is. But now I understand why he looked a little sad. He really didn't think David was his, but he loved him anyway. Because David was a part of me." Maggie bit her lip, hoping she could keep from breaking down in front of J.D. "I'm sorry I'm so emotional. This was supposed to be a celebration of Eric."

"I don't mind."

Gathering her thoughts, Maggie took the bundle of envelopes from the box, fingering the red ribbon binding them. "Eric wrote these to me, but never mailed them. He mostly wrote down his thoughts, kind of like a journal. The letters answered a lot of my questions and might answer some of yours."

J.D. hesitated.

"There's nothing explicit," she assured him.

He grasped her hand tightly. "You don't mind if I read these?"

She placed her palm against his rough-textured jaw. "No, I don't mind. I can't think of anyone I would rather share them with."

CHAPTER SEVENTEEN

J.D. ACCEPTED THE LETTERS as if they were made of glass and might shatter in his grasp. His hands shook slightly, and he couldn't seem to steady them.

"I'll go check on David, give you some time alone." Maggie stood and left the room.

He was grateful for her tact and generosity. She seemed to realize he didn't have prurient interest in knowing the details of her physical relationship with his brother. But he did have a driving need to figure out who his brother had been.

The first letter was written shortly after Maggie had told Eric she was pregnant. The child couldn't possibly be his, or so he'd thought. Eric hadn't missed the irony of his deep sense of betrayal at the hands of a woman he thought he loved. But if the impossible had happened and the child was his, where did that leave him? He'd never intended to leave Nancy. Though he occasionally strayed, Nancy had always represented home and he couldn't, no, *wouldn't* give up that sense of security. He'd always loved her as much as he was capable.

J.D. paused, shaking his head at his brother's self-absorption.

The next letter dated several months later was much the same, except now Eric was considering how to stay connected to the child if it turned out to be his.

There were a few others recording the progression of Maggie's pregnancy and Eric's confusion. He desperately wanted to be a father, but he knew it was unlikely.

J.D. heard Maggie slip back into the room. She sat next to him, but was silent while he read. When he finished the last letter, he turned to her. "He never believed David was his child?"

She shook her head. "Like the rest of the family, he believed what the doctors had said."

"But he decided to see you through the pregnancy as best he could. Ironic, and in some convoluted way, kinda noble. He didn't ever confront you with his suspicions?"

"Once. Shortly after I told him I was pregnant. He insisted the baby wasn't his, but I thought he was scared and in denial." Maggie frowned. "He never told me he was sterile, or supposed to be sterile."

"I wonder if things would have turned out differently if he'd known David was his? Would he have left Nancy? He seemed to have loved both of you, as best as he was able." J.D. ran a hand over his head. "What a mess."

Maggie placed her hand on his forearm. "I'm glad I know the truth. It'll make it easier to be kind when I talk to David about him. And I guess it makes me feel a little better, too, that he wasn't just using me." She turned her head, but not before he saw tears shimmering in her eyes. "But it makes me so damn angry, too. Why couldn't he have believed me? Doctors aren't infallible. Eric cared about me, but he wasn't willing to have faith in me despite what he'd been told. That isn't the way love's supposed to be."

The grief in her voice was painful to hear. "Aw, sweetheart, you deserved to be loved unconditionally." He put his arm around her and drew her close. She rested her head on his shoulder. "He'd probably lied so much to the people he loved that he couldn't quite understand how to trust."

Maggie raised her face to him. Her eyelashes were wet. "*You* believed me before you had proof."

"I'm just an extraordinary guy, I guess," he joked, refusing to face the real reason he saw the absolute goodness in Maggie.

He tilted her chin with his index finger. Intending to plant a kiss the tip of her nose, he surprised himself by kissing her on the mouth. A nice, friendly, getting-to-know-you kiss. At least that's what he figured, until her scent enveloped him and her lips parted. Groaning, he deepened the kiss and lost himself in her response. He was only half-aware of pulling her into his lap, his heart thundering in his ears.

She pulled away from him, her eyes wide. "I'm not sure this is a good idea."

J.D. flushed. "I'm sorry. I shouldn't have done that."

Maggie scooted out of his lap and stood, collecting the scattered letters and photographs. She grabbed the box and practically ran from the room.

"Maggie, wait."

But she was long gone. J.D. felt like the biggest jerk alive. She'd trusted him, confided in him, wanted to share with him. And what had he done? He'd practically sucked out her tonsils.

Smooth, McGuire, really smooth.

So much for being the more sensitive and evolved McGuire brother.

MAGGIE WAS OUT OF BREATH when she shut her bedroom door behind her. Resting her back against the door, her legs gave out and she slowly slid to the floor.

Maggie covered her eyes with her hand and groaned. This was what she'd wanted, wasn't it? But now that J.D. had taken a decidedly nonplatonic interest in her, she wanted the old J.D. back, the safe J.D. The pseudo–big brother watching out for her, helping her, making her feel secure. Maggie pressed her hand to her mouth, preventing a hysterical laugh from escaping.

The worst part was that her relationship with him could never go back to that safe, protected place. So where did they go from here?

Her lips tingled just remembering the kiss. She'd thought fireworks only happened with first love, but she'd been wrong. His kiss had pushed all rational thought from her head. All she'd wanted was to get closer to him. To feel his naked flesh beneath her fingers. To feel the coarse texture of his chest hair pressed against her breasts. To welcome him inside her and never let him go.

In the heat of the moment, she'd forgotten he was Eric's brother. He was just J.D.—an intense, sexy guy who played for keeps. A man, who, if he told you he loved you, meant it. Exclusively.

The air-conditioner fan came on, and Maggie shivered from the chilly blast. She'd made a monumental mess of things by running out on J.D. He deserved better than having her act like a scared kid.

Maggie went to the bathroom to splash water on her face. Patting her cheeks dry, she decided she owed J.D. an explanation. How in the heck could she explain her retreat without sounding like an immature teenager?

One thing was sure. Maggie had to try. She tiptoed past the playpen, holding her breath as David stirred in his sleep. She prayed for just a few more minutes to make things right with J.D. But David sat up, rubbing his eyes. He surveyed the room till his gaze came to rest on her. His face lit up as he smiled from ear to ear.

"Hi, sweetheart. Did you have a good nap?"

He held out his arms to her, and she lifted him out of the playpen.

"Let's get you changed, then Mommy needs to talk to Uncle J.D."

When she ventured downstairs a few minutes later, all was quiet. "I wonder where J.D. is?"

David babbled a suggestion, but it wasn't much help.

"I bet he's in the workshop. That's always where he goes when something's on his mind."

David started fussing and she realized he was probably hungry. "I'll get you some yummy rice cereal and then we'll track down Uncle J.D."

Maggie fed David and wiped off his face and hands. Lifting him from the high chair, she plunked him on her hip and marched out to the shop. Sure enough, the whine of a power tool came from the workshop.

J.D.'s profile was strong, intense. She watched the deft way he turned a table leg on some sort of machine that cut grooves. His movements were controlled and confident.

He glanced up and saw her standing there. Shutting off the machine, he removed his safety glasses. "Hey, about what happened—"

"I need to explain."

Frowning, he said, "I was out of line."

"No, you weren't." She resisted the temptation to glance down at her shoes or the wall or just about anywhere except his face. "I enjoyed every second of it and that scared me."

He raised an eyebrow. "That's a good kind of scared, right?"

Maggie scraped her hair off her forehead and laughed. "I wish I knew."

"So where does that leave us?"

"I don't know. I'm open to suggestions, though."

"A date, maybe? Dinner and a concert at the park tomorrow?"

Maggie exhaled her relief. Suddenly, things didn't look nearly as difficult. "That would be wonderful. And we could take David."

"Huh-uh. No babies on dates. At least not first dates," he amended. "I imagine my grandmother would be more than happy to babysit David tomorrow evening. It'll give her an opportunity to remember just how all-consuming babies can be. Maybe then she'll quit pestering you to leave David with her during the day."

"She doesn't pester me."

"No, but she pesters me."

"Oh, I see. She thinks you can talk me into it?"

"Something like that."

She found it interesting that Edna believed Maggie could be manipulated so easily. "Does she think I'm putty in the hands of any McGuire man?"

He flushed. "Um, I don't think so. She's pretty tuned in to the people around her and she figured I was attracted to you."

On her hip David bounced, jabbering and holding his arms out to J.D.

"Come here, buddy." J.D. brushed sawdust off his shirt and hands before taking her son.

David reached up and patted his face.

J.D. grinned, his eyes alight with amusement. "Must've had a good nap. You were one crabby kid earlier." He glanced at Maggie. "I thought for sure he hated me."

"Oh, it's not personal. He's always that way when he's overtired. Now that he's had a long nap, a dry diaper and a big bowl of cereal, he's a happy camper."

"Wouldn't it be nice if life were that easy for the rest of us?"

"No kidding. But then again, I'd miss out on tomorrow night." She stepped closer. "And I'm looking forward to it." Standing on tiptoe, she planted a defiant kiss on his mouth.

David crowed and bounced in J.D.'s arms, apparently greatly amused.

"And you can tell your grandmother I intend to exercise my free will and date her grandson. Not because it's convenient for her, but because her grandson is an incredible man."

J.D. threw his head back and laughed. "I think maybe Grandma's met her match. Let's go to the house and call her."

MAGGIE TWIRLED IN FRONT of the mirror and laughed aloud. It was wonderful to feel so alive again.

She fingered the gauzy fabric of the retro seventies dress she'd found in a vintage clothing store downtown. With tiny green flowers on a cream background, it had long, loose sleeves cut on the diagonal, the point reaching below her wrist. She pulled the gathered neckline low on her shoulders, peasant style. With her hair loose, she felt like a gypsy princess. Small gold-hoop earrings completed the effect.

David stood in his playpen, very vocal in his encouragement. He'd evidently sensed her excitement and knew something wonderful was about to happen.

She combed a few curls into place, grasped her purse and lifted David out of the crib. "You get to go see your great-grandma. She'll probably stuff you with cookies and cobbler and all sorts of sugary stuff."

David made a grab for an earring as they descended the stairs, but she was too quick for him. He let out a frustrated screech when she caught his hand and told him no. "You can save that temper for Great-Grandma, because it doesn't work on me."

"It works pretty well on me, though," J.D. said from the foot of the stairs. "The kid's got a heckuva set of lungs."

Maggie laughed. "Wait till your grandmother starts him on a sugar buzz. He'll make the Tasmanian Devil look tame."

J.D. chuckled, his eyes warmed with appreciation as he viewed her from head to toe. "Paybacks are a mother, huh? Or a great-grandmother to be precise. I suppose you plan on instructing her that absolutely under no circumstances should she allow David to have sugar? That way she'll shovel cake and cookies at him the minute we get in the car?"

Maggie smiled. She liked the easy way J.D. teased her. "No, *I'm* not manipulative, though it's very tempting." She hesitated. "All kidding aside, are you sure she's up to watching an active baby?"

J.D. grasped her shoulders. "Maggie, I would never, ever allow David to be endangered." He leaned down and kissed her son on the forehead, then kissed her lingeringly on the lips. "The evening will be good for him, good for her. And I'm hoping very good for us. Now let's go."

He grasped the portable crib with his left hand, slung the bulging diaper bag over his shoulder and grabbed the car seat with his right hand. "He's only going for one night. You're sure he'll need all this?"

"Oh, yes, those are only the bare essentials. You're sure Edna offered to keep him overnight? I thought she was worried about propriety. But I guess David might seem like a chaperone of sorts, limiting our chance of...intimacy."

"Honestly, I think that's what she's hoping for. Propriety kinda went out the window in light of a matchmaking opportunity."

"She wasn't interested in matchmaking before. Why the change?"

J. D. shrugged. "She'd like nothing better than to keep David close. What better way than if you and I fell for each other?"

"You don't mind that she's trying to manipulate us?"

"Hey, she had a good excuse—she didn't want us

to disturb her or the baby after ten. It wasn't a curfew I thought we'd make. Besides, it's only manipulation if she gets us to do something we don't want to. I'm looking forward to having you all to myself for a candlelit dinner complete with scintillating conversation. Then I plan on kicking back to listen to jazz under the stars. But I don't have plans beyond that, so don't worry you're being set up for seduction."

Maggie was instantly remorseful. "I'm sorry, I didn't mean that you were being manipulated by Edna. Well, maybe I did, but I should have known better."

He tipped his head to the side. "I can't blame you for being cautious. I'm willing to earn your trust."

"Thanks," she whispered, hoping her melting heart wasn't reflected in her eyes.

"Do you want to drive?"

"You know where we're going, so why don't you go ahead and drive."

They were at Edna's before Maggie knew it. Though it was difficult to leave David, Maggie felt light and carefree as they drove to the restaurant.

J.D. reached across the console and grasped her hand. "I love seeing you smile like that."

She leaned her head back. "I haven't felt this way in, well, forever. I'd almost forgotten what it was like to do something just for fun. That probably sounds strange to you."

"Not at all. I can see how devoted you are to David.

You probably forget to take care of yourself. And that includes fun."

Maggie glanced sideways at him. "How about you? Do you get much of a chance for fun while you're slaying dragons and protecting the McGuires?"

He was silent for a moment. She wondered if he might ignore her question.

"You know, I never gave it much thought. It's just what I do. I can make time for fun, but I think, until you and David came into my life, I'd forgotten how to play."

She squeezed his hand. "When was the last time you did something just for fun?"

"Before you and David? Hmm, that's a tough one. Probably not since my mom and stepdad died."

"Really?"

He nodded. "'Fraid so."

Maggie's heart contracted at the starkness of his reply. "So tonight's a first for both of us, isn't it? Maybe we'll learn to play again. Together."

CHAPTER EIGHTEEN

J.D. TOOK MAGGIE to the best surf-and-turf restaurant in town. He'd made reservations, so they were immediately shown to their table.

"I know you're not a vegetarian, so I figured it was pretty safe to bring you here. It's one of my favorite places."

"This is wonderful."

J.D. pulled out Maggie's chair for her, bemused by his desire to treat her like spun glass. He hadn't felt this way about a woman in how long? A decade, at least. Or maybe never.

Their table was secluded, just as he'd requested.

The candlelight played over Maggie's bare shoulders, leaving a deep shadow between her breasts and highlighting the sprinkling of freckles across her chest. A small, gold locket caressed her collarbone.

Reaching across the table, he fingered the necklace, wondering if Eric had given it to her. "Does this have special significance?"

Her eyes were dark and mysterious in the dim light. "It was my sister's. I have a picture of my niece, Emma, on one side, one of David on the other."

He nodded, unsure of what to say.

Maggie grasped his hand. "It's okay. I can talk about it. But this is a night for fun."

The waiter arrived and handed them menus. They ordered shortly afterward—steak and lobster for him, filet mignon for her.

"This is a wonderful place, J.D." She gestured toward the paneled oak walls, deep booths, subdued lighting.

"I wanted to bring you some place special."

Out of the corner of his eye, he saw Belmont and his wife enter the restaurant. He hoped Belmont didn't spot them. Dinner for four wasn't J.D.'s idea of fun. At least not tonight.

He pretended to be engrossed in the menu, but heard his name being called. Glancing up, J.D. sighed. The couple approached rapidly, Belmont's wife pulling him by the hand. Grace loved to gossip and probably couldn't wait to spread the news of seeing J.D. and Maggie on a date.

"I hope we're not disturbing you," Belmont said. "But my wife insisted on saying hello."

J.D. nodded and managed a tight smile.

Belmont cleared his throat. "This is my wife, Grace. Grace, you already know J.D. of course. And this is Maggie, um, McGuire."

The two women shook hands and traded polite greetings.

J.D. didn't want to encourage the couple, but he couldn't be rude. "Grace, how have you been?"

"Fine. Did Belmont tell you what I'd like the gazebo to look like?"

"He suggested I work directly with you. I meant to call and set up an appointment. Would you like me to swing by your house tomorrow afternoon?"

"That would be lovely." She tucked her hand in the crook of her husband's arm. "We're renewing our vows in September and I would love to have the ceremony in the gazebo with a few close friends."

Maggie smiled up at the woman. "That's so romantic. How long have you been married?"

"Twenty-four years." The woman's voice was strained when she said, "We just couldn't wait for our silver anniversary."

Belmont adjusted his tie and cleared his throat. "Yes, couldn't wait."

J.D. was glad that Belmont and Grace had reunited after separating several months prior. Rumors had been flying fast and thick about infidelity on both sides. Darrell Holder, McGuireville's self-appointed queen of gossip, swore he'd seen Belmont checking into a Fayetteville hotel with an especially hot-looking young guy, wink-wink.

J.D.'s curiosity got the better of him. "Grace, your hair's especially nice tonight. Who styled it for you?"

Grace smiled. "Thank you for the compliment. I'm going to a new salon in the city."

Nodding, J.D. figured she'd changed stylists about the same time she and Belmont had separated. Maybe Darrell had told the hotel story one time too many.

Belmont wrapped his arm around his wife's waist. "We'll see you two later. Come on, dear." He propelled Grace away from their table.

"What a strange couple," Maggie commented. "They're not doing a very good job of pretending to be happy, so why renew their vows?"

"I imagine it's more for show than anything else. Now, enough of Belmont and Grace." He was relieved to see their salads had arrived, along with a glass of wine for each of them.

"To fun and first dates," he toasted.

Maggie raised her glass. "To dates and fun."

MAGGIE HELPED J.D. spread a blanket on the grass while she looked at their surroundings. Blankets dotted the huge open field and up a gently rolling slope. Children raced and giggled, high-school couples cuddled and families enjoyed the relaxed atmosphere.

"What a lovely idea." She folded her legs to sit on the blanket, arranging her skirt around her. Tipping her head back, she gazed at the stars twinkling in the night sky. She breathed in the fresh air and felt her worries float off on the breeze. Everything seemed right when she was with J.D.

"I thought it might be fun." He handed her a tube of lotion. "Here, you might need this."

Maggie giggled. "Insect repellent, how romantic."

He grinned. "What can I say? I'm a practical guy at heart. Besides, those mosquitoes will gobble up that soft, pretty skin of yours."

Tracing his finger down the inside of her arm, he chuckled when she shivered.

"Or I could apply it for you?" His voice was low.

Maggie felt her face flush at the thought of his hands massaging lotion into her skin. But in her fantasy he didn't stop at only the exposed areas. She was tempted to call his bluff. The only thing that stopped her was the number of families in the immediate area.

Glancing around, she said, "Um, no, I think I can handle it."

J.D. grinned. "Coward."

He was absolutely right. She was in over her head and it scared her to death. Because the responsible Maggie who devoted herself to her son and her work was tempted to revert back to fun Maggie. She reminded herself that her initial time with Eric had been intoxicating, but it had ceased being fun shortly after she'd become pregnant.

Fortunately, the band took the stage and started tuning up. It made conversation difficult.

J.D. sat beside her, their knees touching.

She enjoyed the easy camaraderie, content to be still and listen to the music. Eric had always been too energetic to sit for any amount of time. J.D. seemed happy enjoying the little things.

It wasn't hard to imagine him here with a family of his own. An adoring wife and several little enforcers roaming around.

Maggie suppressed a pang of envy. Everything she'd wanted in life, it seemed, was right here in this town.

J.D. bumped her with his shoulder. He leaned over close to her ear. "Whatcha thinking about?"

"I was wondering how David's doing." The excuse made her feel guilty because she'd only fleetingly thought of her son. The unexpected freedom was just so darn exhilarating.

"We can call when they take a break, okay? I've got my cell."

She nodded.

The band started their first set and Maggie lost herself in the music and J.D.'s nearness. It was heavenly.

When the band took a break, the quiet was almost eerie. Then people started talking, children resumed playing and a black Lab raced by, his leash trailing behind. A thirtyish man and several of the kids were in hot pursuit.

"Sorry, J.D.," the man hollered as he hurdled the corner of their blanket.

Maggie threw back her head and laughed. "You didn't tell me there was entertainment during intermission."

J.D. leaned close, a lilt to his voice. "I'll tell Mike you appreciated the show. But there are lots of other ways to entertain ourselves."

Glancing at the people around them, she detected a few couples kissing in the dark.

When she turned back to J.D., she was surprised to find that his face was only inches from hers. He closed the distance and kissed her. It was a kiss as hot and passionate as any of the teenagers making out in the shadows.

Maggie leaned into him, needing to feel the warmth of his body next to hers.

He cradled the back of her neck and murmured her name.

Then they were sent sprawling by the impact of a locomotive, or at least it seemed like a locomotive.

Maggie sat up, trying to catch her breath when a huge black beast slurped her chin.

J.D. got to his feet. "You okay?"

"I think so. Except for dog slobber."

"You are referring to Jethro, here, I hope?" He grabbed the leash and ended Jethro's reign of terror. "Not me."

"Definitely Jethro." J.D. was a lot more persuasive with his tongue. Maggie's face warmed at the thought.

"Good. You had me worried for a second."

Jethro's adult pursuer jogged up, bending over at the waist while he caught his breath. Finally, he was able to straighten. Sticking out his hand, he said, "Thanks, man. Jethro could have been in the next county by the time I caught up with him."

"No problem." J.D. handed over the leash. "How's

business these days?" He turned to Maggie. "Mike is the best body man in the state."

"Pretty good. By the way, how'd your grandmother like the repairs to her Lincoln? Belmont said everything looked okay, but I want to make sure your grandmother was satisfied."

J.D. frowned. "What repairs?"

"Oh, shoot, I thought you would have figured it out by now. She hit a fence post. I kinda wondered why she bothered having it fixed. I mean, with all the other dings and dents on that car, what's the point? But she was afraid you'd find out and wouldn't let her drive anymore. Hope I didn't let the cat out of the bag."

"No problem. You said Belmont okayed repairs?"

"Yeah. He picked up the car for her. His wife dropped him off."

"I'll look into it. Thanks for letting me know."

Jethro took advantage of his owner's inattention and bounded away, jerking the leash from Mike's hands. The man cursed under his breath and took off after the dog. He waved over his shoulder.

"I'm sure it was nothing." Maggie tucked her arm in his.

"Huh? Oh, yeah, probably nothing." He unclipped his cell phone and gave it to her. "Do you want to call and check on David?"

"Yes, thanks. You look worried though."

"I'm just not sure what's up with Grandma." He recited Edna's phone number and Maggie entered the numbers.

Edna sounded unperturbed when she updated Maggie. The conversation was brief and left Maggie staring at the phone.

"What'd she say?"

"They're having a wonderful time. David is bathed and ready for bed and she suggested I not call again tonight. She doesn't want the phone to wake her up."

"Nothing to worry about then."

Maggie suddenly wished they'd included David in their outing. She didn't feel complete without her son.

"Come on, sweetheart." He pulled her close. "You've got to have some time away from each other every once in a while. And I promise you, my grandmother would never allow anything to happen to David."

Maggie rested her head against his shoulder. "I suppose you're right."

"I know I'm right. Now let's kick back and enjoy the rest of the concert. It looks like the band is coming back."

Taking his advice, she leaned back against his chest. When he wrapped his arm around her, she felt like all the pieces fell into place. The only thing missing in her life up to this moment had been J.D.

THE CLOSER THEY GOT to home, the more J.D. fidgeted, unable to keep still. Drumming his fingers on the steering wheel, he wished the Toyota were a five-speed. Shifting would have given him some way to keep his hands occupied.

Oh, he knew darn well how he wanted to keep his hands occupied. He wanted to take Maggie upstairs to his room and explore every inch of her body. But he was supposed to be more sensitive, more evolved than his brother. That complicated seduction enormously.

First, he had to be sure he wanted a future with Maggie. Having a one-night stand with her after what Eric had done would be cruel. He knew he wanted to be with her, but couldn't say how long.

"Is something wrong?" Maggie asked.

"No," he answered quickly. "Not at all."

They continued in silence until they reached home.

"I had so much fun tonight, J.D. Thank you."

Swiveling to meet her gaze, he wished his brother had never met Maggie. But then J.D. would have never met Maggie.

He leaned over and kissed her on the lips. No tongue, no tonsils. Just a quick kiss to show her he cared. When her lips parted, he steeled himself to refuse the invitation.

Pulling away from her was hell, but he was exceedingly proud of his self-control.

He got out of the car and went around to open the door for her.

She was very quiet as they walked to the house.

He'd remembered to leave the porch light on. The house was bathed in a welcoming glow.

Maggie's shoulders shimmered in the light. Her skin looked soft and delicate.

His fingers itched to pull the neck of her dress down over her shoulders to reveal her slender back. He could imagine tracing the length of her spine with his tongue. Then turning her around to trace her small, perfect breasts.

He almost groaned aloud, but caught himself in time. Instead, he muttered a curse under his breath.

As they climbed the steps, Maggie reached out and grasped his hand, as if they'd had a thousand dates and returning home together was as natural as breathing.

J.D. knew his self-control was slipping. His body told him there was only one suitable ending to such a terrific evening. But how could he seduce Maggie, a guest in his house, his almost-sister-in-law, and not wonder if she felt some sort of obligation.

She stopped on the porch and turned to him. Raising her chin, she held his gaze. "Talk to me, J.D. Tell me what I did wrong."

He pulled her close, resting his chin on the top of her head. "Aw, sweetheart, you did everything right. That's the problem."

"Then why are you pulling away from me. You closed yourself off the minute we started home."

Shrugging, he had no idea how to explain it to her.

"J.D., I think you've always been honest with me."

He cleared his throat. "I've always tried."

"You're not trying to be honest now? What's different?"

She pulled back, looking up into his face. Her eyes were huge and luminous in the light.

"The difference is that if you were anyone else, I'd be doing my damnedest to seduce you."

"So the problem is you don't want to seduce me?"

He made an impatient noise. "Of course I want to."

"Then seduce me."

"It's not that simple. You were my brother's lover, you're the mother of his child. You've been treated badly and you're very vulnerable. The last thing I should be thinking about is sleeping with you."

Maggie stepped forward. She gently put her cupped hands on his face. "I may be vulnerable, but I know I can trust you. I want to be with you tonight. So don't think. Just seduce."

"That's not me." He threw his head back and squeezed his eyes shut. "I always think about the repercussions."

"Then I guess it's my job to convince you to quit thinking."

She went on tiptoe and nibbled his lower lip, then placed tiny kisses along his jawline. Unbuttoning the top two buttons of his shirt, she slid her hands inside.

J.D. sucked in a breath.

"Please, J.D.? I need you tonight."

He looked down into her big, green eyes and knew he was a goner.

CHAPTER NINETEEN

MAGGIE HOPED SHE WAS DOING the right thing. She'd never seduced a man before; Eric had been the aggressor in their relationship.

She only knew that she needed J.D. He made her feel alive again and she was so very tired of feeling numb.

"Please hold me?" She twined her arms around his neck and kissed him, willing him to acquiesce. Pressing her body to his, she sighed with pleasure when he put his hands on her waist and pulled her close.

But it still wasn't enough.

"I need you, J.D. Please stay with me tonight?"

His voice was thick when he said, "Sweetheart, there isn't anything that I'd like more."

She took him by the hand and led him upstairs where she opened the door she knew led to his bedroom.

Once inside, her nerve faltered. Should she rip off her clothes and jump on the bed? Rip off his clothes and jump on the bed? Or simply push him to the floor and have her way with him. She giggled at the mental image.

He smiled with bemusement. "What's so funny?"

"Now that I've got you here, I'm not sure how a seductress is supposed to proceed."

J.D. grasped her hand and placed a surprisingly erotic kiss on her palm. "Maggie," he sighed. "There's no seduction needed. You don't know how badly I've wanted this."

"You could have fooled me." She shivered as he kissed and nibbled his way past her wrist, working his way to her shoulder. Maggie caught her breath when he reached the curve of her neck. "You...didn't seem interested."

"Oh, I was interested all right." He nudged her toward the bed. "But it wouldn't have been responsible to pursue you."

"How about now?"

J.D. kissed her deeply, sensuously and decidedly without thought of consequences.

She murmured his name and inched closer.

He pulled her hard against him. "I want you, Maggie." His voice was hoarse.

Running her palms over his back, she reveled in his strength. The fact that he was a man she could trust was more potent an aphrodisiac than she would have ever imagined. "I want you, too, J.D. But I want to make sure you know I don't hop into bed with just anyone. I have...feelings for you."

That didn't come out right. Sure, she had feelings for him. Every cell in her body lusted after him, screamed for her to move things into high gear.

"I mean, I care about you."

He rubbed her chin with his thumb. "I care for you, too. Probably more than you know. But are you sure this is what you want?"

She nodded, unable to speak.

"I need to see all of you. Is that okay?" His gaze was intent.

"Yes." Maggie stepped back and untied the ribbon holding her dress closed. Tipping her head to the side, she paused, unsure.

J.D. made an approving noise low in his throat. He reached up and touched the curls draped over her shoulder, his fingers brushing her collarbone.

His touch was so gentle, so tentative, her heart melted. She pushed the neckline of the peasant dress down and waited for his reaction.

"Beautiful," he murmured. "You are so beautiful."

He skimmed his palms over her shoulders, and she sucked in a surprised breath. Who knew work-roughened hands could be so erotic? She put her hands over his and guided them to her breasts.

His caress was gentle, but his calluses scraped against her nipples.

Maggie groaned at the exquisite sensation. She pushed her dress down over her hips, where it slid the rest of the way to her feet. Then she stepped out of her panties.

J.D.'s jaw tensed, as if he were trying to maintain self-control.

"J.D.," she whispered, "I need you. Now."

His fingers fumbled in his haste to remove his shirt, revealing the gorgeous sinews and muscles she had suspected were beneath his clothes. Reaching up, she traced his biceps with her fingernail, sucking in her breath as she watched goose bumps appear on his golden flesh.

Meeting his gaze, Maggie murmured, "You're beautiful." She unbuttoned his pants.

He removed his pants and white briefs in quick succession.

Maggie realized she'd underestimated the beauty of his body. Shadow played across his muscles as he moved to the nightstand and pulled out several condom packets. He pressed one into her palm. "Help me with this?"

She ripped it open. "With pleasure."

THE SUN BARELY PEEKED through the blinds when J.D. felt Maggie stir next to him. His body was ready, willing and able to repeat their lovemaking, but Maggie needed her sleep. Besides, he didn't want her to think he was waiting to pounce on her the second she awoke.

So he rolled over and went back to sleep. But Maggie's sweet little body tormented his dreams. He awakened once, his hand curved around her breast, his thumb rubbing her nipple.

Her low moan stopped him cold.

Was it a conscious invitation, or only an automatic response to stimuli? Her deep, even breathing told him it was the latter.

The next time he'd awakened, his fingers were between her legs, teasing her, exploring her, readying her to accept him. His erection throbbed against her rear end. It took him a lot longer to get back to sleep after he rolled over that time.

His last dream was the most erotic yet. Maggie's soft hands caressed the length of him, she teased his nipples erect with her kisses. Then slid her tongue lower, tracing the line of hair to his belly.

Groaning, he tried to move, but didn't have the energy.

The tender, wet kisses trailed lower still, until she took him in her mouth. In his dream, he could see her red hair fan across his thighs, feel the silk of her curls trail across his stomach.

When he thought he couldn't stand it a moment longer, he grasped her head, stilling her motion, running his hands through her gorgeous hair.

Cold air hit him where her mouth had once been. He whimpered in frustration. Had he been less turned on, the chill would have had the same effect as a cold shower. But he was past that point.

The bed dipped near his waist.

A rustling noise reached his ears.

Then Maggie's hands stroked him again, rolling a condom down his erection.

He tried to open his eyes, but they were heavy and refused to obey.

Slowly, very slowly, slick heat engulfed him. His

body jerked. Every molecule within him screamed for release.

The woman in his dream murmured encouragement as she rode him, setting a torturously slow pace. His hips lifted from the bed in a futile effort to take control. But it did no good. She simply laughed, contracting her muscles around him. He thought he might die.

He grasped her hips and plunged deeper.

Her laughter turned to a moan that sounded an awful lot like his name.

On his next thrust, she clenched around him and quivered.

There was no way in hell he was gonna sleep through this. It was either the best wet dream he'd had since he was thirteen or it was no dream at all.

Opening his eyes, he caught his breath at the sight of Maggie straddling him, her lips parted her eyes half-closed.

He whispered her name.

She opened her eyes.

Her expression was wild and beautiful as she climaxed.

AFTER AN EARTH-SHATTERING orgasm, consciousness crept over Maggie by degrees. She was resting on J.D.'s chest, his heartbeat slowing beneath her ear.

Maggie was content to lie there for the rest of her life. Her breathing slowed, contentment seeped through her body.

J.D. asked, "You okay?"

She nodded. "Never better."

He smoothed her hair, his motions slow and lazy. "Maggie?"

"Hmm?"

"I think I'm falling for you."

Glancing up at his face, her heart warmed at the emotion she saw. She rubbed her thumb along his jawline. "I'm glad. Because I fell for you a while ago."

She rested her ear against his chest. Just the sound of his steady heartbeat relaxed her. As long as J.D. cared for her, things would be fine.

"You ever think of moving here?" he asked.

"My school's in Arizona...."

"Could you transfer?"

"I don't know. I'd have to look into it." She rolled off him and shoved tangled curls away from her eyes. "But, J.D., I made big changes in my life for a man before and it was disastrous. I'm not sure if I'm ready to move cross-country."

"We don't have to decide now."

"No, we don't." Maggie couldn't begin to contemplate life without J.D. in it. But it scared her silly to consider making the kind of sweeping changes he'd suggested. Her life was safe now. Not nearly as exciting as when Eric had been there, but she'd had enough excitement. And David thrived in the apartment in Arizona.

She sat up abruptly. "David. What time is it? When do we have to pick him up?"

"It's okay." J.D. pulled her back down. "We've got plenty of time. Grandma invited us to brunch at noon."

MAGGIE'S HEART WAS LIGHT as J.D. grasped her hand. They were a few minutes late for brunch, but the time had been well spent.

"I can't wait to see David. This is the longest we've been apart since he was born." She practically danced up the steps to the front door.

"I kinda miss the little crumb-catcher, too." J.D. wrapped his arm around her waist and pulled her close. "But I have to admit I sure enjoyed the time alone with you."

Raising her face, she met him halfway in a bone-melting kiss. She lost herself in his strength, his scent and the perfection of being held by him.

J.D. raised his head for a second and Maggie regained a small fraction of her ability to function in the real world.

There had been a noise….

"I said ahem."

J.D. released her.

They turned in unison toward the open door.

"Um, hello, Grandma. How long have you been standing there?"

"Long enough. I told David I thought I heard some-one at the door and found you two making a spectacle of yourselves."

"Hey, remember those Confederate widows, Grandma." He grinned and winked.

"Come inside before the neighbors figure out what you've been up to."

J.D. ushered Maggie through the door.

"Where's David?" Maggie asked, eager to see her son.

"In the sunroom, dear."

Maggie and J.D. hurried ahead of her.

David let out a squeal from the playpen when he saw them enter the room. He grinned, raising his arms to be held.

Maggie scooped him up and planted kisses all over his soft little neck and face. "I'm so glad to see you." She turned to Edna. "Did he miss me?"

"He cried a bit before bed. You must spoil the child."

"It's normal for a child his age to have separation anxiety."

"What smells so good?" J.D.'s tone was overly hearty.

"Some of your favorites for breakfast." She beamed. "Just like when you were a little boy. Eggs Benedict, bacon, sausage, grits and hush puppies."

"It sounds wonderful," Maggie murmured.

J.D. leaned close, his voice low. "Yeah, all Eric's favorites."

Edna didn't seem to hear. She held out her hands to David. "Come to Great-Grandma, sugar."

David batted her hand away.

"I'll just get him settled." Maggie glanced at the beautifully appointed mahogany table. "Where's the little chair I brought that clips to the table?"

"Oh, we don't need that. David can sit on my lap."

Maggie shot J.D. a worried frown.

"Grandma, I'll go get the clip-on high chair. Where is it?" J.D.'s tone didn't invite argument.

Edna frowned. "It's in the sunroom, by the playpen."

An uncomfortable silence settled on the dining room as they waited for J.D. to return.

Maggie bounced David on her hip. "Mommy missed you." She kissed the top of his head.

"Here we go." J.D. returned with the chair. "Where do you want Maggie to sit?"

"There, on the right." Edna's words were stilted.

"I'll put David here." He clamped the chair to the table. "And I'll sit on the other side. That way we can tag team him and both of us can eat."

"He would have been fine in my lap," she muttered under her breath before she gestured toward the sideboard. "Please help yourselves. I'll hold David while you fill your plates." She pried him out of Maggie's arms before she knew what had happened.

Maggie suppressed rising anger. Edna was old and accustomed to getting her own way. She could humor the woman for an hour.

When Maggie set her plate on the table and turned to get David, she found Edna already up and loading her plate, the baby on her hip.

"Thank you for holding him." Maggie stepped in front of Edna and held out her arms. Her son leaned toward her, but Edna ignored her.

"You're a guest, dear. Please sit down. I'm fine."

Maggie glanced at J.D. for guidance. He shrugged.

She reluctantly took her seat and watched the stubborn woman complete her task.

Edna's smile was triumphant as she set the plate on the table and sat down, planting David on her lap.

Maggie told herself it was a small thing. A silly power play, but it still bothered her.

J.D. stood. "Here, I'll put him in his chair."

Edna's eyes snapped, her cheeks flushed. "Nonsense, James David. Sit down."

"I mean it, Grandma." His tone was strained.

Maggie knew how hard he tried to please his grandmother and regretted that she'd put him in the middle. Touching his arm, Maggie murmured, "It's okay. Really."

J.D. took his seat, but didn't look happy about backing down.

And Edna looked absolutely furious.

J.D. flinched almost imperceptibly at her glare. He unfolded his cloth napkin and placed it on his lap.

They ate in silence for a few minutes; the only sound was that of utensils scraping against china.

Edna regally inclined her head. "David is such a good little boy. Just like Eric at the same age. Except Eric was sickly. My, David is such an eater."

Maggie smiled, but it felt stiff and forced. "Yes, he is a good boy." Her face thawed when she looked at her son. How could she fault the woman for praising her child? "Did he eat all the baby food I sent?"

Edna scooped a small portion of grits and fed them to David. "No, the boy needs to eat real food. You should have seen him light into the leftover mashed potatoes and gravy."

J.D. turned to Maggie. "Didn't you say you were trying to limit his table food? Something about food allergies?"

She nodded slowly. "That's what the experts recommend. But I imagine a little grits would be okay."

"Of course it's okay. The little tyke loves them. He'll grow faster if you feed him nutritious food."

"I feed him the food his pediatrician recommends."

Edna sniffed. "Doctors think they know everything. They thought Eric couldn't father a child and look how wrong they were about that."

J.D. frowned. "I ran into Mike Tanner at the concert last night. He wanted to know if you were satisfied with the repairs to the Lincoln."

Edna stiffened. "I don't know what he's talking about."

"He said Belmont asked him to fix it for you. Apparently you didn't want me to know about it. Something about me taking your car away."

"He must be mistaken."

J.D. sighed.

Maggie watched as David grabbed a piece of bacon off Edna's plate and gnawed on it.

She jumped up and pried the bacon out of David's hand. "Edna, he might choke." She grasped the baby under the arms and lifted him from the woman's lap. "Grits are one thing. They're soft and easy to swallow. Bacon is not."

"He was just fine," Edna protested.

The doorbell rang and she excused herself to answer it.

Maggie took the opportunity to place David in his seat.

"I'd like to leave as soon as possible," she whispered to J.D. "Your grandmother is making me very uncomfortable."

J.D. nodded. "She's not herself today." He glanced in the direction of the living room. "And that bit about the car, I'm wondering if her memory is starting to go."

"There's one way to find out. You can look at the Lincoln when we leave. See if there's any new bodywork."

"I think I'll do that. Now eat up, so we can get out of here."

The murmur of Edna's voice alternated with a baritone. The conversation went on a few minutes and then Edna returned, followed by a uniformed older man Maggie didn't recognize.

"Sheriff Andrews, please help yourself to the buffet." She gestured toward the sideboard.

"No, thank you, ma'am. I'm not staying. Like I explained, I just need to borrow J.D."

Edna frowned. "Surely he can finish his meal."

"No, ma'am. I have a search warrant." He handed

some folded papers to J.D. "I need you to let me in to your architectural firm."

J.D. tossed his napkin on the table and stood. "On what grounds?"

"Your partner is being investigated for the murder of Eric McGuire."

CHAPTER TWENTY

MAGGIE SQUEEZED J.D.'s arm. "It'll be okay," she said, as they watched several deputies paw through his life's work.

He ran a hand over his head in frustration. "I called the sheriff. He assured me they would be as careful as they could, but he couldn't guarantee there wouldn't be damage."

"Oh, J.D." She pressed her forehead to his upper arm. "This is horrible."

"I can't believe Roy would do something like that. I've known him since high school. He used to hang around our house all the time."

"Maybe it's all a mistake." Maggie couldn't force more than halfhearted enthusiasm in her voice. A couple of Roy's drinking buddies had come forward and said Roy had admitted to arguing with Eric the night he'd been murdered. He'd also commented later that Eric had gotten what he deserved.

J.D. wrapped his arm around her shoulder. "The one good thing to come of this is things are looking better for you now."

"I wish it happened a different way, though."

And she wished the possibility of clearing her name didn't mean she might lose J.D. right when she'd found him. The sheriff had said he would advise her attorney of the new development and it was possible she would be allowed to return to Arizona. She longed to get back to school and graduate, but her joy, her heart, would be with J.D.

J.D. glanced down to the child carrier where David slept. "If you think they'll wake him up, I can drop you two off at home and come back."

"We're not going anywhere. David's fine and I intend to be here with you."

He kissed her on the lips. "Thank you."

Maggie got the feeling very few people had stood by J.D. in the past, at least not in any way that counted. The thought made her sad. "No thanks necessary. I wouldn't want to be anywhere else."

"We need to talk when this is over." J.D. cupped her face with his hand. His gaze was intent.

"Yes, we do." Only she had no clue what they could say. Her school was in Arizona, his family and roots were in Arkansas.

Maggie needed to keep her mind busy, so she wouldn't obsess about their future, or possible lack of a future. "They think the murder weapon is here?"

"No. My bet is they're just being thorough. The only knife Roy keeps around here is his pocketknife.

The coroner's report indicates the murder weapon was probably an eight-inch deboning knife."

"Do you know where Roy would hide something like that?"

J.D. shook his head. "Roy and I don't talk so much anymore."

One of the deputies shouted that he'd found something in Roy's office. Maggie wanted to get closer, but a deputy instructed them to stay in the reception area.

Sheriff Andrews brushed past them, holding an evidence bag.

The color drained from J.D.'s face. He grasped the deputy's arm. "Did you find something?"

"Box cutter and a pocketknife, but nothing even close to the murder weapon. Maybe the guys at his house will have more luck."

"God, Maggie, if it was Roy, how could I have been so completely unaware?" J.D's shoulders slumped.

She felt his defeat as if it had been her own. She ached to comfort him, but didn't have any wise words to offer. So Maggie opted for the truth. "Sometimes we see only what we want to see. I'm the master at that."

MAGGIE WAS GRATEFUL to be busy at work the next day. It helped take her mind off J.D.'s troubles and her own.

David, however, was not happy to be there. He was teething and fussy and wanted everyone to know about it.

Finally, about midmorning, Maggie poked her head

into Jack's office and asked, "Is it okay if I take a break now? I'd like to take David for a walk. Maybe a change of scenery will soothe him. I'm sorry he's making such a racket today."

"Go ahead and take a long break—you've worked hard, you deserve it. The voice mail can pick up any calls. Don't worry about David, he's not bothering me. And Mr. Snyder hasn't complained a bit." He grinned and winked.

"I would worry if Mr. Snyder *did* complain. Someone at the hospital would have a lot of explaining to do."

"Go, get some fresh air." He shooed her toward the reception area.

"Thanks, boss."

Maggie was smiling when she turned to find a woman standing in front of her desk, frowning. She wore a navy-blue suit, no makeup and lank brown hair pulled back in a neat ponytail.

"May I help you?"

"I'm looking for Maggie McGuire."

"I'm Maggie."

The woman held out a business card. "I'm Stephanie White from the Department of Children and Family Services."

Maggie accepted the card and died a little inside. But on the outside, she remained businesslike. "Yes, Ms. White?"

"We've received a complaint of child neglect

regarding—" she referred to a file folder "—David McGuire. Is this David in the playpen?"

"Yes, he's my son. He's fine."

"You understand we have to investigate each and every complaint. I'll need to examine David and then interview you."

"This can't be happening." Dizziness washed over Maggie. She braced her hand on her desk to keep from falling. "There's some mistake."

"I'm sure you're probably right." The woman smiled, transforming her face to near-beauty. "But I need to follow procedure."

The woman went to the playpen and talked to David in a soothing tone. "Hey, sweetheart. Can I hold you?"

He glanced at Maggie, as if looking for reassurance.

"It's okay. She's a, um, friend."

Putting down her file and briefcase, the woman picked up David and settled him on her hip. "You are a big boy."

She turned to Maggie and said, "He's certainly not malnourished."

"No. He gets plenty to eat."

"The complaint indicated he wasn't being fed."

A niggling suspicion started in the back of Maggie's mind as she recalled brunch at Edna's. Surely J.D.'s grandmother hadn't filed a complaint because of their disagreement over table food?

"He's teething?" Ms. White asked as she peered into his mouth.

"Yes. It makes him a little crabby."

"Well, that's certainly normal."

Maggie started to relax, but then realized the woman probably tried to develop a rapport with all her clients. The social worker who'd taken away her niece, Emma, might have seemed nice, too.

"I need to remove his shirt." Ms. White quickly and efficiently removed the little shirt with the Winnie the Pooh emblem.

David started to cry. This definitely wasn't his idea of fun. But then again, it wasn't Maggie's idea of fun, either.

Checking him front and back, Ms. White put his shirt back on and handed him to Maggie. "He seems to be in excellent physical condition."

"He *is* in excellent physical condition. I follow my pediatrician's instructions to the letter."

Ms. White glanced around the room. "Are the plants real?"

Maggie paused, wondering where the question led. "No, they're silk."

"I don't see electrical-outlet covers."

"David is either in his playpen or I'm holding him. I don't allow him on the floor."

They discussed Maggie's work and child-care arrangements extensively, including the location of dangerous chemicals. Maggie promised to provide her with the phone number of David's pediatrician in Arizona.

Ms. White closed the manila folder and slid it into her briefcase. "I should have a report ready by Friday. I'll be in touch. Oh, and if you plan to vacation or move back to Arizona before Friday, please advise me."

Maggie nodded. "Um, yes."

Her mind was spinning as she watched the woman exit the office. She had to figure something out. They couldn't possibly conclude she was an unfit mother. But what if they did? They could take David away just as they'd taken Emma.

What would she do?

Maggie paced, trying to calm her rising panic. Grabbing her purse from the bottom desk drawer, she asked Jack for an early lunch and headed to the only place where she felt safe—J.D.'s.

Pulling into the drive, she was relieved to see his truck parked in the detached garage. He'd said he would work at home today, since he'd been at the office most of the night putting things back in order.

She removed David from his car seat, planted a kiss on the top of his head and used her key to enter the house.

"J.D.?" she called.

He emerged from his den, dark circles beneath his eyes. Black stubble covered his jaw and head. It was the first time she'd seen more than a hint of what his hair might be like.

"What's wrong?" he asked.

Maggie flew to his side. "Someone reported me to the Department of Children and Family Services for neglect. They sent a caseworker to check on David."

J.D. wrapped his arms around her.

For the first time since Stephanie White had introduced herself, Maggie allowed herself to fall apart. Her knees trembled; she shook as if with cold.

"It's got to be a mistake," he soothed. "Here, let's put the crumb-catcher in his playpen for a minute while we sort this out."

J.D. took David from her arms and placed him in the playpen. Then he tickled her son under the chin with his favorite teddy bear. David kicked his feet and giggled, grabbing on to the teddy and hugging it tight.

Maggie's eyes clouded as she watched J.D. with her son. What a warm, wonderful man. His strength wasn't in his muscled build, but in his character.

"J.D., I have to go. Help me pack up our stuff and I'll be out of here before the social worker knows I'm gone."

"Hey, don't do anything rash. First, tell me everything that happened, then we'll put our heads together and figure something out."

"You don't understand. They might take David. I couldn't live with myself if that happened."

J.D. grasped her arms. "Listen to me, Maggie. You're not alone. Your sister made a mistake when she didn't ask for help. Your situation is different. I'm here for you. So are a lot of other people who care about you and David. I'll stand beside you."

Maggie stifled a hysterical laugh. "Oh, yeah, and who do you think called DCFS?"

J.D.'s eyes narrowed. The muscle in his jaw twitched. "You think my grandmother reported you?"

"I don't know." She was desperate for a way out. "I'm so scared I can't think straight."

"Okay, calm down. Take a couple deep breaths."

She did as he asked and it helped a little.

"What did they tell you specifically about the complaint? Was Grandma's name mentioned?"

"No, she didn't name the person who complained. But whoever it was said I'd neglected David, that I didn't feed him enough. And she seemed very interested in the reception area at work. Wanting to know if the plants were real, where the chemicals were kept, why there were no protective covers on the electrical outlets."

J.D. let go of her arms and paced. "I don't want to believe Grandma would do something like that. But I didn't want to believe Roy would kill my brother, and apparently, he did." His eyes were dark with hurt and confusion.

"It's the food that makes me think it was your grandmother. She was so insistent he needed table food to grow properly. Even the caseworker said he seemed healthy."

He stepped close, his voice low and hoarse. "I'll find out who it is and I'll stop them." The warm, sensitive man she'd grown to love suddenly seemed a very dangerous stranger. The enforcer, just like the night they'd met.

"No, J.D., don't." She grasped his arm. "Don't do something that could destroy your relationship with Edna."

"We have a right to confront her."

"And what if it wasn't Edna? Maybe a clerk in the grocery store or someone who came in to consult with me or Jack?"

"Then Grandma will understand our concern." His mouth tightened. He tipped her chin with his finger and held her gaze. "I won't allow anyone to hurt you."

Maggie rested her hands at his waist. "You're the first person in this whole world to stand up for me, no matter the cost. However this all turns out, I want you to know how special you are to me."

"Aw, sweetheart, that's what love is all about. United we stand, divided we fall."

"Love?"

"I haven't told you?" His grin was wicked. This was the teasing side of J.D. that sometimes took her by surprise.

"No."

"You're sure?"

She laughed, her breath catching in her throat. "Believe me, I would have remembered."

"I love you, Maggie. I think I've loved you since the first time I saw you on that podium, making one heckuva scene. I remember thinking you looked like an avenging angel."

Maggie absorbed his words and held them close to

her heart. J.D. had seen the best and worst of her and loved her in spite of it all. Maybe even loved her *because* of it all.

"I love you, too, J.D. I love being with you and the way you make me feel that everything is possible. You accept me for who I am in here." She touched her chest above her heart.

He kissed her. His mouth, his scent, his tongue, they were all familiar and oh, so welcome.

Leaning closer, she wrapped her arms around his waist, losing herself in his world for just a few moments. Then, she reluctantly pulled away. David had to come first. "We'll go talk to Edna together. Maybe you could call her and arrange for us to stop by her house after I get off work. Much as I'd like to spend the afternoon with you, I have to get back."

"And if she asks for a reason?"

"Tell her we're craving pie." She winked.

J.D. raised an eyebrow. "A grilling, huh?"

Maggie nodded. "And not the barbecue kind."

CHAPTER TWENTY-ONE

J.D. ALMOST GROANED ALOUD when he saw the sheriff's cruiser parked in the drive at his grandmother's house. His stomach already churned from thoughts of how she might have betrayed the woman he loved.

He couldn't reconcile that type of manipulation with the strict but honorable woman who had raised him.

Glancing at Maggie in the passenger seat, he was amazed at her calm exterior. But she fidgeted with her hands, until he stilled them with an affectionate squeeze. "It's gonna be okay."

She smiled wanly. "Yes, it has to be."

"I'm sure we'll clear this up."

"I hope so."

"If it was grandmother, she can call the DCFS people and explain that she was mistaken. Everything will be fine." His assurance sounded hollow even to him.

"If everything will be fine, then why is the sheriff here?"

"Maybe they found the murder weapon at Roy's house. It's not unusual for law enforcement to keep the family apprised of progress on the case."

Maggie nodded and glanced in the back seat. "How could anyone look at David and think he'd been mistreated?"

"No rational person." And that's what bothered him. Grandma's uncharacteristic behavior of late. Had Eric's death unhinged her? Or was there something else going on?

"I'll get David," Maggie said and got out of the car.

He watched her bend to remove David from the seat and couldn't help but remember the first time he'd seen her do that. Her T-shirt had ridden up, revealing a narrow strip of pale skin. He'd longed to touch her, just as he longed to touch her today.

Stepping behind her, he placed his palm on the bare strip of skin.

She turned and smiled at him, her eyes alight with love. Then she straightened, holding David.

God, he loved her so much it hurt. What would he do if she went back to Arizona and didn't give him a second thought?

He shook off the doubts. They could talk later about their future. But now, they needed to make sure no one tried to separate Maggie from her son.

His throat was dry as he knocked on the door.

The sheriff came out first, his expression grim. "Hello, J.D., Maggie." He placed his hat on his head and left.

His grandmother stood in the doorway, her pallor gray. "Come in."

"What was the sheriff doing here?" J.D. asked.

"He, um, told me that Roy is being questioned about Eric's murder."

Surely, that was old news by now. But he didn't call her on it. The conversation was going to take a difficult turn as it was.

She cleared her throat, darting her gaze at Maggie. "Please go make yourselves comfortable in the sunroom while I get you some pie."

"That won't be necessary," Maggie said. "We just came by to ask you a couple of questions."

Grandma froze. "Questions?"

"Yes." Maggie glanced at J.D.

He nodded. If she wanted to take the initiative, he'd be more than happy to provide backup.

"Maybe we ought to sit down." Maggie suggested.

"Certainly." His grandmother gestured toward the living room. He couldn't recall ever having actually sat on the furniture in that room.

He ushered Maggie to the couch and sat next to her. The cushion was stiff and unyielding.

Grandma lowered herself slowly to a chair. She seemed older today. Weary? Afraid?

J.D. couldn't quite put his finger on the change.

Maggie sat David on her knee. "Edna, a social worker came by work today to check on David's welfare. Do you know anything about that?"

"Why would I know anything?" Her gaze shifted from Maggie to J.D.

Maggie glanced at him for reassurance. He put his arm around her shoulders.

"The caseworker said someone was worried that I neglected David. That he didn't receive proper nutrition. After our discussion at brunch the other day, I thought it was possible you might have misunderstood and been concerned about David's welfare." Maggie's voice was calm, yet firm.

"No, of course I didn't file a complaint." Grandma's cheeks flushed with indignation. "Now that we've clarified that situation, I'd like to speak to J.D. alone."

J.D. said, "Maggie can hear anything you have to say to me."

"This is different." Her voice cracked slightly. Her lips trembled.

J.D. got a bad feeling in the pit of his stomach. He'd never seen his grandmother quite this distraught before, except when she'd been told Eric had been murdered.

"Maggie, why don't you and David go outside. I'll be there in a minute." He rubbed her arm.

She nodded and rose, holding David, whom J.D.'s grandmother didn't seem to notice. Maggie left the room and J.D. heard the front door click behind her.

"What is it, Grandma?"

"I've always taken care of you, James David. Even though you weren't my own flesh and blood, I took you in when your mother and my dear son died." Her eyes filled with tears.

"And I've always been grateful."

She nodded. "You've been a good boy. Now I need to ask a favor."

"You know I'd do just about anything for you."

"Yes. I need you to say you were with me the night Eric died. That you came over here after you dropped Maggie off at the hotel and we spent the evening together."

J.D. couldn't have been more shocked if she'd asked him to fly her to the moon. "What's going on?"

"I was here by myself after Belmont dropped me off, so I have no one to verify it."

"That's never been questioned. Why now?"

She wrung her hands and stood. "It seems that Roy is spreading vicious lies in an effort to save his own neck."

"What lies?"

"He says he saw me at the racetrack that night, entering Eric's motor home around the time they think he was killed." She paced, her voice high-pitched. "Of course it's nonsense. But people might misunderstand. It won't be an issue if you confirm you were here with me."

"But I wasn't, and the police already know where I was. You brought me up to tell the truth, Grandma."

"I'm asking you to fudge the truth just this once." She sat next to him and took his hands in hers. "Please? For me?"

J.D.'s heart ached with the knowledge that she would sacrifice his integrity. "Grandma, nobody is going to think you murdered Eric. It's ridiculous."

She hesitated for a split second. "Of course it's ridiculous. But innocent people have gone to jail before."

He gently removed his hands from hers and stood. "I'm sorry. I just can't do it." He strode out of the house, his heart breaking.

It was the sight of Maggie and David waiting for him near the car that kept him from sliding into a pit of self-doubt. He owed his grandmother a lot, but he wouldn't lie for her.

As he approached Maggie, David raised his arms and leaned toward him.

J.D. gladly accepted the child, breathing in his sweet scent and total innocence. "Hey, buddy." His voice was husky. This was real. This was right. What his grandmother had asked him to do was wrong.

"Do you want to talk about it?" Maggie's eyes were warm with concern.

"She asked me to lie for her. I told her no."

"What kind of lie?"

He shook his head. "Not now. I need to look into something. Come with me to the garage?"

"I'll help you any way I can." She slipped her hand into his.

The interior of the garage was dark. J.D. felt for the light switch. The bare bulb cast an eerie glow, like something out of a horror flick.

He went to the passenger side of his grandmother's car and ran his palm down the length of the door. "The dent's been repaired."

"But Edna denied having had it fixed. Maybe Belmont did it as a favor for her, kind of a surprise?"

"Maybe. But I doubt it." What had happened to the woman who had preached honor to her grandsons as they grew? Of course, it appeared J.D. had been the only one listening. "Man, I have one screwed-up family."

Maggie placed her hand on his arm. "All families are screwed up. Some just hide it better than others."

He tipped his head back and squeezed his eyes shut. Hopelessness threatened to consume him.

Then he felt David's small hands softly patting his face.

Opening his eyes, J.D. realized he held hope in his arms. "No, not all of them. I've got to believe we can change the pattern. I believe you and I can still be good parents for David and create a healthy family if we want it badly enough."

Maggie's voice was low. "I'd sure like to try."

J.D. wrapped an arm around her shoulders and pulled her close. "Me, too."

MAGGIE FOUND J.D. sitting on the porch. She glanced up at the stars and inhaled the fresh air. "I gave David his bath and put him to bed."

"Good. Do you want to sit?" He motioned toward the other rocking chair.

Part of her wanted to accept his offer, be right there for him. But the other part of her couldn't quit turning over Edna's request. They needed answers and they needed them now.

Slinging her purse over her shoulder, she asked, "Would you mind if I go for a drive? I'll only be gone for an hour or so."

"Let me give you my cell to take, just in case anything happens."

He unclipped his phone and handed it to her. It was still warm from his body heat. For some reason, that made her feel connected to him.

She smiled. "I'll be back."

He was still sitting on the porch when she pointed the Toyota toward town. The drive was reminiscent of her first night in McGuireville.

She shivered, thinking that someone had brutally murdered Eric while she'd been driving out to the track. If Maggie hadn't stopped for directions, she might have walked in on the killer and been murdered, too. David would have been orphaned.

Her heart ached for J.D. Edna had given him a stable home when he'd desperately needed one, then yanked it out from under him today. How could she do that to him?

Maggie suspected Edna was more concerned about survival than J.D. at the moment. And that's what she intended to prove.

Pulling into the parking lot, Maggie noted it wasn't nearly as full as the last time she'd been there, when the Saturday-night crowd overflowed the lot.

She drove to the back of the lot, looking for the area where she'd been parked. The entrance to that portion was narrow, with chain link fencing on either side. On busy nights, the gates were thrown open so people could park in the field beyond.

Maggie parked to the side and switched off the engine. She grabbed a flashlight from the glove box and got out, carefully inspecting the first post. Nothing. The second post, however, showed traces of black paint.

Her heart plummeted. She'd hoped to be wrong. If her suspicions were correct, J.D. was about to have his heart broken.

Maggie reset the odometer before she left for town.

J.D. was still on the front porch when she returned. Rocking and thinking, thinking and rocking. He smiled as she approached, but she could tell his mind was far, far away.

She pulled the second rocker close to his and sat down. Leaning forward, she braced her elbows on her knees. "J.D., we've got to talk."

J.D. sighed. "Can it wait? I've got a lot on my mind."

"It has to do with your grandmother and Eric's murder."

"What do you mean?"

"This is really tough for me to ask, but has the thought crossed your mind that Edna might have... murdered Eric?"

"She loved him."

"Sometimes the line between love and hate is blurry. And you said she'd been acting a little different lately."

"Different isn't the same thing as going on a murderous rampage."

"I didn't say she went on a rampage. J.D., when I went to the races that night, I noticed someone had hit one of the fence poles between the main lot and the field out back."

His expression was bleak. "And Grandma had that new dent on her door, the one with silver paint. I suppose the poles are painted silver?"

Maggie nodded. "And there's some black paint on the pole. It's about the right height."

"And she had extra miles on the Lincoln."

"She did? I checked the distance so I could work on my own time line. It's twenty-five miles round trip from your house. Add on an extra, what, two miles, to her house?"

"That's about right."

"Then that would account for approximately twenty-seven extra miles on the car. Do you remember how many miles she was over?"

"Twenty-nine. That could be about fifteen trips to the grocery store in one week, or an unexpected trip to the racetrack." J.D. rested his head in his hand. "What am I going to do, Maggie?"

She wrapped her arm around his shoulder. "It'll be okay. I'll be here with you."

They sat in silence for what seemed like forever. Finally, J.D. said, "I guess I'll go talk to the sheriff first thing tomorrow morning. It's not like she's going anywhere tonight. And God help me if I'm wrong."

God help him if they were right.

Maggie stood, extending her hand to him. She would comfort him the best way she knew how. "I'm going upstairs. Come with me?"

He slid his hand into hers and slowly rose.

CHAPTER TWENTY-TWO

MAGGIE PROPPED HERSELF on one arm and watched J.D. sleep. It was a restless, fitful sleep, but at least he slept.

She longed to reach out and smooth the grooves around his mouth, run her hand over the dark stubble on his head. But she didn't. He needed whatever rest he could get.

Slight snuffling, rustling noises came from the baby monitor by the bed. She'd had the presence of mind to bring the monitor to J.D.'s room the night before.

A good thing, since David was waking and would be demanding attention soon.

Sighing, Maggie decided she would take a few more minutes for herself, enjoying the sight of the hard muscles in J.D.'s arms and shoulders.

But soon her mind turned to other things, and she began to wonder if Edna could have killed Eric. Why? Unfortunately, Edna was the only one who could answer that question.

Baby gibberish came through the monitor and Maggie turned it off. She smiled, imagining David lying in his crib, playing with his toes and talking to himself.

She calculated quickly. She might be able to tiptoe into her shower without David being the wiser. Five minutes would have to do.

She was showered, dressed and in the process of feeding David cereal when J.D. emerged, his head and face freshly shaven, wearing chinos and a short-sleeve T-shirt.

"Why didn't you wake me?" he asked, his voice still husky with sleep.

"You needed your sleep. The little human alarm clock woke me earlier than I would have preferred."

"Hey, buddy." He chucked David under the chin.

J.D. poured himself a cup of coffee and pulled up a chair. He straddled the chair, resting his arms on the back. "Do you want me to call you at work after I've seen the sheriff?"

"Work? No way. I'm with you today."

He raised an eyebrow.

"What? We stick together during the tough times. That's what love's all about."

His smile was sheepish as he recognized his own words, tweaked to her liking. "You don't have to, but I wouldn't mind the moral support."

"I've already called Jack and told him I have a family emergency. He's expecting me tomorrow."

He leaned over and kissed her. David and the rest of the world faded as he showed her how much he loved and needed her. Or at least that's how she chose to interpret it.

She was breathless when he broke off the kiss. His slow smile told her he knew exactly the effect he had on her.

"Grab some breakfast, Romeo. It's going to be a long day. There's cereal, muffins, fruit and whatever else you can scrounge up."

"You're right. I have the feeling it's going to be a *very* long day." He sipped his coffee, his face unreadable.

J.D. SWITCHED OFF THE ENGINE and stared at the house he'd once called home.

In the rearview mirror, he saw the sheriff pull in behind him. They'd agreed J.D. would talk to his grandmother first, then Sheriff Andrews would execute the search warrant.

J.D. wished like hell he could be anywhere else at the moment, but he owed it to his grandmother to offer moral support, even if his worst fears were true. He wished Maggie were there, but he'd dropped her off at home. This was bound to be a gut-wrenching visit and there was no reason to subject David to it.

Slowly, he exited the car and walked up the drive. His tread was heavy as he climbed the porch steps. When he got to the top, he turned to see the sheriff standing by his patrol car waiting. It was a courtesy J.D. fervently appreciated.

He knocked on the door.

When there was no answer, he knocked again.

Where the hell was she? Grandma always answered almost immediately. Had she left him holding the bag? Or maybe hurt herself? His heart hammered at the thought.

He raised his hand to pound on the door one more time when it opened.

His grandmother stood before him, her head held high. "J.D., I didn't know you were coming by."

"May I come in? We need to talk."

She glanced over his shoulder at the patrol car, but opened the door for him to enter.

"What's this all about?" she asked.

"I think you know what this is about. I brought the sheriff with me because I've found out some things that worry me."

"What could I have possibly done to worry you?"

"That's what I want to know. How did you get the extra miles on your car? Where did that dent in the door come from? And why have only the one dent fixed?"

"You know I don't pay much attention to that car." She waved away his concern.

He cleared his throat. "And then you asked me to lie so you'd have an alibi. It doesn't look good."

"Nonsense."

J.D. glanced out the window to see another patrol car pull into the drive. "Grandma, we don't have much time. I thought about this a lot last night. Whatever you have or haven't done, I'll stand beside you. You don't have to go through it alone. But I won't lie and I won't stand in the way of justice."

Her chin quivered as she gazed out the window at the cars. "Are they arresting me?"

"No. But they have a search warrant. And I wanted to be here with you while they searched. Can I signal them to come in?"

Nodding, her eyes filled with tears. She wiped them with a tissue and straightened her spine. It saddened him to see the acceptance and fear on her face. "Let them in."

J.D. opened the front door for the sheriff and several deputies. Putting his arm around his grandmother, he was worried she might collapse as she received the search warrant. As it was, she merely leaned heavily on him. He stood by her as the uniformed men trampled through his childhood home, and he was still there two hours later when three deputies went into the yard with metal detectors. J.D. was the one who caught his grandmother as she crumpled to the ground after hearing a knife had been found.

He helped her to a chair, saddened by the irony of where the knife had been found, buried at the foot of a granite statue—a Confederate soldier.

"Why, Grandma?" he asked, remembering how Eric had always been her favorite.

She covered her face and wept. "I didn't mean to, but he caused so much pain. I saw him there asleep and I thought how maybe it might be better if he weren't here anymore. And I thought of all the ways he'd embarrassed the family and brought shame to the McGuire name. I was angry, so angry."

Her eyes pleaded with J.D. to understand. "Why couldn't you have been a McGuire, Jamie?"

Grasping her hand, he didn't know what to say, except, "Why couldn't you love me anyway?"

When she didn't answer, he walked out the door.

IT WAS WELL PAST DUSK when J.D. arrived home. His heart lifted a bit at the sight of a welcoming light shining through the window. He'd been driving aimlessly for hours, thinking.

Trudging up the steps, he stopped for a moment to admire the old house—the graceful columns, the red-brick mellowed by age, and best of all, the two people inside. He pressed his face to the glass and saw Maggie putting supper on the table. David was supervising from his swing.

As if sensing his presence, Maggie turned and saw him. Her smile was all encompassing, reaching clear down to his soul.

She ran to the door and opened it, her cheeks flushed a rosy pink. "What are you doing standing out there? You belong in here."

And J.D. realized she was right. He was no longer the lost little boy on the outside looking in. He belonged inside with Maggie and David, the two people who loved him just the way he was.

EPILOGUE

Maggie waddled onto the dais and sighed. She was forever making a scene at family reunions it seemed. This was the Rossi family reunion, held just outside Boston, and J.D. was having a wonderful time reuniting with long-lost cousins, aunts and uncles. Maggie would have had a wonderful time, too, except that her ankles were swollen and her belly felt as if she carried a baby elephant, though her doctor had assured her she didn't.

Still, she loved seeing J.D. in the midst of this laughing, loving family. He'd grown his hair out and she had a hard time telling the back of his head from the rest of the raven-haired Rossis. It was too bad she had to interrupt his fun.

"Excuse me," she yelled. But this was a boisterous reunion and her voice didn't reach the front row. Shrugging, she went to the podium and grabbed the microphone.

"I'm looking for my husband."

A few people looked up, but most were too involved in conversation to pay attention. "I said, I'm looking for my husband." This time her voice was loud enough to shake the crystal chandelier. "I know he's out there somewhere. J. D. McGuire, where are you?" She sighed when he didn't appear. There were more Rossis than she could count.

Maggie tried again. "Would someone please find J.D. and tell him his wife's water just broke and she needs a ride to the hospital. And whichever nice aunt is pinching David's cheek, would you please hand him over to his daddy?"

J.D. emerged from a crowd at the back of the room, amid much back slapping and joking. He grinned from ear to ear. "I'm here, sweetheart."

As he moved to the front of the room, the many aunties passed David toward J.D., as if the boy were at one giant rave concert. Two-year-old David giggled with delight, dodging kisses along the way. He was obviously a happy, healthy child—something even DCFS had acknowledged shortly after Edna had been arrested. Though the case had been quickly closed, it had taken nearly a year before Maggie was able to quit worrying the authorities might take David from her.

But now, everything looked rosy. Swollen ankles and baby elephants aside, Maggie thought it was about the best family reunion she'd ever attended. Definitely worth taking a mini-vacation from Tinker & McGuire mortuary, where her diploma from Arkansas State University Mountain Home was proudly displayed in her office.

J.D. and David joined her as a contraction doubled her over.

"Come on, let's get you to the hospital, sweetheart." J.D.'s voice was calm, but his eyes were dark with concern.

NEARLY TWELVE HOURS LATER, Maggie held J.D.'s hand as Faith Rossi McGuire was born. The nurses cleaned her up and handed her to her daddy.

Tears dribbled down Maggie's face as she watched J.D. cradle his daughter in his big, strong hands. Tears crept out of the corners of his eyes, too.

"Now I have the two best girls who like to cause a scene at reunions," he murmured, smoothing a hand over Faith's red baby fuzz.

The nurse took a photo of father and daughter with the camera Maggie had provided beforehand.

J.D. PRESSED THE PHOTOGRAPH to the glass divider the next time he visited his grandmother at the Women's Correctional Institute. She had improved a great deal since she'd started receiving the right medication for depression. Her condition had nothing to do with her crime. The defense and prosecution doctors both agreed she'd known the difference between right and wrong when she'd killed Eric.

Thankfully, the prosecution had asked for the minimum sentence due to her age. He'd probably also realized a jury would have looked at her and seen their own kindly grandmas.

J.D. wasn't sure she would ever come to terms with what she'd done. He wasn't sure he would, either.

Grandma gazed at the photograph for what seemed like forever. Finally, she clasped her hands together and exclaimed, "Oh, she's every inch a McGuire."

J.D. shook his head, thinking some things never changed. But this time, he was grateful to be on the outside looking in.

* * * * *

Watch for Nancy's story,
coming in November 2005
from Harlequin Superromance.

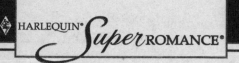

If you enjoyed what you just read,
then we've got an offer you can't resist!

Take 2 bestselling love stories FREE!

Plus get a FREE surprise gift!

▰▰▰▰▰▰▰▰▰▰▰▰▰▰

Clip this page and mail it to Harlequin Reader Service®

IN U.S.A.
3010 Walden Ave.
P.O. Box 1867
Buffalo, N.Y. 14240-1867

IN CANADA
P.O. Box 609
Fort Erie, Ontario
L2A 5X3

YES! Please send me 2 free Harlequin Superromance® novels and my free surprise gift. After receiving them, if I don't wish to receive anymore, I can return the shipping statement marked cancel. If I don't cancel, I will receive 6 brand-new novels every month, before they're available in stores. In the U.S.A., bill me at the bargain price of $4.69 plus 25¢ shipping and handling per book and applicable sales tax, if any*. In Canada, bill me at the bargain price of $5.24 plus 25¢ shipping and handling per book and applicable taxes**. That's the complete price, and a savings of at least 10% off the cover prices—what a great deal! I understand that accepting the 2 free books and gift places me under no obligation ever to buy any books. I can always return a shipment and cancel at any time. Even if I never buy another book from Harlequin, the 2 free books and gift are mine to keep forever.

135 HDN DZ7W
336 HDN DZ7X

Name	(PLEASE PRINT)	
Address	Apt.#	
City	State/Prov.	Zip/Postal Code

Not valid to current Harlequin Superromance® subscribers.

Want to try two free books from another series?
Call 1-800-873-8635 or visit www.morefreebooks.com.

* Terms and prices subject to change without notice. Sales tax applicable in N.Y.
** Canadian residents will be charged applicable provincial taxes and GST.
   All orders subject to approval. Offer limited to one per household.
   ® are registered trademarks owned and used by the trademark owner and or its licensee.

SUP04R   ©2004 Harlequin Enterprises Limited

COMING NEXT MONTH

#1278 STRANGER IN TOWN • Brenda Novak
A Dundee, Idaho, book

Hannah Russell almost killed Gabe Holbrook in a car accident. Gabe's been in a wheelchair ever since, his athletic career ended. He's a recluse, living in a cabin some distance from Dundee, and Hannah can't get over her guilt. But one of her sons is on the high school football team and when Gabe—reluctantly—becomes the coach, she finds herself facing him again....

#1279 HIS REAL FATHER • Debra Salonen
Twins

Lisa never had trouble telling the Kelly brothers apart. Even though they were twins, they were nothing alike. Joe was quiet, and Patrick the life of the party. Each was important to her. But only one was the father of her son.

#1280 A FAMILY FOR DANIEL • Anna DeStefano
You, Me & the Kids

Josh White is trying to care for his late sister's son, but Daniel's hurting so much nothing seems to reach him. The only person the boy responds to is Amy Loar, Josh's childhood friend. Amy has her own problems,but she does her best to help. Then Daniel's father shows up and threatens to sue for custody, and the two old friends have to figure out how to make a family for Daniel.

#1281 HIS CASE, HER CHILD • Linda Style
Cold Cases: L.A.

He's a by-the-book detective determined to find his niece's missing child. She's a youth advocate equally determined to protect an abandoned boy in her charge. Together, Rico Santini and Macy Capshaw form an uneasy alliance to investigate the child's past, and in the process they unearth a black-market adoption ring at a shelter for unwed mothers. The same shelter where years earlier Macy had given birth to a stillborn son. At least, that's what she was told....

#1282 THE DAUGHTER'S RETURN • Rebecca Winters
Lost & Found

Maggie McFarland's little sister was kidnapped twenty-six years ago, but Maggie has never given up hope of finding Kathryn. Now Jake Halsey has a new lead for her, and it looks as if she's finally closing in on the truth. The trouble is, it doesn't look as if Jake has told her the truth about *himself*.

#1283 PREGNANT PROTECTOR • Anne Marie Duquette
9 Months Later

The stick said positive. She was pregnant. Lara Nelson couldn't believe it. How had she, a normally levelheaded cop, let this happen—especially since the soon-to-be father was the man she was sworn to protect?